From the Award-Winning Author of Blood Line...

2015 Killer Nashville Silver Falchion™ Reader's Choice Award
2015 Readers' Favorite Gold Medal in Fiction-Action
2015 eLit Gold Medal in Popular Fiction and
Silver Medal in Mystery/Thriller/Suspense

"***Bloody Truth* is smart, deadly, and lightning-fast.** It reveals the back stage intrigues, double-crosses and unscrupulous corruption of global politics today." –Alan Rinzler, *Contributing Editor*

"***Bloody Truth* is intrigue, thriller, espionage and counterintelligence at its best,** bound up by family interactions and relationships unusual for a genre that typically features only a lone wolf or two at the helm of disaster. " –D. Donovan, *Midwest Book Reviews*

"**Readers will most certainly fall in love with the compelling characters, the exciting drama, and the surprises that are never lacking in the well-crafted plot.** The dialogue flows naturally and readers can easily get the feeling that they are part of it, but the real fun happens in those nail-biting moments of roller-coaster action and the insanity that creates our fictional heroes." –*Romuald Dzemo for Readers' Favorite*

"John J. Davis has written a series that is not only fresh and riveting, but in many ways it is also **a throwback to the golden era of mysteries—the type many of us cut our teeth on when we were young—think James Bond and Nancy Drew blended and stirred.** ...A suspense thriller that defies genre. In *Bloody Truth*, **Davis has done what few authors have accomplished in many years; he has written a suspense thriller that can be read and enjoyed by the entire family, and for that, he is to be applauded.**" –J.M. LeDuc, *Author of* "Sin", *for Suspense Magazine*

BLOODY TRUTH

A GRANGER SPY NOVEL

JOHN J. DAVIS

Be sure to visit www.johnjdavis.com for insider information, character bio's and author updates. Subscribe to *The Granger Report* for exclusive news and events.

BOOKS BY JOHN J. DAVIS

Granger Spy Novel Series:
Blood Line
Bloody Truth
Book Three (Coming Soon)

BLOODY TRUTH

A GRANGER SPY NOVEL

JOHN J. DAVIS

SIMON & WINTER, INC.

Simon & Winter
Inc.
www.simonandwinter.com

Library of Congress Control Number: 2015909688

For more information or to book an event or interview, contact
Simon & Winter, Inc. at info@simonandwinter.com.

Printed in the United States of America

First Printing, 2015
ISBN 978-0-9903144-3-1
www.johnjdavis.com

§

My wife and my inspiration, Rebekah.
My daughter and my toughest critic, Leecy.
And for their unwavering support, my dad and Cindy.

Special Thanks To

Alan Rinzler
Chris Coleman
James von Scholz
Jimmy "T"
Jesse & Dedo

BLOOD LINE
Book One of the Granger Spy Novel Series

The sudden explosion of breaking glass and splintering wood reverberated inside the house like a clap of thunder. I was awake instantly, and the rush of adrenaline coursing through my veins propelled me out of the bed and into action.

"Valerie!" I yelled at my wife, who was already leaping out of the other side of the bed. "That should've set off the alarm."

She was rounding the end of our bed just as I flipped on the overhead lights and opened the door of our room. There was someone in the hallway, but the beam from a high-powered LED flashlight blinded my eyes before I could look away.

I heard a voice.

"Back the fuck up! Keep your hands where I can see them."

I felt the round end of a small pistol barrel poke me in the chest before I could blink my eyes and begin to see the revolver in one hand, the flashlight in the other.

"Both of you back up, hands in the air, and stay right where you are."

I raised my hands and backed up until I bumped against my bedside table. Then the guy swung the pistol and hit me in the face hard enough to get my attention, but not enough to hurt me.

He aimed his gun at Valerie again. "Not another step."

My vision had recovered, and I could see the intruder was wearing a black ski mask, t-shirt, jeans, and boots. He was about five-feet, seven inches, and thin, about 160 pounds, so I had a distinct size advantage, being six-feet and two hundred pounds. But he had the gun, a revolver of some kind. That was actually another plus for me since the hammer wasn't cocked. Getting it ready to fire would take all the time I needed.

He started moving the gun in my direction again when I heard the scream.

"Daddy!"

Finish reading **Blood Line** by *John J. Davis*.

Real family; real events;
fictionalized for their protection.

CHAPTER

ONE

THE BLACK SEA

The explosion shredded the walls and roof of the Quonset hut, ripping through the vintage World War II-era Russian building and catapulting me across the gravel road, slamming me into the chain link fence encircling the naval base. The twelve-foot high security fence buckled and stretched out grotesquely under the force of my weight, but didn't break. The fence snapped back into its original shape and pitched me down into the ground with a force that knocked me nearly unconscious. Landing hard on my back, I struggled to breathe. Burning debris was raining down around me like hundreds of flaming arrows stabbing into the ground. Shielding my face and rolling to my right, I tried pushing up on my knees.

Engulfed in a cloud of black smoke, I gagged on the taste of blood, the smell of burnt hair and flesh, and the noxious fumes coming from the remnants of the burning building. Throwing up, I wiped my mouth on my sleeve and tried to stand, but my legs buckled and I fell to my knees. Two hands appeared in the smoke like apparitions— grabbing, lifting, and dragging me to my feet.

It was Hodges and Valerie. Given my condition, I was glad to see them both. They were upright and obviously in better shape than me, and he was big enough to lean against if I needed to.

Coughing, trying to clear my lungs and head and steady myself on legs that felt numb, I faltered, stumbling forward a few steps before regaining my balance. With my pulse rate slowing, I began my self-assessment. Starting at my feet, I tried flexing and extending every muscle and every joint of my six-foot, 200-pound frame, while checking my surroundings. Feeling only minor pain and discomfort in my lower extremities, I looked behind me, seeing the shell of the burning metal building. The jagged edges of twisted metal, backlit by fire, stood as stark reminders of what might have happened to me.

I was lucky to be in one piece. I was lucky to be alive.

I touched my ribcage, wincing. Closing my eyes to the pain radiating from my left side, I knew one or more ribs were cracked, maybe broken.

Focusing on the job meant pushing the discomfort aside. I opened my eyes to see my daughter, Leecy, standing in front of me. She was saying something, asking me a question, but I couldn't hear her because of the ringing in my ears. I tried reading her lips, but narrowing my focus made things worse. A shockwave of pain rolled over me, bending me down at the waist. I tried to fight it. We needed to move. I needed to move.

Straightening and gritting my teeth against the pain, I placed my hands on top of my head, and closed my eyes as I took in a deep breath, filling my lungs with fresh sea air. I came rushing back into the moment.

"Can you hear me, Ron?" Hearing my wife's voice, I opened my eyes and thought I was seeing double, but I wasn't. Valerie was standing next to Leecy, and the only discernible difference between the two olive-skinned, dark-haired, black-eyed beauties was Leecy's height. She was one inch taller than her mother's five-foot, seven inches. Val took a step toward me and reinserted my earpiece before gently slapping my cheek. "Ron Granger, can you hear me?"

I blinked my eyes a few times before responding. "Yeah, yeah, I hear you," I answered, feeling my feet firmly under me but reaching out placing a hand on her shoulder anyway. "I'm just a little dizzy."

"Anything broken?" Leecy asked.
"No," I answered, shaking my head.

"Liar," Val said. "I saw you wince when you touched your ribs."
Smiling a half smile, I said, "Yeah, well Leecy asked if anything was broken, and I think the ribs are just bruised."
"You mean cracked?"
Eyeing my wife warily I started to respond, but Hodges cut me off.

"Look guys, we can do a full workup on his injuries when we get back to the plane, but right now we need to get out of here. I'm pretty sure that's a siren I hear, and it's heading in our direction."
"Maybe so," I said, "but it's only one siren. No reason to panic yet."
"I don't care if it's one or a dozen sirens," Hodges said. "It means military police are coming. We need to move right now."

"He's right, Ron," Val said. "Think you're up for a run?"

"Yeah, sure," I said, lying again. "Lead the way."

I fell in line behind Hodges as Valerie and Leecy led the way. Staying close to the buildings and away from the illuminated fence line, we sprinted between the shadows, covering the first six hundred yards in less than five minutes. I thought we were making good time.

"Ron, you okay?" I heard Val's voice ask me through my earpiece.

"Hanging in there."

"Catch your breath," she said, her back to the building we were hiding behind. "We've got to hold here for the truck to pass. Then we move."

"Roger that," I said, hearing the blare of an approaching siren, thinking it odd how long the response to the explosion was taking.

"Here it comes," Val said.

"Troop transport vehicle?" I asked.

"Coming into view now and, no, it's not a transport truck; just an MP vehicle carrying two passengers. Let's move. You okay with picking up the pace, Ron?"

"Do your worst," I answered, pushing off the wall and giving chase.

"Okay, but remember, you asked for it. No more pausing between shadows. Full sprint the rest of the way."

I was lagging behind the otherwise tight formation as we covered the remaining six hundred yards to the exfiltration point, but I'd decided after seeing the meager response to the explosion our covert tactics were overkill. I didn't think anyone cared if that building blew up or if we were on the Naval Base at all. But I ran anyway.

The freezing November night air was fighting with the hot smoke I'd inhaled and just when I started to think I couldn't run any longer I reached the blind spot at the apex of the curve in the fence line.

Ryan and Franks stood on the other side of the fence.

"How'd you two get here so fast?" I asked between deep breaths.

"Just following orders," Ryan answered.

"Is that right?" Val asked, climbing over the fence with Leecy.

"You said, and I quote," Ryan responded, "'rendezvous at the exfiltration point,' and that's what I did."

"Hodges," I said, ignoring Ryan, "you're going to have to give me a little boost."

"That's right, Hodges," Val said, dropping to the ground on the other side of the fence. "Help the man with the broken ribs."

I was about to comment when suddenly Val slammed Ryan to the ground with a leg sweep and stood over him with a boot on his throat.

"You'll answer for what you did one way or another."

Ryan rolled away and struggled to stand up.

"And you'll answer for striking a fellow agent. I have witnesses."

Landing in a crouch position next to Leecy after Hodges helped me over the fence, I stood slowly to face a now-standing Ryan and said, "No, that's not what striking a fellow agent looks like. This is what striking a fellow agent looks like," and dropped him with a weak left jab. "You can call it even now. Unless, of course, you want more."

Laughing and nodding his head, he leaned on his elbow then stood, wiping his bloody lip on the back of his hand.

"Don't like your lady fighting your battles for you so

you sucker punch me?"

"If you think that..."

"That's enough," Val interrupted. Addressing Ryan again, she said, "You know what you did, and you'll own it."

"Or what?" Ryan asked.

"Or nothing, but trust me; you'll own it. Now let's move out."

"I did nothing wrong," he said to the back of Valerie's head.

But she wasn't listening. She was running, issuing orders. "We still have a thousand yards to cover. Let's move. Double time it."

I ran past Ryan and said, "Keep telling yourself that."

***

A thousand yards later, we were all stripping off our makeshift Russian Military Police insignias and replacing them with proper NATO designations. With Franks behind the wheel of the NATO marked sedan, driving toward the Sevastopol International Airport, we were almost home.

"Wakefield, are you receiving me yet?" Val said, cupping her hand over her ear. "Come in, Wakefield."

Everyone heard Wakefield's voice coming in loud and clear over our earpieces.

"Roger that. Status?"

"Inbound," Val responded. "All present and accounted for."

"Roger. ETA?"

"Less than ten."

"I take it you saw that explosion?" Wakefield asked.

"Affirmative."

"Tell me that wasn't us."

"We suffered minor injuries."

"That's not good. You didn't answer my question."

"ETA now eight minutes," Val said, turning off her earpiece.

"Damn it," I heard Wakefield saying just before turning off my own.

We rode in silence for the next three miles. Something was eating at me. I was missing something. Not seeing something obvious.

Ryan broke the silence.

"Why didn't you tell her what happened?"

"Are you talking to me?" Val asked.

"Yeah, I'm talking to you. Why didn't you tell Wakefield what happened?"

"Unlike you, Ryan," Val answered, "I respect the team."

"What does that mean?"

"It means it's not my place to tell on you. You'll have to own what you did or not, but I won't relieve you of that burden."

"I didn't ask you to."

"Good, then we understand each other."

The lights of the airport were coming into view. Checking my watch, I saw that Franks had made the return trip in less than twenty minutes. He parked the sedan next to the CIA Gulfstream with his customary aplomb and the doors flew open.

Seeing me struggle getting out of the rear of the sedan, Wakefield said, "Damn it, Valerie, you greatly understated the severity of the situation. Minor injuries, my ass. He looks like hell."

"Yeah, I know," Valerie said, helping me up the stairs of the plane.

"Zach," Wakefield called inside the plane, "what's the status of the real NATO plane?"

"They're on the ground in Kiev and not scheduled to depart for eight hours. We're good to go, and our pilots have us cleared for takeoff."

"Get those tail numbers changed once we're airborne."

"I'm doing it now."

"Everyone prepare for takeoff," Wakefield instructed, closing the door to the Gulfstream. "We'll debrief once we're clear of Russian-controlled airspace."

As the plane lifted off, I caught sight of the blue lights of a Russian patrol vehicle arriving at the airport. I wanted to laugh, but held it in as Val, who'd signaled it was time to take a look at my wounds, began helping me strip off my sweater and carefully remove my undershirt.

"Lean over, I want to look at your back first."

"How bad is it?"

"Minor burns, but that's not what's causing your back pain."

"Really?"

"Nope, you've got about fifty small fragments, some metal some wood, embedded in your skin."

"Well get them out."

"Keep your pants on, big boy, I will," she said. "Bring me the field medic kit, Leecy." She turned back to me. "Sit up and let me check your rib cage." Palpating the already-bruising lower left quadrant of my torso, she said, "Good news, you're just deeply bruised. No cracks, but I'd need an x-ray to be one hundred percent."

"Thanks, Doc," I said.

"I'm going to dose you with a painkiller, give you a tetanus shot, and wrap your ribs, and you should be ready to go."

We'd been in the air about thirty minutes when Wakefield asked, "Val, you about done playing doctor?"

"Yes, all done. Debrief?"

"Not yet. First, we need to watch the news. I've just received an email alert. There's a breaking news story coming out Moscow. Putin is going to be holding a press conference."

"So it's made the news already?" Val asked.

"If by 'it' you mean the explosion, then you're correct. Zach!" Wakefield called over her shoulder.

"Yes?" Zach asked.

"Get the TV tuned to a news station." Wakefield stood, addressing the team. "Everyone eyes front and pay attention."

Sitting upright, I took a couple of deep breaths to loosen the bandage wrapped around my ribs before settling back into my chair in time to see the flat screen TV mounted on the bulkhead wall come to life.

A dark-haired, English-speaking MSNBC reporter faced the camera.

"Two months of ceasefire may be coming to an end tonight," she said. "A large explosion at the Russian-occupied Black Sea Military base in Sevastopol destroyed what high-ranking Russian military officials are reporting was a warehouse containing humanitarian aid packages destined for Eastern Ukraine. These same officials are laying the blame for this unprovoked attack squarely at the feet of pro-nationalist Ukrainian forces. However, the newly elected Ukrainian President denies these claims, saying they are false and unsubstantiated. President Vladimir Putin is said to be weighing in on this horrific turn of events live from Moscow." Placing a finger on her ear and nodding, she added, "We're going live to Moscow and President Putin now."

"What in the hell is she talking about?" Hodges asked.

"That's all bullshit," Ryan added. "The warehouse was full of wooden pallets, nothing else."

"So what does this mean?" Franks asked.

"It means," Leecy answered, "the Russians not only rigged that building to blow, but they also released the false intelligence about pro-Ukrainian forces operating in the area which was the basis for bringing NATO inspectors to the region in the first place. Our taskforce took the bait, sending us here to stop what was going to happen regardless of what we did or didn't do."

"Maybe so, but we were sent here to prevent the explosion, and I hope we didn't actually cause it," Wakefield said, interrupting Leecy. "Quiet," she added, "Putin's coming to the podium."

Wearing his customary dark suit, light gray shirt and blue tie, standing behind a podium, nodding and looking grim, Vladimir Putin began speaking in Russian.

"Valerie?" Wakefield asked. "Will you translate?"

"Sure," Val said. "He's saying the unfortunate event in Sevastopol should be viewed as an act of war by the Nationalist Ukrainian government, justifying the need for the troops he's amassed at the Eastern Ukrainian border, and allowing him to move those troops deeper into the region. But he says he's instead calling for calm and asking the media not to rush to judgment. And though he feels it's justified to strike back, he is willing to give the peace process time to work. He understands the frustrations the Ukrainian people have with their government and the results of recent elections, but Russia is not to blame for their problems. Russia is here to help its Ukrainian neighbor, not harm it. The proof of that pledge lies in the burned remnants of humanitarian aid that lie scattered across the grounds of the Naval base and floating in the dark waters of the Black Sea, rather than in the hands and mouths of the people in the Eastern Ukraine. And that's why he's calling for an emergency session of the UN Security Council in Geneva."

"So now Putin is a statesman?" Ryan interrupted.

Valerie continued, ignoring Ryan's outburst.

"Putin is sending his newly-appointed Deputy Chairman of the Government to Geneva. He insists this is not a slight to the process that he himself is calling for, but simply that the Chairman of the Government, Prime Minister Medvedev, has taken ill. He's assuring the world that Mr. Medvedev's second is a more-than-capable substitute. Now the reporters are asking questions about the qualifications of this newly-appointed member of the government."

"Okay, Zach," Wakefield said, standing to face her team, "that's it. Shut it down." She walked toward the aft section of the plane. "A little more than three hours ago I stood here and conducted a pre-mission briefing. I remember it very clearly, and I came away thinking each of you knew your roles and mission objectives. Yet here we are dealing with the fallout of this colossal failure. Who wants to tell me what went sideways out there?"

Silence.

"Okay, that's how you want to play it? Then let's go at the issue from another angle. Let's run it down. We'll take it from the top."

"Is that really necessary?" Ryan asked.

"You're damn right it is! Didn't you just hear the news report? Furthermore, don't you realize the incalculable size, immeasurable weight, and unyielding force of the pile of shit that is coming down on our collective heads when we arrive back at Langley? Screw ups like this one are career enders."

"Yes I did," Ryan said, "and I get it."

Looking down at him, reaching the tail section of the plane, she continued. "Then we obviously need to run it down again, don't we? Don't you think we need to find out where we screwed up?" Wakefield asked, pacing in the aisle of the plane. Suddenly, she stopped, choosing instead to grip the headrest of an unoccupied seat with such force that the veins in her forearms began to throb visibly beneath her skin.

"I see your point," Ryan said, dropping his eyes from hers, looking instead at the floor of the plane.

"Zach!" Wakefield barked. "You're up!"

"I hack the Federal Air Transport Agency in Moscow," Zach said, "and change our plane's tail number to the one they're expecting the NATO team to arrive in, so we're in the clear and expected at Sevastopol airport. We'll be early, but that can be explained as a surprise inspection, which is very common."

"Ryan, what's our cover?" Wakefield asked walking toward Ryan.

"Our cover is that of a NATO peace keeping delegation inspecting the region. We're following up on Russian troop movements along the border and the Russian claims of pro-Nationalist Ukrainian forces active in the area during the cease fire."

"Good," she said, nodding in agreement. She turned and walked toward the front of the plane, placing a hand on

Leecy's shoulder. "Leecy, tell me the mission objective."

"Our mission objective is to find and disable the bomb and/or bombs the joint taskforce—consisting of NSA, DIA, and our own CIA intelligence officers—believe pro-Nationalist Ukrainian forces have planted to destroy a warehouse located on the Naval base. The intelligence reports indicate the warehouse being targeted is a staging area for smuggling weapons to the rebels in Eastern Ukraine. If we can disable the bombs, preventing the attack on Russian controlled soil, we can avert a possible escalation of Russian troops in Eastern Ukraine and preserve the cease fire agreement."

"Hodges and Franks," Wakefield said, stopping next to their seats, "Game plan?"

"After we land, we drive off in one NATO-marked sedan," Hodges said.

"Yep, that's right," Franks agreed, finishing the thought for his partner like an old married couple might do. "We're using the plan provided by the joint taskforce officers. We're to deviate from the preauthorized, in-country travel route submitted to the Russians and the Ukrainians by NATO, and instead of inspecting the region for signs of troop movements, head directly for the military base."

"We hide the NATO vehicle inside a vacant barn," Hodges said, picking up the story, nodding his head as he often did when he talked. "It's located on Ukrainian government-owned land. An abandoned farm."

"The farm," Franks finished, "shares a property line with the Military base."

"So far, so good," Wakefield said, turning to face all of us from the front of the plane. Looking down at Valerie, seated next to me in the first row, Wakefield continued.

"The team will be short on time. We need to be in and out so as not to overlap with the real NATO plane. From the moment our wheels hit the tarmac, you'll have just two hours to locate and dismantle the bombs. Now, Valerie, you're up. You're at the target location. Walk me through what happens next."

"The joint taskforce intelligence reports indicate one of four buildings as being the possible target. We clear each one with half the team through the front entrance and the other half through the rear entrance. If we encounter any explosive devices, we disarm and remove, then we double-time it back here."

"And double-time is exactly what you'd need to do."

"Roger that," I said, getting into the spirit of the reenactment.

"You bet your ass roger that," Tammy Wakefield said, fully immersed in the rehashing of the pre-mission debrief. "If we're still on the ground when the real team arrives, all hell will break loose. No amount of explaining our unauthorized presence on Russian-occupied soil will save us. So," she paused, just as she'd done earlier, mimicked confirming the time on her watch, then continued. "Get in, get the job done, and get back to the plane ASAP. And remember: don't, under any circumstances, use lethal force. Zero body count on this. We need to be like the Army Rangers and leave no trace we were ever here. Are you hearing me, Ron and Valerie?"

"Roger that," I said again.

"Copy," is all Val offered in reply. She wasn't as enthusiastic about this little song and dance of Wakefield's as I was.

"One last reminder before we land," Wakefield said

taking her seat and going as far as buckling her seatbelt, "Val's in command."

I recalled the groan that emanated from Ryan's seat in the rear of the plane when Tammy said that the first time, but I didn't hear it this time.

"Is that a question, Agent Ryan?" Wakefield asked replaying the moment I was thinking about.

"No, just exercising my God-given right to be displeased about the unit's command choice," Ryan answered.

"You've spent the past year making me aware of your constant displeasure, Ryan. Maybe you should give some consideration to seeking reassignment."

"'And leave the agencies premiere Actionable Data Deployment Team,'" Tammy said in her best Ryan impression. "'Not a chance.'"

"Then I suggest a change of attitude," she continued in her own voice, "'cause it's long overdue."

"'Working on that, Ma'am,'" she finished, adding Ryan's last words for him. Then standing and breaking from the past, she asked, "Is that about how the pre-mission briefing went, Leecy?"

"Yes, it is," Leecy answered.

"Then what?" Wakefield asked before answering her own question. "Oh, yes. We landed, and you drove off in the NATO-marked sedan wearing your coordinating black UN uniforms and carrying identical black backpacks. Just like clockwork. So what happened? Where'd this all go south?"

"I think knowing we might have to handle explosive devices," Val answered, "may have put some team members under stress. Add to that, we were really pressed for time on this one."

"Valerie," Wakefield said, easing up beside Val's seat on the plane, "really? You guys were under stress? Let's go to the recordings from your earpieces and hear exactly just how stressed everyone was. Play it, Zach."

The overhead speakers mounted in the plane's fuselage hummed and cracked to life. Ryan's voice came in loud and clear.

"Don't worry about that, Old Man," he was saying, addressing me in his usual way. "This is an easy in and out."

"Easy?" Valerie was heard questioning. "Best guard against that type of thinking; it only leads to lapses in concentration. This is just the type of mission that can go sideways on us."

"Yeah, I hear you," Ryan's recorded voice said. "But why don't we worry about that when we get where we're going, and see if we have anything to worry about before we get all worked up over nothing."

The playback ended.

"That's all we've got before you guys were out of effective range for the earpieces," Wakefield said, "and it doesn't sound like anyone's under stress to me. Sounds to me like you were all as relaxed as seasoned operators should be, if not a little complacent." She paused, looking each one of us over, then asked, "What happened next?"

"Right," Val began again. "I remember saying we were about one kilometer away. I reminded Hodges and Franks to keep a lookout at the front and rear entrances after we breached a building. And I reminded the entry team that if one of them located an explosive device to hold and advise me before attempting to defuse it."

"Leecy, take me to the arrival at the barn," Wakefield

said.

"We parked the sedan in front of the empty barn the taskforce had located for our use," Leecy answered, "and switched out our UN insignias for the Russian Military Police insignias. We armed ourselves with the standard issue weapon for Russian Military Police, so if we encountered anyone on the base we'd look legit, as long as no one looked too closely, that is. Once we were ready to go, Val said to move out."

"I don't see the reason things went so badly," Wakefield began. "It's clear each of you knew what your role was and what to do. Your commander reminded you of a few last minute details that might slip your mind in the heat of the moment. So what the hell went wrong, Valerie?"

"I don't know," Val answered. "We were clearing the inside of the last building, having found nothing inside the first three, and... I don't know."

"I don't know?" Wakefield asked. "Is that right, Leecy, you don't know what happened?"

"I heard Mom, I mean Val, give the all hold, then..." and her voice trailed off because she, like her mother, wasn't about to burn a teammate. As new as she was to this business, she knew the team took the fall together and the team got the glory together.

"Is anyone going to tell me what went down out there?" Wakefield asked, her tone intensifying with her ever quickening pacing, "Hodges, how 'bout it?"

"Yeah, fuck it. I'll tell you what happened," Hodges said, nodding his head. "Now, I didn't see it, mind you, because I was keeping lookout at the rear door, but I heard Ryan say he'd located a device. Val gave the hold call. Then, I heard Ryan say the bomb was active. Next thing I know, Granger is being catapulted through the door of the building like a human torch."

Wakefield stopped pacing in front of Ryan and asked, "What do you have to say?"

"Look," he said, standing to address his boss, "the building was full of wooden pallets. The other three buildings consisted of a machine shop, office space, and empty barracks. Someone rigged that Quonset hut to blow because they knew we were coming."

"No one knew we were coming," Wakefield said.

"Well that's my guess. I mean it's not that hard to fathom, is it?"

"That's a load of crap, Agent Ryan," Wakefield barked. "And you know it is."

"Whatever. I located the bomb and did what we'd been trained to do. I followed Standard Operating Procedure. I did exactly what our commander would've done, and had she been the one to cut the wire, the results would've been the same. I don't see the problem here."

"Oh, I see. You think you're in charge of the team, and not Valerie. You think because you received a ninety-minute refresher course on disabling bombs before this mission that you know all there is to know about bombs. Is that it?"

"We all received the same refresher course, yes."

"That's right, you did. But riddle me this, Batman, were you trained by the Mossad in how to build and disable bombs? No? Valerie was. And that's why I put her in charge," Wakefield said. "But it's a moot point, and it doesn't excuse the fact that you walked through a direct order from your unit commander to hold your position, does it? Had Valerie's order to hold been obeyed, we wouldn't be having this conversation, and I doubt you'd have a busted lip, and Granger wouldn't have broken ribs."

"Yeah, my busted lip is something else I..."

"Not interested in hearing it, Agent Ryan," she said, cutting him off before turning and walking toward the front of the plane. "I'll make sure to note your bonehead mistake in the report I need to file with Langley. Meantime, I suggest you guys get to work on team chemistry and find a way to work with each other more effectively. Like it or not, Ryan, Val will continue to be in charge in the field. This is your last chance to get onboard with the program or find yourself out on your ass."

Wakefield retook her seat and I stood up. Every muscle in my body ached. Walking toward the bathroom at the rear of the plane, I caught Ryan's eye, but he just looked away from me and neither of us said a word as I walked past him.

Washing my face and hands clean of the smell of smoke and patches of dried blood, I watched the soot-colored water fill the small sink and thought about how lucky I was to have escaped with only minor injuries. Drying my hands and face with paper towels, and combing my hair with my fingers, I stared at the reflection of my bandaged torso, remembering the last time I'd been wrapped up like this. It was my last official mission as a CIA agent. The only difference between that time and this was that I'd been shot twice back then, not blown up.

Exiting the bathroom and hearing Wakefield calling the team to attention, I leaned against the closed bathroom door to listen.

"Good news and bad news, people," Wakefield began. "Good news is the taskforce agrees with Leecy's assessment that the bomb Ryan activated would've exploded regardless of our actions. They believe Putin or someone in his administration planned to blame pro-Nationalist Ukrainian forces all along. To what end, we don't know yet for sure, but the thinking is it's to justify any Russian action in the region that can defeat the continuing Nationalist resistance to the Russian incursions." Pausing, she dropped her head, exhaling a deep breath before continuing, "Now, the bad news. We've been dropped to one step above taking temperatures for Ebola screenings at Ronald Reagan International airport. We're tasked with offering assistance to an Interpol operation in Brussels."

"You're joking," Ryan said.

Ignoring him, Wakefield finished. "Seems Interpol's budget cuts have left them short-staffed, and in this new age of law enforcement cooperation, we've been volunteered."

"Brussels," I said, intrigued by the idea of returning to familiar stomping grounds. I asked, "What's the operation?"

"Arresting a team of hackers."

"Ouch. We've officially hit the bottom of the barrel," Franks said.

"No, we haven't," Wakefield countered. "Ebola screening is next if we screw up again."

"For real?" Leecy asked. "You're serious?"

"Yes, I am," Wakefield answered. Turning toward the cockpit, she continued. "I'll update the pilots on our new destination. Run your gear checks and get some rest. We'll be on the ground in two hours."

Closing the cockpit door behind her, Wakefield retook her seat, and I slid into the seat next to her.

"You know what we should do while we're in Belgium?"

"Eat some mussels and fries?"

"Yeah, maybe," I answered, trying not to laugh. "But in all seriousness, I was thinking we should shoot down to Overjise."

Closing her laptop and turning to face me, she just stared at me with those crystal clear blue eyes, saying nothing, but encouraging me to continue.

"It might be a good idea to see an old acquaintance who might know something that can help us dig ourselves out of this hole we're in."

She still said nothing; she just smiled and continued to stare at me like she knew something I didn't know, which was usually the case.

"You know, Jens in Overjise. Jens has his hands in every illegal thing going on in Europe. Nothing happens that he or his people don't know about."

Smiling that all too familiar cat-that-ate-the-canary smile of hers, she finally told me.

"Ron, Jens is being arrested by Interpol, and we're assisting."

CHAPTER

TWO

JENS HANNE

I saw headlights speeding toward us as our plane taxied down the runway. A black Mercedes Sprinter van raced alongside us on the private airfield's tarmac, located a few kilometers southwest of Brussels, Belgium.

"Who the hell is Jens?" Leecy asked me as the plane came to a complete stop, and Tammy started moving toward the exit.

"You'll find out soon enough," I said, helping her open the door of the plane.

"Agent Wakefield?" a voice asked from the darkness.

Appearing in the wash of the van's headlights, I saw a tall, slim, black man in a well-tailored suit, looking like he'd just stepped out of the display window of a Savile Row shop. He extended his hand toward Tammy as she stepped onto the tarmac and said with a very British accent, "Allow me to introduce myself. I'm Robert Jeffery Leeds, the Eastern European Station Chief with Interpol. It's a pleasure to make your acquaintance."

"You're it?" Wakefield asked, eschewing any pleasantries.

Unfazed by Wakefield's lack of decorum, he answered. "Budget's taken a bit of a shellacking the past few years. Not a surprise, really, given the status of the global economy and all that. Some of our member countries have been delinquent with their annual contributions and staffing is, as you well know, the first cut. Unfortunately, when the economy goes south, crime rates go north, and we're spread pretty thin right now. We certainly appreciate the assist."

"So, you're it?" Tammy asked again, standing in front of the van and looking around the tarmac for more Interpol agents.

"Yes," he answered, nodding and smiling at all of us now assembled behind Tammy. "I'm it, as you say, but from what I'm seeing I don't believe even I'll be needed."

Tammy looked over her shoulder at me, giving me the look and nod that said *now's your chance.*

"Robert?" I asked. "May I call you Robert?"

"That's perfectly fine," he answered, smiling an ultra bright smile and extending his hand. "I know you Americans like to keep things informal, and to whom am I speaking?"

"Ron Granger," I said, shaking his hand. His grip was as firm and as confident as his eye contact was direct. I made the rest of the introductions and then asked, "Tell me what you know about Jens Hanne?"

Looking at his watch, a stainless steel Rolex, he said, "Why don't I bring you up to speed on the road? We do have a schedule to keep. That is, if we plan to use the cover of darkness."

We listened to him as he drove, outlining the mission details, and what he knew wasn't much. Interpol's Computer Forensic Division, or the I.C.F.D., in conjunction with the FBI and the Secret Service, had spent the past ten months back tracing the hackers responsible for the attack on Sony, Target, and JP Morgan Chase and that work led them to Jens Hanne.

"With cyber crime at an all time high," he said, "there's a priority on bringing hackers to justice. That's why our officers are spread so thin, we're working directly with the US government on this one."

"I see," I said.

"These types of operations have become a global law enforcement effort, so when I reached out to my contacts in the US with what we had on Jens, I expected to have FBI or Secret Service joining me, like when the FBI lured that Romanian hacker to Boston for arrest earlier this year. I had no idea they would send a CIA tactical team on this mission but, like I said, I welcome the assist."

"Yeah, well, we'll go where we're ordered," Tammy said. "But back to Jens. He's an old...what would you call him, Ron?"

"I'll tell you what I'd call him," Valerie answered for me. "I'd call him a killer. He shot Ron twice some years ago."

Eyeing me in the rearview mirror, Robert asked, "Is that so?"

"Yes," I answered, "but that was a long time ago. To answer your question, Tammy, I'd call Jens a valuable resource."

"Care to elaborate?" Leecy asked from the seat behind me.

Prompting Robert to comment to Wakefield who was seated next to him, "Your team doesn't seem to be on the same page."

"They're fine, just an outspoken bunch," she said,

looking in Robert's direction before answering Leecy's question. "Jens is the fourth generation of a well-connected criminal syndicate that's been active in Europe's underground crime scene since the nineteen hundreds. Jens took control of the family business in early 2003 after...let's just call it an internal power struggle, which landed him in the boss's chair, which is where he's been ever since."

"I know it's your job to know this stuff," Zach said from his seat next to Leecy, "but why is this one bad guy on the tip of your tongue, Wakefield?"

"He wasn't on the tip of my tongue. I was briefed during the flight that he was wanted by Interpol."

"Jens Hanne was Wakefield and my last mission together,"

I said.

"One we failed at," Wakefield corrected. "You're forgetting that."

"Well, we did get half the job done."

"And as Valerie has already mentioned, Jens shot you twice."

"Oh, I see," Leecy said. "So this is the time Wakefield saved your life. And to think, I didn't have to wait till 2035 for you to tell me after all."

"No, that's something else entirely," I corrected my daughter. "Wakefield said shot, not almost killed. Anyway, what's important is Jens can help us."

"Help us?" Robert asked. "How can he help us? We're charged with arresting him."

"That's right, Ron," Wakefield said. "Jens can't even help himself."

"I understand what we're here to do, but I think the intelligence on this is all wrong," I argued. "Years ago, I spent months learning everything about Jens and his family's organization so I could get close to them, and I'm telling you these guys aren't hackers. They're into the black market. Clothes, music, movies, anything they can make pirated copies or cheap knock-offs of and sell. They did do a little weapons smuggling, and they're definitely involved in prostitution and drugs, but not computer hacking."

"I'm sorry, Ron," Robert countered, "but the intelligence is spot on. There's no doubting it."

"Yeah," Ryan said, speaking for only the second time since his dressing down on the plane. "We're here in the first place because the intelligence we were given about the Ukraine turned out to be not so 'spot on' as you say. I'd question everything at this point."

"Jesus, really?" Hodges said.

"That's your story now?" Franks added.

"Seems your team is all over the place," Robert said, glancing at Wakefield. "What am I to make of that?" With his eyes back on the road he continued, not waiting for an answer. "Nasty business when the intelligence you're told to trust is a shambles, but you made it out all in one piece. All of you, that is, except for Ron, who from the looks of him was in a bit of a dust up."

"Yeah, he was tossed around a bit," Wakefield said, staring through the windshield, "but he's tougher than he looks."

"Where's this conversation going?" Leecy asked. "Why do I get the feeling Dad wants to talk face to face with a guy that shot him twice?"

"That's exactly what I want to do," I said, looking over my shoulder at my daughter sharing a bench seat with Zach and Hodges. "And for the last time, Jens wasn't trying to kill me."

"I don't think this is a good idea," Val said.

"Why not?" I asked, turning my head to look at her. "Setting aside the shooting, we have leverage over him with this Interpol thing hanging over his head, and we should use it."

"Use it how?" Tammy asked.

"Look, we know the guy's connected. There's not much happening that's illegal in Europe or Asia that he or his people don't know about. Why not give him a chance to help himself by sharing some of that knowledge with us?"

"That's Interpol's call, not mine," Tammy answered.

"Ron, you want to bring him in," Robert began, "and then turn him out in exchange for information on a bigger fish?"

"Not exactly, no. I don't want to bring him in at all. Bringing him in is a waste of time," I said. "An added step to the process that we don't need."

"You can't be serious," Val interrupted.

"You bet I'm serious," I said. "I know him. I know the layout of his residence. I know what to expect. It's the fastest way to achieve the desired results because he's not the hacker, but he'll know more than your computer forensic guys know, Robert, or ours."

"Getting shot again or worse?" Val asked, then calmly added. "That's what I know, and it's a risk you shouldn't take. You're hoping Jens will get our team off the bench. But it's not worth risking your life."

"Granger's right, but also wrong," Ryan interjected. "If this Jens guy is really as connected as Ron and Wakefield say he is, he's worth talking to. But Ron's busted up and in no condition to take lead on this. If we want to get back in the game, I should be the one to take point."

"As always," Wakefield said, "your thoughts are duly noted."

"Okay, hold on a tic," Robert said. "Regardless of which one of your boys it is, let's say I agree to this meeting with Jens. How do you approach him? What's the plan?"

"Well," I began, and then paused, looking around at Ryan, who averted his gaze, falling silent. "Robert, you've told us we're driving to Overjise, so I guess Jens still lives in the same place. I'll just approach him like I did in 2003."

"And how was that?" Robert asked.

"I was sent to kill him before, not talk to him, but I'm mainly talking about how to gain entry to the residence. The rest of it, I'll make up as I go along."

"That's what I've been saying," Val said. "He knows that. He knows you were sent to kill him. Why wouldn't he just put two bullets in you on sight?"

"I agree," Robert said. "It sounds like a suicide mission. I don't think I can sign off on this. Sorry, but you'll just have to interrogate him after the arrest."

"No, it's not a suicide mission," I said, leaning forward between the front captain's chairs. "Look, I've got a history with the guy, and I know him. If we arrest him he'll go deaf and dumb on us. I'll concede that maybe my history with the guy isn't on the best of terms, but he owes me in a way. I'm the reason he's in the position he's in. I killed his boss."

"Yes, that's true," Wakefield agreed, "but you were supposed to kill Jens, too."

"He doesn't know that. He shot me before I got the chance to shoot him, remember?"

"Oh, I remember," Val chimed in again. "I remember you were out of action for months, and I don't want to go through that again."

"It's been so long since all that happened," Wakefield said. "And Jens dropped below the CIA radar after that mission. I think Ron going in is a risk worth taking."

"Wow, talk about flip flops," Valerie said.

"What can I say?" Wakefield rejoined, "Granger's persuasive."

"I have a question," Leecy said, breaking the tension inside the van. "Who was Jens' boss?"

"His father," I answered.

"His father?" Leecy said. "What in the..."

"Yeah, I know how it sounds, but trust me, it's complicated."

"You're going to walk back in there?" Val asked me, squeezing my hand.

"What's it going to be, Robert?" I asked, ignoring Valerie, but squeezing her hand to let her know I understood her concern. "I need you to trust me. I know this guy, and I know he's not the hacker."

"Sounds a bit reckless to me, honestly it does," he answered. "But I'll go for it on two conditions: one, you'll have thirty minutes, and two, you go in wearing an earpiece so we can monitor the action."

"Deal," I said.

Flipping down the TV screen mounted in the roof of the van, I said "Zach, can you put the satellite map view of Jens' house on this screen?"

"No problem. I'll just need a few seconds."

"If memory serves," Wakefield said, turning in her seat to face us, "Jens might, like his father before him, want to conduct any unpleasantness in the empty barn." I pointed to the roof of the longest of the three buildings on the screen, showing everyone the barn as Wakefield continued laying out her plan, "Leecy, you and Val can access the barn from the adjoining vacant lot. If I remember correctly, the loft had excellent sightlines to the main floor of the barn, as well as the secure courtyard. In addition to that, you two will have the high ground. I think one of you positioned fore and one aft it will work just fine. Any questions?"

"Terminate or incapacitate?" Leecy asked.

"Incapacitate, and I'm surprised you'd ask that question, knowing the strict protocols the team has in place for engaging any opposition. I want you both firing bean bag rounds only."

"Doesn't sound like much of a plan to me, Wakefield," Ryan offered. "Shouldn't you deploy the healthiest and most qualified agent at all times? Or at least send in the entire team?"

"No," I answered for her. "We need to keep this operation simple. We don't want to spook him. I'll make the approach alone. Val, you and Leecy give me a ninety-second head start before following me inside the secure compound. The rest of you hang back and listen. If you hear things starting to go sideways, come riding in like the cavalry."

"What about your earpiece?" Leecy asked. "Won't it be found if they search you?"

"It's part of the deal, but I don't think they'll search me that thoroughly."

"From what I'm seeing on the satellite, there's construction nearby," Zach said. "We can set up in the van two blocks south of the compound and not be noticed."

"I see," Val said, glancing at the flat screen. "Tell me, how old are these images?"

"Six weeks, but I can task one of our satellites in the

area to photograph on the next pass. Problem is, that's five hours from now."

"No, don't do that," Wakefield said. "We need to be in and out before the sun comes up. Let's trust the data we have and make changes once we're on site. Jesus, Ron," Wakefield said, spinning around to face me, "I just remembered Jens knows you as Peter Heely. We don't have any credentials for you to show."

"I don't think that matters given what happened on our last visit," I said, exchanging my vomit-stained black tactical sweater for a clean, long-sleeve black Under Armor HeatMax fitted shirt and black wool sweater. "I think he knows I'm not who I said I was, but I'll stick to that cover anyway, even without the papers."

"All right," Robert said. "I can't say this plan is brilliant. Not one for this spur of the moment thing, but I'm on board. We should be there in fifteen minutes; best make ready."

"So," Leecy asked, prepping her weapon, "when do I get to hear the full story on this Jens guy shooting you?"

"I told you over a year ago," I answered. "Anything related to my early days at the CIA is classified until 2035."

***

The black Mercedes Sprinter van exited the highway, slowing for the off-ramp before turning toward the city center and increasing speed. I told Robert where to drop me, and the team how I planned to approach the compound. We synchronized our watches. It was 3 a.m., giving me three hours till sunrise, which was more than enough time.

I was comforted knowing Val and Leecy would be

watching my back. Val was carrying her Glock 17 in a back holster, and shouldering a sawed-off 12-gauge pistol-grip Mossberg pump-action shotgun loaded with beanbag rounds. She'd borrowed the weapon from Hodges.

Leecy was sitting close to the window and next to Zach. I watched her checking her Sig Sauer P320 before holstering it on her left hip. She preferred a left-handed draw even though she was right-handed. She shouldered the twin to the shotgun Val had, which she had borrowed from Franks.

I could see in the early morning darkness that Overijse had grown in the past decade and was no longer a small country town. Robert was stopping at the petrol station I'd used as my drop point for my first visit to the Hanne compound.

"Here we are," Robert said, eyeballing me in the rearview mirror, "You're certain about this?"

"One hundred percent," I said. "From here I go on foot. Val, you, and Leecy ride with the others to the spot Zach picked out two blocks south of the house. If the satellite images are true, you'll have a clear view of the compound and be able to see me enter the courtyard using night vision goggles. Just mark my route and follow me inside."

I winked at Val before closing the door to the van and watched as she, Leecy, and the team sped away. Alone in the darkness, I starting walking the three remaining blocks from the petrol station to the compound, hoping this plan of mine didn't blow up in my face.

***

The white wall around Jens' courtyard marked the beginning of the property, and it ran the length of the block. I noticed a new addition to the security wall: a heavy-gauge black metal door was built into the wall where there had been an open pass-through before. Other than that, the place was unchanged. Walking past the metal door and turning right at the corner, I walked by the automatic gate securing the driveway. I continued toward the far corner of the adjacent field, leaving the wall and the compound about half a block behind me.

"Here we go," I said, then climbed over the fence and trotted back toward the compound and the wall of the barn facing the empty lot. Climbing the tree I'd used years before, I gained access to the roof of the barn. Moving silently over the roof, lowering myself onto the beam where the old pulley wheel was still hanging, I dropped inside the open loading door of the loft. I waited a ten count before moving toward the ladder and down to the main floor of the barn. I listened carefully, but all was silent. Reaching the open barn door on the first floor, I looked out into the inner courtyard toward the main house, realizing all too late that I wasn't alone.

The business end of a Russian-made PP-19 Bizon—or Bison, as it was more commonly called—a 9-mm submachine gun that can fire seven hundred rounds a minute, appeared out of the shadows. I could see the gun and the man aiming it at my chest clearly. He was standing in the moonlit courtyard directly in front of me. His well-muscled arms and shoulders, straining against the confines of his clothing, easily handled the heft of the weapon. His dark hair was closely cut, and his crooked nose pointed at the deep red scar cleaving his left cheek in half.

I knew I was in trouble. This wasn't this guy's first day

on the job.

"Let's go," he said, gesturing me back inside the barn. "This way."

His Dutch-accented English was clear enough, but not great.

"Back inside barn," he directed. "On your knees, hands behind your head."

The lights came on inside the barn, and I could see it wasn't just a barn anymore; I was standing in the middle of an apartment. On my left stood a king-sized bed, and on my right rested a large wooden chopping block, beyond which was a sink full of dirty dishes and a kitchenette. I kneeled down on the bare cobblestone floor in the small living room space across from a small plaid couch, smelling the steamed cabbage and ham the man holding the gun on me had enjoyed for dinner, getting ready to make my move. But I stopped when two more men, the same size as my captor, walked through the open courtyard door carrying Bison's of their own.

"What you doing here?" the man with the scar asked.

"I'm here to see Jens."

Laughter erupted from all three men, echoing off the plaster walls and wooden ceiling beams. Then one of the other men said, "You're out of luck. Jens is dead. You won't be seeing him tonight, or anyone else ever again."

"Ron," I heard Valerie in my ear. "We're here, and we've got two of them in our sights, but the one at your three o'clock is behind a beam. We don't have a clear shot."

"Ron," Wakefield added, "we're breaching in five seconds."

"Hold on, fellas," I said, spreading my arms out to the side, talking to my team as much as I was addressing my captors, "there's no need for any of that. No need for any killing tonight. Let's just slow down a bit, okay?"

"No," the man with the scar said, looking me over, pulling up my sweater and patting me down while the other two trained their weapons on me. "So why are you sneaking in here asking to see a dead man?"

"I know it does seem odd, but Jens and I go way back. I mean, went way back, and this was a little thing we liked to do to each other. Just a little game we played, but since he's dead," I said, standing suddenly, "there's no reason for me to stick around, so I'll be on my way."

The sound of the guns' slides being pulled back stopped me in my tracks, and one of the two men in front of me said, "Funny guy, this one, but it's no joke you breaking in here. No, I don't think you leaving here ever. I think we deal with you like we dealt with funny guys in old days."

"Oh, really?" I said, smiling at him and his friends with the big guns, holding my hands out to the side. "And how was that?"

"Dad," Leecy said, "still no shot on the guy at your three o'clock. We're moving to a better position."

Wakefield added, "I'll give you thirty seconds to talk your way out of this jackpot then we're coming in and making the arrest."

"Come on," I said, "we've got all the time in the world. Tell me how you dealt with funny guys in the old days."

I looked over my shoulder as the man with the scar circled me, answering my question.

"We'd bring them to the pig farm way out in the country and feed them to the pigs. Happy now? You like knowing how you're going to die. That's enough talk. Back down on your knees."

"Repositioned, ready to take the shot," Val said. "Can

you handle the guy on your six?"

"No," I said, stopping Val and my execution for another precious few seconds. "Wait. Just slow down and listen to me. Jens and I were old friends. He wouldn't want you to kill me."

"Maybe," the man behind me said, jamming the barrel of the gun into my back, causing me to wince in pain and fall to the floor on my stomach, "but I don't know you. I don't care you say you knew Jens. He's not here; he's dead."

"Well," I said, pushing up off the floor and turning slowly on my knees to face him, "allow me to introduce myself. I'm Peter Heely."

"Nice to meet you. Now, time for you to die, Peter Heely," he responded, shoving the gun into my chest, then stopping and saying to his friends. "I have better idea for him. Grab him and put him on chopping block."

The other two men did as the man with the scar instructed. I was laid out on my back on top of the chopping block, staring into the single light bulb hanging by a wire.

"We don't have a clear shot of the man at your feet," Leecy said.

"Breaching now," Wakefield said. "We're coming up the driveway. We're at the gate."

"Okay, okay, easy, hold on, don't do anything rash," I said looking from side to side. "Hold on a second."

I saw the rectangular shape of the meat clever rising above his head, and said, "Wait a..."

"That is enough," I heard a woman's voice call out in Dutch, causing the man to drop the cleaver and back away. "I never thought I'd see you again," she continued in

English.

Sitting up on the edge of the chopping block, I saw a tall, beautiful, red-haired woman wearing an open gray silk bathrobe over a gray silk pajama top and pants with fluffy white heels standing in the open doorway of the barn. Backlit by the moonlight, her silhouette left little to the imagination.

"All hold," Wakefield ordered.

"Holding," echoed in my ear.

"I'm sorry," I said, hopping off the chopping block, "but do I know you?"

"You should, darling; I put two bullets in your back," she answered, crossing the floor and extending her hand to me. Taking her hand, I searched her face for some sign of recognition, but she was standing so close to me I was distracted by the hint of her perfume and couldn't really see her.

Then touching my right trapezius muscle with a long, delicate finger, her nail painted a deep rich shade of red, she continued.

"One bullet exited here, and one," she ran her finger down my arm, drawing a line to my hip, stopping on the bullet wound in my right oblique muscle, "bullet here. They didn't kill you, obviously, but I so hoped you'd remember."

I stared into deep pools that I now realized were the dark blue eyes of Jens Hanne and asked, "Jens?"

"Yes, dear, it's me, but you can call me Jenny."

I didn't move. I just stared at Jenny.

"My God, you're gorgeous."

She smiled before turning away from me and walking toward the door, gesturing for me to follow her.

"Thank you. I know; isn't it marvelous? And to think, I have you to thank for it."

Leaving the barn with one of the three henchmen in tow, I saw that the interior courtyard remained exactly as it had been on my previous visit. Two large concrete watering troughs separated the garden area at my three o'clock from the stone patio at my nine o'clock.

The pea-gravel path I was following lead to the patio, which was connected to the house Jenny was entering ahead of me. The path snaked away behind me toward my ten o'clock, terminating at the garage. The white wall I'd passed on the street filled in the gaps between the buildings.

Research for my previous mission here told me that decades before, the area inside the walls would've been used to house the cattle or sheep that grazed in the neighboring fields, keeping them secure during a time of war or civil unrest, hence the name secure courtyard. During that first mission, I recalled thinking the intended use of the courtyard would not apply to the people I was about to kill, and now I wondered if it would apply to me.

"Go," my large escort said, nudging me in the back with the tip of the Bison.

The foyer resembled the entrance to a medieval castle. Large slabs of stone covered the floor and walls, and thick wooden beams crisscrossing the ceiling were in stark contrast to the pale plaster they supported.

I heard a beep behind me as my escort passed through the doorway. A metal scanner was built into the door's frame.

"In there," he said, nudging me to my left with the nose of the Bison.

Walking beneath a stone archway into a formal dining room, I saw Jenny seated at the round wooden table, watching me admiring her home. On my left, heavy maroon-colored drapes hung from the ceiling, framing either side of the one large window in the room.

The stone entryway floor gave way to large slabs of wood that also covered the walls. A heavy round wooden table was in the center of the room, and I counted twelve wooden chairs. Each chair was appointed with a thickly padded leather seat.

"Knights of the round table," I said, walking around the table, looking out the window. I could see Jenny sizing me up in the window's reflection. She was smiling much like Wakefield smiled, like she knew something the rest of the world didn't know. There was no sign of the men with the Bisons now, or of anyone else in the courtyard. I didn't know what to make of that.

I turned away from the window, sat down next to Jenny, and said, "Well, aside from the obvious, I see nothing has changed."

"Only me, darling. Only me," she said, leaning toward me. "Listen, Peter...that's what you were calling yourself back then, right? Peter?"

"I still am." And she was right. She'd changed a lot. No longer a man; she was a woman. A beautiful woman.

"Well, Peter, the day you showed up here and killed my father was my death and subsequent rebirth," she said, smiling and touching my knee before waving her hand dismissively. "Oh, I know, I shot you. I had to. You know, for appearance' sake. But I was careful not to do any real damage. And you look just fine to me," she added before sitting back in her chair and crossing her legs. "Oh yes, darling, that day was the best day of my life."

"Glad to know I could be of service," I said, looking at the archway entrance to the room for the man with the Bison before asking, "Tell me what you're up to these days?"

"Just like that?" she asked, smiling slyly. "No foreplay,

no romance, and no intricate dance? You can't just ask a girl such a direct question." She paused, pushing her hair behind her ears. "But given our history, I think I may understand why you would want to get right to the point. Before I answer, you must understand that my personal security, and security of my organization, is a concern for me. With that said, what do you want to know?"

"By 'security,' do you mean like the beeping sound I heard when I entered?"

"Yes, darling, like that and other things. That beeping sound indicates two things: that a metal object is present and that I have a complete picture of you," she said, looking me up and down. "But enough about that," she said, changing the subject. She leaned forward, placing a hand on my knee again, and looked at me quizzically. "I never thought I'd see you again. And here you are, sitting at my table. When I saw you smiling at my men on the security cameras, I thought you knew, but you didn't. How could you, really? So that means you came here to see a man, a man that shot you twice, and that takes a special kind of man." She leaned back into her chair, draping her arms on the armrest, looking at me less doubtfully and more impressed. "Now why would you do that...unless...you need something, don't you? What do you need? How can Jenny help you?"

"Beauty *and* brains," I said, smiling at her.

"No need for flattery, Peter; I owe you. Go ahead, ask away and if I can help you, I will gladly do so."

"Fair enough," I said, leaning back in my chair. "Tell me this: are you still into the same things as before?"

"Exactly the same, and doing them the same way. Oh, we tried computers and going high tech, but once the hackers became more prevalent, we went back to pen and paper, and only when it's absolutely necessary. My people are trained to rely on their memories. I teach them to use their brains," she said, tapping her temple with her finger. "Can't be too careful with our information. The only real technology we use is the scanner that's built into the entryway doorframe and a handful of security cameras around the property. Otherwise, we stay off the grid, so to speak."

"You're telling me you and your people don't use any computer technology of any kind? Not even smart phones?"

"That's right, Peter. Why do you ask?"

"I ask because Interpol thinks you're the head of a huge international hacking organization, and they're waiting outside your gates to arrest you."

Laughing a soft, seductive, and somewhat dismissive laugh, she said, "Idiots. All of them are idiots. They couldn't track a bleeding man across white carpet."

"Maybe so, but it's true, Jenny. That's why I'm here."

"You're Interpol?"

"No, I was arrested on charges similar to the ones they have against you and used my knowledge of you and your organization to make a deal. I told them they were barking up the wrong tree with you, but they don't believe me; they trust their intelligence reports."

"So," she said, shifting in her seat and tucking her legs beneath her, "why are you here?"

"I'm here to save my neck, and in doing so, save yours," I said. "I told them you could give them something or someone else in exchange for leaving you alone. I told them there was no way you're a hacker," I leaned forward, elbows on knees, and asked, "Can you help me?"

"Tell me something first, Peter?"

"Anything."

"Are they listening to us right now?"

"Yes, they are. As a matter of fact, they're parked in a black van a couple of blocks south of here. Check it out if you don't believe me."

She snapped her fingers and the man with the scar materialized out of the darkness.

"Check it out. If there's no van we kill him."

"But I thought you said you owe me?" I protested.

"I do," she said, waving a dismissive hand at me, "but they work best if they think they might get to kill someone. Now, Peter, tell me what it is Interpol thinks I've done."

"They have evidence linking you to the hacks on Sony, Target, and JP Morgan Chase."

This time the laughter was loud and more angry than dismissive. Shaking her head from side to side, her long red locks fell into her face. Looking at me from behind the curtain of hair, her gaze turned hard as she said, "I knew doing business with that lady in Cologne would bring trouble to my door."

Her man entered the room nodding. "You want I should kill the people in the van?" he asked.

She waved him off, shaking her head, and he disappeared around the corner before she continued.

"I make one business decision based on a shared bond of womanhood and all that sentimental crap, and it lands me in Interpol's lap. Are all of you listening?" she asked, looking around at the walls and ceiling. "I only brokered the deal for the machines; I didn't use them to hack anything. The person you're looking for is Tia Reins. She's a lying little bitch."

"Tia Reins? So she's a hacker?"

Jenny composed herself by pushing her hair behind her

ears again, adjusting her sitting position, and crossing her legs.

"The best in Europe. She undoubtedly made it appear as if I were the one responsible for the hacks on the American companies. She's that good."

"And you say she's in Cologne?"

"Yes, and you should avoid her, Peter; she's not playing by the rules. Well, not any rules I'm aware of, anyway. No honor among thieves, you know? Tell me, are you in so deep with Interpol you have to help them with her, too?"

"Afraid so. My debt has yet to be paid in full, but your help makes the burden lighter."

"Well listen to me, Peter Heely. What I tell you now I tell you because she's implicated me, and I realize, albeit a little late, everything I'd heard about her is true. Honestly, I didn't want to believe the stories, but in light of present circumstances, I'm reconsidering. I don't want you to make the same mistake I made by trusting her, understand?"

"Yes, I follow."

"Now, I was told, and subsequently failed to believe, that Tia and her father, a man named Heinrich Laird, are very dangerous."

"Come on. They're hackers. How dangerous can they be?"

"No, he's not a hacker. I don't even think he knows what day it is. He's old and reclusive, like your country's Howard Hughes. No one's seen Laird since his wife was murdered. He lives on the top floor of the building that once housed his company, CCP."

"Slow down. One thing at a time. First, his wife was murdered?"

"Yes. Back in his day, Laird was a top mergers and acquisitions man, with degrees from Oxford and Cambridge and connections all over the world. He quickly amassed a fortune and a reputation for doing anything to make money. Story goes, he crossed a man named Ross Kleberg, a German businessman. Kleberg hired some men to kill Laird, but Laird's wife was killed by mistake." Holding up a hand to stop the question she saw forming on my lips, she said, "I don't know how the wife died, but I know something else."

"What?"

"Laird, so distraught over the death of his wife, sought revenge. He would have it, though it would take ten years to see it through."

"Why so long?"

"Granted, this is a story, a rumor really, but I was told Laird sent his then ten-year-old daughter, Tia, away to boarding school because she was the embodiment of his dead wife, and looking at the child was too painful. But the schools weren't normal schools. Tia was trained in the martial arts, learning Aikido first, and then mastering the ancient art of Ninjutsu. She also studied economics, finance, and apparently took to computers like a duck to water. When she returned home after her ten-year absence, her father sent her to exact revenge for her long dead mother."

"You're joking. That's completely absurd."

"Doubt me at your own peril. I've met her, and like I said, I now realize what I was seeing in those jet black eyes of hers. It wasn't compassion, or the recognition of the bond of womanhood we share, fighting our way through this male world. No. It was quite the opposite. On the day we made the deal for the computer components, I realize now I was seeing only death."

"Wow," I said, leaning back in my chair. "That's some

story. Let's say I believe you, and the father is some recluse and the daughter a hacker and a killer. I still need to answer to Interpol. Where do I find them in Cologne?"

"Wait, Peter; there's more. You must understand this Laird was once quite a brilliant man. Some say he was just a misunderstood genius. Others think he got what he deserved. I fall in the latter category, but CCP made a fortune before Laird's wife was murdered and he's been sitting on it ever since. Like a miser, he counts his pennies and checks the balance sheets daily. He's quite the paranoid, and fears for his life, choosing to operate in total secrecy. His daughter is his protector, but in addition to her, I saw three other men on the day I met her. One of the men I recognized as a former MMA fighter. Tia's a serious threat in her own regard, and her bodyguards are serious men. Don't underestimate her or them."

"Believe me, I won't. I know better than to underestimate any woman. Now, if Laird is tight with his money, tell me about this deal you brokered for the daughter? How'd she pay for the components? Does she have money of her own? Is Laird involved with whatever the daughter is doing?"

"All I know about the deal is I was contacted last year by intermediaries. I was told someone was seeking help in acquiring some very fancy computers and other components. I thought it sounded like an easy payday and charged my people with acquiring the merchandise. We were successful, and so I set the delivery date. When I learned the buyer was a woman, I thought hey, a kindred spirit, you know? I had my people do a little digging on the buyer, and they turned up everything I just told you."

"So, why didn't you believe the stories? You're a cautious woman."

"I'm very cautious, and I did believe the stories until I saw her at the exchange. There she was, this beautiful, tiny Asian woman, maybe Japanese. I just couldn't believe she was capable of the things I'd been told. Looks can be deceiving, and I of all people should know that. Anyway, she had the cash, and I made the deal. I don't know where she got her money, but I doubt dear old Dad made her a loan."

"Anything else on the daughter?"

"Other than she's the one Interpol should be after, not me."

"But there's no proof of her involvement in any of the hacks being investigated. All evidence points to you, not Cologne."

"Check your so-called evidence again," Jenny said. "It's leading you away from the real target. I guess she's so good at what she does she's fooled the computer nerds at Interpol. Is that really so hard to believe and accept?"

"No, it's not," I said, extending my hand and standing. "Thank you for your help."

She stood, her robe falling open, her silk pajamas clinging to her skin.

"Leaving so soon?"

She moved a step closer, her breast pressing against my body, stroking my arm with her hand. "Is that enough for your Interpol agents in the van or do you require more?"

"Can you tell me her address in Cologne?"

"I can do that. You'll find her office in the city center at thirty-three Portalsgasse, but must you go? Do you have to leave so soon?"

"Yes," I said. "But thank you again. Consider us even."

"Oh, how I wish you wouldn't leave so quickly!"

"Like you said, I needed help. You've helped. I don't want to involve you further."

"Are you worried about me because I'm a woman, Peter?"

"No, I know you can take care of things. I just don't like the idea of bringing trouble to your door to save my own neck, but I did, and I'm sorry for that."

"I'm glad I didn't kill you. I knew I was right about you."

"Right about what?"

"You're a good guy, Peter Heely. I thought so back then, and now I know for sure. Peter Heely, or whatever your name really is, come see me anytime. If I can help you, I will."

I leaned down and kissed her on the cheek.

"Thank you."

"Why, Peter," she said, blushing.

"I just wanted to thank you properly."

"Before you go, there is one more thing I should tell you."

"What's that?"

"After my people acquired the hardware, I was contacted by a Russian looking to make a deal. He offered me twice what Tia was going to pay. I don't know if that helps, but I thought you should know."

"Yeah, I think it does help. Thank you."

"So long, Peter Heely. My man will show you out. Oh, and if you do call on me again, just ring the bell next to the black iron door, okay?"

***

Back inside the van, speeding toward the airfield, Valerie

spoke first.

"Sounds like you've cultivated a valuable asset."

"Yeah, Dad," Leecy said. "Jenny was everything you said Jens would be, and more."

"That's great work, Granger," Wakefield added. "I thought we were going to lose you, but in the end, we got more than we thought we'd get from her. Robert was able to track down the components Jenny sold to Tia."

"That's right," Robert broke in. "Turns out, the timing of the deal she made with Tia coincides with the theft of twenty prototype computers special-built for MI5 to use in the war against cybercrime. They were stolen last year. I informed the home office, and they agree you're on to something here and have given the go ahead, as have your boys back in Langley."

"What's so special about this stuff?" Zach asked.

"Don't know, really. It's rumored to be next generation processors, or chips, coupled with some new really powerful security software, apparently very hush-hush."

"Oh," Zach said. "I see."

"Whatever," I said. "What did they make of the Russian angle?"

"Nothing new, I'm afraid. The Russians have long been rumored to be involved in all the hacking business. Just last week, a report surfaced that Russian hackers read your President's emails. Stories like that pop up every other day but eventually die out, because there's nothing to support the allegation."

"I'm guessing that's what we're going to have to do if Jenny's going to be cleared?"

"Spot on," Robert said. "We'll wipe Jenny's slate clean when you deliver this Tia and, if possible, make the Russian connection."

"I knew there was a catch."

"That's not the only catch," Valerie informed me. "We've got seventy-two hours, then they arrest Jenny and her crew."

"With that in mind," Wakefield said, "our plane is being prepared for takeoff and we'll be wheels up and in Cologne before sunrise."

"I must say," Robert began, eyeing me in the rearview mirror as he spoke, "just brilliant work in there. I guess there's something to be said for experience and all that. I don't know if a younger, less seasoned agent could've kept it together under those circumstances. How'd you manage?"

"He's the great and powerful Ron Granger," Ryan said from the back of the van. "Half-breed assassin. CIA legend. I thought everyone in this business knew that."

The tension was palpable. We'd grown accustomed to his occasional outbursts and voicing displeasure with his position within the team but to do so in front of a non-team member was a serious breach of protocol.

Robert diffused the tension; smiling a smile so bright it illuminated the dark interior of the van.

"Now that you mention it, I have heard of Ron Granger. So, that's what you look like. Forgive me for saying so, but based on your reputation I thought you'd be more, well, Native American-looking."

"Don't give it another thought," I said, looking over my shoulder in Ryan's direction, but he was looking out the window. "You can't believe everything you hear anyway. But to answer your question, I manage by trusting my teammates, as any good agent should."

"You mean trusting your wife and daughter," Ryan chimed in again. "The rest of us just sit back and watch most of the time."

"Ryan!" Wakefield barked. "Remember where you are, who you're with, and the reason we're here."

"Ten-four, Boss."

"The infamous Granger clan," Robert said, glancing back at us in the rearview mirror. "Stories about you three have been making the rounds in the intelligence community for over a year now. Pleasure to finally put faces with names."

"Like Ron said, don't believe everything you hear," Valerie said.

"We're just doing the job," I said.

"Wakefield's the real glue," Leecy added. "Can't have a great team without a great leader."

"Why don't all of you run a gear check, okay?" Wakefield said. "We'll be boarding the plane in fifteen minutes. Police the van and leave nothing behind. Ron?"

"Yes, Tammy?"

"Wash that puke-stained sweater in the sink of the airplane as soon as we're airborne or throw it in the trash."

"Yes, Boss."

***

Washing my sweater in the sink, I decided saying nothing to Ryan was the best choice for the team and what little remained of the team dynamic.

As I pushed open the bathroom door, I saw Wakefield huddled with Ryan and walked quickly past them toward the front of the plane.

"Wakefield wants to talk with us," Valerie said as I retook the seat next to her. "Got concerns. She's having Ryan move to the front of the plane so we can talk privately in the rear. She asked that all earpieces be turned in to Zach. So whatever we're about to discuss is serious, and off the record."

Touching my shoulder, Wakefield said, "You two come with me."

Following Wakefield down the aisle, we handed Zach our earpieces. I noticed Leecy seated next to him and wanted to say something. Now wasn't the time, but I did recall having talked to Valerie before about Zach and Leecy's burgeoning relationship.

At the time, Valerie explained it was only natural for the two youngest members of this elite CIA squad to find something in common with each other.

I'd understood that. They were both just a couple of kids. Zach was a nineteen-year-old graduate of MIT, and Leecy was a soon to be eighteen-year-old graduate of Yale. She'd accomplished that feat while attending part-time and taking online courses between missions. Those two kids were anything but normal or average; they were exceptional, but it didn't mean I had to be enthusiastic about what I saw happening. They were too young to get involved on a serious level. I made a mental note to have a talk with Zach.

"Have a seat," Tammy said, gesturing toward the couch in the aft section of the plane.

She sat down in the chair opposite us and began.

"I've given serious thought to the upcoming operation in Cologne. Taking the information Jenny gave us into consideration, I'm thinking about benching Leecy for the duration of the mission."

I tried to resist the urge to defend my child.

"Justification?" I asked, as softly as I could.

"Till recently, our unit has been the most successful A.D.D.T. unit in the field. We've batted a thousand, but our missions have been devoid of one vital component."

"A real threat," Valerie said.

"That's right," Wakefield said, nodding in agreement. "We've done our job accessing the data and assessing it. We've been proactive, and preempted threats before they could take shape thanks to our tactics and technology, but this time the threat is real. It's dangerous and deadly, that is, if Jenny is to be believed."

"I fail to see the problem," I said. "That's the job, isn't it? Take down the threat?"

"Yes, but setting aside Leecy's preternatural abilities and intellect, we're left with a kid that's months shy of her eighteenth birthday."

"Still don't see the problem."

"Jesus, Ron, why are you making this so difficult? When I was her age I was in high school. I think we need to take that into account before we send her into a situation where she might engage a trained killer."

Valerie stepped up.

"This type of mission is exactly what Leecy's been preparing for. To bench her now would be unfair."

"Rather than focusing on her age," I added, "why don't you justify your concern by telling us she's not ready because she's deficient in some area of her development or training? Why don't you do that? Because you can't. She's more combat ready than Hodges, Franks, and Ryan combined, and scored higher on her marksmanship skills than Valerie. But if you can point to a deficiency she has that I'm unaware of, I'll agree with your plan."

"I'm sorry," Tammy said, leaning toward us, "did I just wake up in a world where you two are in charge of this team? No, I don't think so. And I don't need to justify my decisions to either of you. This meeting was a courtesy, nothing more, because of our history," she paused, glancing at me. "I'll take your comments under advisement when making my final decision as to Leecy's status, but know this: whatever I decide will be final."

"I apologize for coming across like I was challenging your authority," I said. "I guess I was a little taken aback by your concerns."

"Me, too," Val said. "I didn't expect that from you. You've never voiced any concern about Leecy before, but I can understand your thinking even if I don't agree with it. I mean, don't forget, I was doing this stuff when I was her age."

"Yeah, I know," Wakefield said. "I know it's in her blood, but she's my responsibility and the agency has big plans for her. I don't want to bring her along too quickly." Holding my gaze with hers, she added, "I know what can happen when people are rushed into situations before they're ready."

I tried to shake off the stare and the comment.

"So, is this coming from you or from your bosses?"

Smiling that Cheshire Cat-like grin of hers, she said, "You know the answer to that and you know my hands are tied if they give me the order, which they haven't—yet."

"What are you going to do?" Val asked.

"That depends on how this thing plays out on the ground, which brings me to my next topic for discussion."

"What's that?" Val asked. "The plan?"

"Yeah, I have a few ideas, but I want to hear what you two are thinking."

"Well you both know me," I said, "and how I like to keep it as simple as possible. I say we stick with what's working and take the direct approach."

"And what's that exactly?" Tammy asked.

"I'll knock on the CCP front door."

"Justification?" Tammy asked, smiling.

"I can pose as Peter Heely, mercenary for hire, using my relationship with Jenny as pretense, and it will double as verification if Tia checks me out."

"That's thin," Valerie said.

"Okay," I said. "Then I can also use Tia and her father's paranoia against them by suggesting through my many underworld contacts I've learned they're being spied on, and who knows, maybe they really are. Maybe the unconfirmed Russian angle works to our advantage."

"Risky," Tammy said. "If you play that game and come up empty handed or they call your bluff, you'll be back on the proverbial chopping block."

"I agree, but I think the odds are in our favor, given what we know about them. Maybe someone is still looking to kill the old man. Maybe the daughter's purchase of the stolen computer components and the money she got from somewhere to pay for the components has landed her in bed with people that want to keep tabs on her. Regardless, if they aren't being spied on and haven't been hacked I can play it out long enough for Zach to actually hack into whatever system they're running."

"That's one too many maybes for my taste," Val said.

"Me, too," Tammy added.

"I concede it's high risk, but I'm not hearing anything better from you two, and given we only have seventy-two hours, we don't have time to stake out the place and find a weak spot."

"That's also true," Tammy agreed.

"You're right. I can't believe I'm agreeing with this," Val said, "but with the time constraints we're under I don't see a faster, safer way to get inside."

"Okay, we'll play it from the hip for now," Wakefield said. "Adjusting on the fly as we progress."

"And Leecy?" I asked.

"I just said nothing's set in stone. We'll have to see what happens when boots hit the ground."

"Okay, fair enough."

"But as a precaution, I'll have Zach secure all three of your identities. So if Leecy and Val join you undercover, they'll just be nameless mercenaries for hire, got it?"

"It's risky, but I don't see that we have another option," Val said.

"We don't," Wakefield said before turning toward me. "Ron, I like the idea of sticking with the Peter Heely cover. Zach will leave just enough information out there in the cyber universe to make it believable, but if Tia digs too deep it could unravel. We don't have the time or equipment to dummy up papers for any of you, let alone create a full-blown legend. You guys okay with that?"

"Understood," I said.

"If you two don't have anything else to add, I'll brief the team."

"I don't have anything," I said.

"Me, either," Val said, standing, "I'll follow you up front."

Watching Valerie following Tammy toward the front of the plane and listening as Tammy began her briefing, I recalled the event Tammy referred to earlier. The one she was thinking about when she said she didn't want to rush

Leecy into anything. I had little doubt Tammy was thinking about the first time we met.

Running the numbers in my head, I calculated CIA Agent Tammy Daniel Wakefield first entered my life twenty-four years ago. Iraq had just ended its war with Iran in 1988, and a year later in September 1989, was engaged in talks with Kuwait in Baghdad regarding border demarcations that failed. This failure to reach an accord highlighted just one of the many differences in the region between Iraq, Kuwait, and Saudi Arabia.

By the time talks were scheduled to take place in Jeddah, Saudi Arabia, US Intelligence reports coming out of the region indicated the tensions between Iraq and Kuwait wouldn't be easily resolved. The US had decided they'd waited long enough and it was time to take preemptive action.

Phase one of Operation Nighthawk, code-named Eagle Eye, was given the green light. Known only by the call sign Alpha, I made a midnight HALO jump from thirty-five thousand feet above Iraq on July 19, 1990, along with one other person, known by the call sign Bravo.

We were told to plant signal beacons—a secondary measure incase dust storms affected the Satellite Guided Missiles—ensuring strategic Iraqi military targets would be destroyed in the bombings carried out by Nighthawk stealth bombers.

When we splashed down in Lake Tharthar 120 kilometers north of Baghdad, Bravo, failing to cut away his parachute before hitting the water, became tangled in the rigging and was pulled below the surface of the lake. I remembered how hard I struggled to cut him free before having to rush to the surface of the lake or risk drowning myself.

While I treaded water above him, Bravo's parachute-entangled body disappeared into the darkness of the deep lake. I remembered wondering who he'd been. What was his name? Neither of us had been wearing dog tags or carrying anything that identified us as US citizens. We were just nameless, faceless arms of our government.

Swimming toward shore alone, I assumed Bravo was like me, at least, I'd hoped he was. Back then, I was alone in the world, and with nothing to lose, had volunteered for the mission during my last month of active duty. Looking back now, I realized the death wish I was carrying around with me at the time. Facing discharge from the army, I'd taken on that mission as an out. I was hoping I wouldn't have to face civilian life.

Once on dry land, I'd stripped off the drysuit, adjusted my ankle length dishdasha, and put on the traditional ghutra headdress. Checking my compass for the proper heading and the contents of my gear bag, I started walking out of the lake basin and up and over the surrounding mountain range. I hiked toward the southwest and my rendezvous with my in-country contact, a CIA agent named Wakefield.

Meeting Wakefield on the road to Ramadi proved to be more difficult than I'd anticipated, and I was running late, but spotted the jeep waiting for me as I crested a hill about thirty meters from the road.

"Wakefield?" I remember calling as I approached the vehicle.

"Identify," came the curt response, and I smiled at the memory of how surprised I'd been that the voice was female.

"Alpha here. Bravo's DOA."

"Body?"

"At the bottom of the lake," I said, climbing into the truck's passenger seat.

"Shame."

"Yes, it is."

"Questions?" she asked me, turning over the engine.

"None."

"Good; that's the way I like it," she said, driving away. "We'll be in Baghdad in a few hours. You know your strategic target location and extraction coordinates?"

"I know I look dumb, but I know what I'm doing."

She looked over at me, smiling that trademark smile of hers, the one I'd come to rely on years later as a CIA operative. "You sure about that, soldier?"

The memory of our first words to each other resembled every word we'd spoken to each other since, in tone, intent, and brevity. I laughed to myself, but that nostalgia quickly vanished when I remembered what happened to me next. Standing up suddenly, hitting my head on the fuselage of the plane, I realized I'd reacted involuntarily to the memory.

"Something to add to the briefing, Granger?" Wakefield asked.

Her question snapped me back to the present moment. "No, just stretching my legs."

Sitting back down, listening as Tammy continued her briefing on the mission we were about to undertake in Cologne, I flashed back on the scene near the ammunition supply depot located one mile from the center of Baghdad. That's where it happened.

I'd planted all but three of the satellite-guided devices I'd been charged with deploying, leaving one inside the munitions depot building, and was on my way to the last three spots when two members of the elite Iraqi Republican

Guard surprised me. The fight that ensued wasn't as quick or as easy as I'd hoped. It had been sloppy, and I'd been careless. Though I'd killed the guards, I'd been stabbed in the thigh and forced to abandon the rest of the mission and double-time it toward the evacuation point.

My inability to recall how I arrived at the extraction point or the CIA safe house has nothing to do with a faulty memory and everything to do with the fact I never made it under my own power.

All I remember was waking up in a bed inside the Baghdad apartment, with my leg heavily bandaged, to learn I'd lost a full seven days and that Iraq was now on the verge of invading Kuwait, having amassed a hundred thousand troops along the border. And Agent Wakefield had saved my life.

Somehow, she'd found me two blocks from the rendezvous point, passed out in a roadside ditch and bleeding to death from the wound in my thigh. She'd brought me to the safe house and nursed me back to health.

Watching her now, standing in the front of the plane addressing her team, a team which included my wife and daughter, I thought how strange fate could be.

Back then, Wakefield and I became trapped in that CIA safe house when the fighting began. The targets I'd affixed with SGMs were being destroyed by the smart bombs the Nighthawks dropped on Baghdad, and all of America watched it happen on their TV sets.

Wakefield and I lived together for almost a month in that tiny apartment. We'd found safety and security in each other's arms while the battle raged around us. We'd made love—a desperate, frightened, raw love; a love born from the circumstance and the death and destruction of war. When we finally left Baghdad and parted ways, I recall her saying only, "Maybe I'll see you again, Alpha."

And I'd responded, "You can call me Granger."

Six years passed before I saw Agent Tammy Daniel Wakefield again. By then, I was married to Valerie and reporting to the CIA farm for training.

*****

"Ron."

I heard my name and snapped myself back to the present moment. "What?"

"Pay attention; I'm about to cover emergency protocols."

"Yes," I said. "Sorry, you were saying? Emergency protocols?"

"That's right. In case of catastrophic event outside our control, stick to the CIA playbook for damage control. Does everyone understand what that means?"

"Yes," I said.

Ignoring me, Wakefield asked, "Zach, what's your damage control initiative?"

"Uh, well, my particular area involves disinformation and clean up."

"A specific example would be?"

"Well, an example would be in the case of a dead agent, I suppose. If the death is public, I'm to monitor local police activity, hack the local system, create a false identity for the dead agent to match the fingerprints the locals will take, and submit it to the IAFIS database."

"Very good," Wakefield acknowledged. "That's an extreme example and one we don't want to deal with on this mission, but it's not realistic to assume everything will go as planned. The protocol is in place for a reason."

Walking down the aisle, looking at each us, she asked, "Any questions?"

The pilot's voice came on over the speaker system, announcing our approach.

"We're on approach for Cologne; buckle up," Tammy ordered, glancing at me. "Granger! What's wrong with you? You look like you've seen a ghost."

"Yeah, I'm on it. Sorry," I said.

CHAPTER
THREE

Cologne, Germany

"Ron, we'll be close by monitoring any activity around the building and the action inside on our earpieces," Wakefield said. "If things go sideways, we'll be there."

"Got it," I said, "but I'm hoping this is an easy in and out. I think we've had enough trouble for a while."

"Agreed."

I nodded at Leecy and Val, saying my silent goodbye before opening the door to the van and walking to the address Jenny had given us. As I stood on the sidewalk in front of the building at thirty-three Portalsgasse, I looked left, seeing Hodges and Franks taking up position on the corner, and right, spotting Leecy and Val strolling arm in arm past the windows of a dress shop.

I heard a click while reaching for the door's buzzer and realized it was the sound of the front door unlocking. Scanning the façade of the semi-attached, three-story concrete building, I found the camera mounted near the roofline. It was aimed at the sidewalk and the entrance to the building, and I said loud enough for my earpiece to pick up, "Camera on the front entrance."

Inside the small, dingy lobby, I saw three doors. There was an old single-door elevator directly in front of me, flanked by frosted glass doors located on the adjacent walls.

Both sets of glass doors opened and two men joined me, crowding into the small space. The man on my right was taller and heavier than me. His bald head was covered with beads of sweat. His t-shirt was soaked through and his hands were wrapped with yellow boxing wraps. His socks sagged beneath his enormous calves. The man on my left was my height, but twenty pounds lighter. Beneath his off-the-rack suit and tie, I could see the outline of a well-muscled man. I thought these two must be the MMA-types Jenny had warned me about.

"What are you doing here?" the suit-wearing man asked me.

"Yeah, you interrupted my training," the larger man echoed, his droplets of sweat clearing away the grime on the floor, revealing the marble beneath. "Who the hell are you?"

Smiling, I extended my hand to the suit wearer, saying, "Peter Heely, and you are?"

Shaking my hand and looking confused, he answered, "Hector."

I offered my hand to the other man and repeated, "I'm Peter...and you are?"

"You don't want to know me." He had to be six foot five, weighing a heavily-muscled 250 pounds.

"What do you mean?" I asked. "Sure I do, 'cause we're going to be working together."

Hector turned to face me after staring at his partner for a long moment. He was running his fingers through his jet-black hair.

"Is that right? I'm not aware of anyone being hired."

"Oh," I said, walking between them toward the elevator,

"I haven't been hired yet, but after your bosses hear what I have to say, they'll hire me. And if you two play your cards right, I'll keep you on staff when they put me in charge."

The elevator doors opened and a third man entered. Japanese, I thought, and about my size, wearing jeans, t-shirt, and cowboy boots. He put a hand on my chest.

"Not so fast."

"Hi," I said, taking his hand off my chest and shaking it. "I'm Peter Heely."

The three men closed ranks around me.

Hector asked, "What is your business here, Peter Heely, and don't tell me some crap about being hired?"

Ignoring his question, I spoke directly to cowboy boots. "And who are you? Or are you like that guy," I gestured toward the man in workout clothes, "and going to tell me I don't want to know you?"

"That's right," he said.

"I'll ask once more," Hector said, his suit jacket flapping open as he pointed his finger at my face, revealing the shoulder holster and gun. "Why are you here?"

Looking at Hector, I answered, "Is this how you treat all your guests? I mean, you did let me inside."

"We don't appreciate people hanging around our front door," cowboy boots said, "so we allow them access and then we persuade them to go away. That is, after we make certain of their intentions for being around our building to begin with."

"I see," I said. I backed away from the three men in an effort to create space, but they matched me step for step.

"So, Mr. Heely," Hector began again as the group of three men stood shoulder to shoulder in front of me. I could smell their collective breath and the stench of sweat from the biggest of the bunch and made my move. Reaching inside Hector's suit jacket with my right hand, I relieved him of his gun.

Shoving the gun in the gut of the biggest man, I said, "You die right here right now if your buddies don't back off."

With a look of shock on his face, he raised his hands shoulder height and said, "Back off, fellas. Just back up a step."

Grabbing the big guy by the arm and pulling him in front of me, I pressed the gun into the small of his back.

"On your stomachs, all of you. Put your hands behind your heads." Jabbing the big guy in the back again, I added, "That means you too, big guy."

"Easy," Hector said. "Just take it easy, Peter. It is Peter?"

With all three men on the floor, I answered Hector.

"That's right, but it's too late to make nice. Shame, really, 'cause I wanted to be friends. But at least now you know who you're dealing with." I kicked the big guy's foot. "Isn't that right, big fella? Now, who wants to tell me with whom I need to talk to about a job?"

Silence.

"Now, fellas, I have to say I'm disappointed. First, you ruin our chances at being friends with the tough guy act. I mean, has that ship sailed, or what?" I said, gesturing with the gun as I walked around the lobby. "And now, no one wants to talk. You three are putting me in a very awkward position. So I'll tell you what I'll do. I'll ask a few questions, and if you answer me, I think we can give being friends another chance, which I prefer. If you don't answer my questions, I may have to shoot someone. Understand me?"

"Put the gun down, and this is a different discussion," the big guy barked.

"Looks like we have our first contestant on *Answer or Get Shot.*" I kicked the big guy in the foot again. "Now, I'm going to start the game with you, and since you won't tell me your name, I'll call you 'Big Guy.'" I moved a step to the left, and kicked cowboy boots in the foot, "And you, you'll be contestant number two, and I'll call you 'Cowboy,' okay?"

Silence.

"Now for the questions. If you don't answer, I shoot Big Guy in the foot, then I'll turn to you, Cowboy, and you'll get a chance to answer. But remember, the same rules apply: I ask, you answer, or I work my way up your bodies till I shoot something that's really important, like, say, the femoral artery in your thigh. If you understand the rules, let me hear you say 'I understand.'"

"I understand," rang out from Cowboy, followed by, "My name is Lee."

"Nice to meet you, Lee, but too little too late, I'm afraid."

Silence.

"First question," I said. "Who do I talk to about a job?"

Silence.

"Last chance to answer before I put a bullet in your foot, Big Guy. Who do I talk to about a job?"

Silence.

I slid back the slide on the Glock to check it, and there was a bullet in the chamber. Releasing the slide, I aimed at Big Guy's foot and was about to fire when the elevator opened, revealing a man wearing a Blues Brothers suit, white shirt, and black tie.

"That's enough of that, sir. My name is Taka." He paused, making a slight bow before gesturing toward the door on my left. "If you don't mind following me?"

I followed Taka toward the door on the left, dropping the gun on Big Guy's back.

Once we were through the frosted glass door, Taka paused in front of an interior solid steel door long enough to unlock it. The room we entered was long and narrow. I figured it was approximately half the width of the building, housing half a dozen work cubicles. Each cubicle contained an old 1980s-era desk and a computer from the early Nineties, and was covered in dust.

Following him the length of the room toward the rear of the building, I passed a wooden door festooned with a nameplate that designated the space behind as *Manager's Private Office*.

Arriving at the back of the room, and almost the literal end of the building, I waited as Taka unlocked another door. This one, also made of steel, revealed a spiral staircase.

"Please take the stairs to the top and enter the room you find there," he said. "No need to knock; you're expected."

Climbing the stairs situated in the center of the five-foot deep by twenty-foot wide rectangular space, I was surrounded by floor to ceiling swaths of red fabric. Once at the top of the stairs, I pushed open a five-inch thick, vault-like metal door. Entering the room, I was now walking toward the front of the CCP building from its rear. The overwhelming odor of incense filled the room and breathing it in reignited the dizzy feeling I'd felt after the explosion.

"Impressive watching you extricate yourself from my welcoming party," a gray-haired man said to me, gesturing at the monitor hanging from the ceiling behind me.

He was wearing a long, red, gilded robe, looking like he'd just been bathed, brushed, and polished. He was leaning against a wide, sheet-covered table on a raised platform in the center of the room beneath a large chandelier. He reminded me of Hugh Heffner at the Playboy Mansion overseeing his stable of bunnies.

"That's something I'll have to keep in mind when dealing with you, I suppose," he said. "I'm disappointed my men failed in their task, but such is life. Is it not?"

"It is not," I said, shaking off the dizziness brought on by the incense, realizing I was walking on a hardwood floor instead of the marble flooring of the floor below me. Then I saw her. She was leaning against a glass block wall that ran the width of the room behind the center platform, and looked exactly as Jenny had described. She was small, maybe five feet tall, and about a hundred pounds. Her black suit jacket, white shirt, black pants, and black leather shoes contrasted nicely against the glass blocks. She didn't acknowledge me in any way; she just stared in my direction.

"I see," the old man said. "Your life, such as it is, you don't consider that disappointing?"

"Hey, things can always be better, but I don't go around crying about it."

I watched her watching me. Then she pushed off the wall, walking in my direction, crossing the floor slowly and deliberately, drawing closer with every step. I saw dark eyes nestled deep within her pale skin, but I didn't see death; I thought I saw nothingness. Her dark hair, hanging loose around her face and on her shoulders, framed her beauty. My second thought was she was much lovelier than Jenny described. She was exquisite.

"Hello, I'm Peter Heely. And you are?" I asked, offering her my hand.

"We'll soon know exactly who you are," the robe-wearing man said, walking down the steps of the platform to join the woman who was now standing directly in front of me.

"Is that so?" I asked.

"Oh, make no mistake," the man, who I realized must be Laird, said. "You're not dealing with hired henchman any longer. You wanted to meet the people in charge? Well you have, and if you don't do what I ask of you, our two faces will be the last ones you ever see."

"Threats?" I questioned, then warned, "I don't like threats."

"My name is Heinrich Laird. This beautiful lady is my daughter, Tia. She's going to take your fingerprints. Please place the four fingers of your right hand on the iPad screen she's holding, then the four fingers of your left hand, followed by your two thumbs."

"Nice to meet you both. You can call me Peter," I said, and I did as he asked, thanking Wakefield for having my ID backstopped by Zach.

"Oh, we'll know what to call you soon enough," he said. "Till then, we can make small talk. Now, tell me something: did you notice the cubicles and computers as you entered the room below?"

Tia walked around me, leaving the room without a word.

"Yeah, I noticed."

"Do you have any thoughts as to their purpose?"

"I assume at one time they had something to do with the work you do here. What *do* you do here, by the way?"

"That's a rather obvious observation, isn't it? But yes, they are the last vestiges of my empire. I keep the room exactly like that, a time capsule, if you will, to remind me to never forget the tragedy that my greed brought upon my family."

"Your empire? What empire? And what tragedy?"

"All in due time, Mr. Heely," he said, walking around me like he was an inspector at a cattle auction. "I share that information with you only as a way of illustrating the point that I never forget anything. Men like you have been trying to kill me for decades." Stopping in front of me, he smiled and said, "You, too, will fail," then continued circling. "No, I don't think you should be concerned with my empire or tragedy. No, right now you should be concerned with one thing and one thing only."

"I'm not here to kill you; I'm here to help you. But what should I be so concerned with?"

"Why, leaving here alive, of course."

"Okay, pal, you know what? You're right; I shouldn't be here. This is a big mistake. And to think I came here to help you. No good deed goes unpunished, right?"

"Very well. Tell me, then, in your last moments on earth, why you've risked your life. I so hope you've got a good reason. I really do."

"I'm a mercenary by trade, and being good at my job, I stumbled across some information you might be interested in knowing."

"I'm listening, Mr. Mercenary," he said. "Do tell."

"That's where this gets a little tricky, see. I have neither money nor empire or job. I'm one of the great unwashed."

He laughed.

"You want to deal for your information?"

"A job or payment, but I'd prefer a job."

"I have men like you downstairs, and I don't even know if what you're selling is worth anything to me."

"I had no trouble getting past your men because they're not trained like me. They're not very good fighters, and I'll bet they're even less skilled at surveillance, counter intelligence, and protection. I can offer you so much more than those muscle heads downstairs. That alone should be enough for you to hire me."

"Your life depends not only on the information you have for sale being something that benefits me, but also on whether or not the information we gather on you matches up with what you've told me." Waving his hands around above his head, he continued, "It's happening while we speak. All those ones and zeros are flying around in cyberspace, connecting the dots of your life, coming together right now, and I'll be notified of your real name and everything else about you shortly. If I don't like what we find, it's bye-bye, Peter Heely, bye-bye."

Looking around the room, realizing the only way in or out was through the door I entered; I eased back in that direction. But I was too late; there was no escape. I heard someone enter the room behind me. Tia was walking past me, showing her father the iPad she was carrying.

"Say's here you served in the US Army," Laird read from the iPad, "and then there's nothing. It's like you don't exist."

"That's accurate," I said.

"I think we might be able to work together. Yes," he said, nodding. "I can use a man like you, but tell me: what have you been doing these last twenty years or more?"

"Surviving any way I can."

"I see. A desperate man does desperate things. Yes, I think you'll do nicely, but first, tell me the information you think to be so valuable."

"We deal for the information first."

He smiled at me before turning and walking toward the center of the room and the raised platform, saying one word. "Tia."

She crossed the room much the same way she'd done before, only this time, the beauty that had shown on her face was nowhere to be seen. A dark cloud of menace had replaced it. The sword was at my throat before I could speak.

"No," Laird said. "I think we'll have the information now, and you'll be compensated with your life."

"Okay, okay," I said, backing away from the sword, with Tia matching my movements step for step like we were dancing some macabre Tango. "I said I'd tell you. Can she back off a little?"

"Tia," Laird said calmly, taking a seat on the table atop the raised platform.

"Check your communications, Internet connections, whatever," I said, rubbing my throat where the blade of her sword had rested seconds before. "Your system is compromised. You're being spied on."

"Impossible," Tia said, spitting the word in my face before pirouetting away and leaving the room.

"Jesus," I said, still rubbing my throat. "Was that really necessary?"

"You need to know I'm very well protected," Laird said, smiling down at me from his perch like some sinister proud papa. "Among the many other skills she possesses, Tia is a master of the katana. If you're to be part of the team, you need to know I'll not tolerate insubordination of any kind."

"Message received."

Tia reentered the room holding a device in her left hand and the sword in her right. The device looked like a square octopus. The central section was a three by three by two-inch thick black box, with five cables emanating from its sides like tentacles. I was as surprised as they were to see it; I was only hoping to buy time while Zach figured out how to hack into the system. My hunches seldom paid off that big, but I'd believed what Jenny told me about Tia, and had hoped someone might find a woman like Tia worth spying on. Looking at the device Tia was holding, I assumed the cables each performed a specific function, and though it was bulky, based on the anger in Tia's eyes, it was undoubtedly effective. But the real question was: who had gotten here before us?

"This," she said, climbing the stairs of the platform and handing the device to her father, "was attached to our communication ports inside the control panel, eavesdropping on all our affairs here. Someone knows a great deal about us, now, and that's not good." She walked toward me, sword ready. "How is it you've come to know about it, and I did not? Are you the one that placed the device in our system?"

"No, I didn't place anything anywhere," I said. "I'm just much better at my job than the security detail you currently employ. Let me guess: you do all the work and security sweeps yourself, and those guys drive your cars and watch your back?"

"My software and hardware is state of the art. I designed the software myself and..." Tia started.

"Yeah, but some of that hi-tech stuff was stolen last year," I said, interrupting her. "It was made special for MI5."

"How could you know that?" she asked me, lowering her sword.

"It's the reason someone like you needs someone like me. I have the contacts and the crew to handle just this type of thing."

I walked toward the platform, leaving Tia standing where I once stood.

"So, do I have a job or not?"

"I can't just create a vacancy for you," Laird said, "but I can engage your services to ferret out the person, or persons, responsible for this breech of our system."

"Not a problem," I said. "As long as when I finish the job, the money's right. I don't normally give away for free what I can get paid to do."

Laird smiled and nodded his understanding.

"I will set aside one million US dollars as payment upon completion. Is that type of money 'right,' as you say?"

"Not bad. For that kind of payday, I can bring two more people in on the job. I have a crew I work with. Like me, they're survivors. They'll be in town tomorrow. I'll pick the best two from the group to work with me on this. Tell me, will I get access to the files on your people?"

"Slow down," Tia said. "We'll need to meet these other people first and then decide."

"Fair enough," I said, turning around to address her. "Will tomorrow before noon work for you?"

"Yes," Laird said. "I can meet your people at say ten o'clock, but I'll need to check them out, of course. Are they amenable to being fingerprinted?"

"Fingerprinting people in my line of work is never a good idea," I said, walking toward the door. "You've run my prints; I came back clean. Trust me when I say the people I work with are just like me except for one minor difference."

"And what's that?"

"They're women, so don't make the mistake of

underestimating them. One is younger than your daughter," I nodded in Tia's direction as I walked past her. She was still standing in the same place as when she'd approached me about the device she'd found, smoldering with anger. "And the other is about my age."

"I see," Laird said, disrobing as he climbed atop the table and covering his naked body with a towel. "Convince them to submit to fingerprinting, and we'll be a big happy family, okay?"

"I'll try, but listen to me and believe me when I tell you: they're killers. If you mess with them, that's just what they'll do—kill you."

Lying down on the table, Laird turned his face away from me.

"Tia might have something to say about that as well as the three bodyguards you met today. That's a lot to deal with, and no one person, or three people, is that good. No, the odds are in my favor. Now leave me, Mr. Heely. I'll see you tomorrow."

FURUKAWA

Leaving the CCP building, I took my time walking toward the crowded shopping district. It was early in the day and the skies were clear, and I didn't want to lose whomever Tia would send to follow me.

Passing Leecy and Val as they window-shopped, I nodded at their reflections and said, "Someone should be along any minute."

"We'll be behind you," Val replied, "and we'll be watching. Is your earpiece working?"

"Yeah, and keep a two-block buffer."

"Roger that," Leecy said. "It's just that we lost transmission after you went inside the building."

"Ten-four."

Entering the vibrant shopping district, the cobblestone streets were alive with sounds of Euro-Techno pop music. The smells of fresh pastry and French fries filled the air. Tourists and locals crowded the streets to overflowing, and I tried to lose myself in the mosh pit of shoppers, diners, and revelers.

"Anything?" I asked.

"Your six is clear," Val said.

"Okay," Wakefield broke in, "care to update us on what happened with Laird and Tia?"

"Sure; looks like I'm clear. Everyone reading me?"

"Check," Wakefield answered. "Sounds like you had an interesting meeting."

"So you heard?" I asked, pausing to window shop.

"We got some of it," Zach informed me. "Are they running some kind of radio frequency jamming device?"

"That's a safe assumption," I said, moving on from the window and walking toward the Cathedral.

"I'm running down the names we picked up: a Lee, Hector, and Taka, but you never got a name to go with the fourth voice we heard before the transmission cut out. Doesn't matter anyway. Without full names or pictures, I doubt I'll come up with anything useful."

"Don't go to too much trouble; I recognized three of them," I said while buying French fries from a street vendor. "Taka is an office worker of some kind. The other three guys are former cage fighters. I've seen them on Pay-Per-View events. Lee was a middleweight champ in the UFC, and Hector fought in the PRIDE fighting organization along with the one I called Big Guy."

"Great," Ryan said. "Guys that really know how to handle themselves."

"Yeah," I agreed. "This won't be a cake walk."

"Ron," Wakefield said, "what happened after you left those guys?"

"I met Tia and Laird."

"Your six is clear," Val said. "Are those two as advertised?"

"Jenny was spot on."

"That can't be all."

"No, there's more," I said, lingering a little too long over which sauce to put on my fries. "I told them I heard rumors they were being spied on, and you won't believe this, but they are. Tia found a device that was tied into their communications inside the building. We've got company on this and we need to know who that is."

"Could be whoever backed her purchase for the MI5 gear," Zach suggested.

"Or another agency like us," Val offered.

"Zach," Wakefield began, "get in touch with Leeds. We'll start running down everything Interpol's got on the possible Russian connection in all this hacking."

"It's somewhere to start," I said.

"Anything else?" Wakefield asked.

"Laird wants to meet my team tomorrow mid-morning."

"Your team? What team? Why?" Ryan asked.

"Haven't you been listening?" I said, turning around and walking in the opposite direction, seeing if I could spot Leecy and Valerie in the crowd. "Laird wants me and my team to find out who planted the device. He thinks someone's after him."

"Great, so I'm going in with you, then?"

I made a left turn into a coffee shop, depositing my uneaten French fries in a trashcan before ordering a black coffee to go. Back on the street, I answered Ryan.

"Not exactly."

"What do you mean?"

"I told Laird my team consisted of two women."

"Ron," Wakefield broke in, "that's not your call to make."

"That's right," Ryan said, agreeing with Wakefield, "I

should be the one going in. I'm the most senior agent on the…"

"Yes," I said, interrupting Ryan, then paused, sipping my coffee before finishing my thought. "We're all familiar with your title and the team's hierarchy as it relates to titles, but all due respect, you're all wrong for this."

"Who the hell do you think you are?" Ryan barked.

"That's enough," Wakefield said. "That's enough from the both of you."

"To answer your question, Ryan," I said, tossing my coffee in the trash, "right now I think I'm the guy who's being followed."

"What?" Leecy asked. "How'd they get by us?"

"He didn't get by you. He was waiting for me to come to him. I just spotted him."

"You want backup?" Val asked. "We're fifty meters back."

"No, it's just one guy. I don't want to spook him."

"Is he part of Tia's crew?" Wakefield asked.

"I'm sure he is, but he wasn't in the building."

"Evade or engage?" Wakefield asked.

"I don't know. Maybe a little of both."

"Don't," Wakefield said. "I repeat, DO NOT, under any circumstances, use lethal force. Do you copy?"

"I hear you, and I understand."

Turning around in the street, standing still, letting the crowd fan out around me, I waited for the baldheaded man to notice I'd stopped walking.

Looking in my direction with a pastry raised to his mouth, the man in the black suit, white shirt, black shoes, and tie froze mid-bite, seeing me smiling at him. I decided to have a little fun, then, and using my half-block head start, I ran.

I entered the Cathedral, joining a sightseeing tour gathering near the front entrance, and watched the doors. The man appeared about a minute after I arrived, looking around wide-eyed.

Seeing another line for the entrance to the Cathedral tower, I left the tour group queuing up for a chance to climb the stairs. Then I noticed 'Under Construction' and 'Do Not Enter' signs at the far end of the hallway on my left, and did just the opposite by entering the restricted area.

I found a set of stairs at the end of the hall and took them down to the basement of the Cathedral. I'd seen signs posted in the shopping district about the renovation project, and knew the basement was being turned into a museum of sorts, with an additional entrance being created.

I ran past the barricades in hopes of finding that new exit, but, instead, I found a dead end opening onto an excavation pit twenty feet below street level. The work was obviously behind schedule, trapping me. Running back in the direction I'd come, I spotted the man tailing me at the top of the stairwell.

I turned and began running toward the pit as fast as I could. I leapt out over the abyss toward the vertical support structure for the construction site elevator. I landed hard against the side of the structure. I felt the shockwave of pain rising from my ribcage and began sliding down the steel. Catching a cross member in my grasp, I stopped the slide and began climbing the scaffolding. Reaching the top, and painfully pulling myself over the plywood security fence, I ran for the train station. I raced toward the ticket booth and bought a round-trip ticket to Buir.

"You'll have to hurry if you want to make it, sir," the ticket lady informed me. "The train is leaving in three minutes."

Running through the station, one arm pinned to my side, and up the stairs leading to the platform, I arrived at the train just in time for the final boarding call. I found a window seat in the empty coach class car and breathed deeply. I watched the platform for the man in the black suit and was just about to relax when, at the last minute, the bald man boarded the train and sat two rows behind me.

Arriving in Buir thirty minutes later, leaving the train hurriedly, I made my way down the stairs to the main station area and into the men's restroom. The room was empty except for the janitor who was leaving just as I entered. I walked into a stall, counted to one hundred and then exited. I was washing my hands when the bald man entered the restroom.

Using the wall of mirrors, I watched him go into a stall. I listened, and realized he was doing exactly what I'd done; he was just standing there. When the door opened, we made eye contact in the mirror.

"You know," I said, smiling at his reflection in the mirror, "I have a rule."

He looked around briefly, as if asking *are you talking to me* before responding.

"I'm to be concerned with your rule?"

Ignoring the question, I continued.

"My rule is: if I see a man once, that's okay, and I saw you in the shopping district when I bought my French fries. You were inside the pastry shop watching me through the window. But at the time, I figured I've got nothing to worry about from you. You're just some guy buying a donut."

He said nothing, just washed his hands, smiling back at me all the while.

"Now, if I happen to see that same man again, I pay

attention. And what happens? The harmless pursuer of pastry shows up outside the coffee shop, donut in hand, where I just happened to be buying coffee."

"Sir," he said, drying his hands under the blower, "might I offer you some advice? Seek professional help. You're paranoid. This is all a harmless coincidence. That's all."

"And now you're here," I said, walking past him toward a hand blower located near the door. "A coincidence? Well, maybe, and you know what? I'd be inclined to agree with you if this, right here right now, wasn't the fourth time I'd seen you today. And this," I paused to lock the door before turning to face the bald man, "is the part you should be concerned with."

Driving a right front kick in the direction of his left hip, I was surprised by his quickness. Partially blocking the kick, but still absorbing enough of the blow, he spun away from the sink.

We ran toward each other. Keeping my elbow low, protecting my ribs, we exchanged a quick succession of punches, elbows, and knees. We locked in a clinch, and both struggled to find leverage.

Gaining a slight advantage, I hip tossed him to the floor and he landed hard on his shoulder. My ribs screamed at me. Moving as quickly as I could into a side headlock, I held on with all I had left until he lost consciousness.

***

"One, two, three dunks," I said, pushing his head into the toilet. "Time to wake up. Rise and shine."

He kicked his legs desperately to free himself. He was

bucking like a horse trying to throw me off his back. Realizing the bucking was an exercise in futility, he stopped moving.

"Why don't we start with an easy question?" I said. "I've searched you and found nothing except a few Euros. What's your name?"

"Furukawa," he said spitting a mouthful of toilet water back into the commode.

"Why are you following me, Mr. Furukawa?"

"She wants to know everything you do, and everything about you."

"Who? Tia?"

"There's no one else."

"Okay, fair enough. I'm going to let you go. Stand up, but if you try to fight me again, I'll do far worse than stuff your head in a toilet. Do you understand?"

"Yes, but only for now. We'll see each other again."

Before I carefully began untangling myself from Mr. Furukawa, I squatted low, almost sitting on his back, forcing his arms skyward to reinforce in his mind the predicament he was in.

"Sounds ominous. Should I be worried about letting you go?"

"No, I said next time," he blurted through gritted teeth. The pain evident on his face and in his words, "But when that time comes, don't count on the element of surprise working for you. I'll be ready."

I straightened my legs and his arms slid off my knees. I leaned against the closed stall door.

"I'll keep that in mind."

He sat on the floor, his back against the commode, wiping his face with his jacket's pocket square.

"She will find out all there is to know about you, and

then kill you."

"Say it isn't so. And to think I was looking forward to working with her."

"Make your jokes, but I'm telling you the truth."

"Okay, say I believe I'm marked for death, what harm is there in telling me what she and her old man are up to?"

"No harm," he said, grinning up at me, "but I don't know anything to tell you."

"Want to try again?"

He laughed and shook his head.

"You Americans think you have all the answers, yet you're clueless. I'm not going to help you, Mr. Peter Heely. You want to know what she's doing, ask her yourself or figure it out. I really don't care which path you choose; all paths end the same. You will be dead."

I could hear the pounding on the locked bathroom door. I was running out of time.

"That's it, then? That's all you got? Threats?"

"Not threats, Mr. Heely, promises. You should reconsider your current course of action. Do yourself a favor and take some time off. Go on vacation. Nothing good will come from involving yourself with Tia and her plans."

"And how is it you're alive?"

"Ah," he said, smiling again, "I proved my worth to her."

"Do I want to know how?"

Grinning up at me, he laughed again.

"Tales for dead men, Mr. Heely. You will know soon enough."

I opened the door to the stall and walked away.

"If I catch you following me again, you'll be the dead man. And while I'm thinking about it, tell your MMA guys to stay away from me, too."

I unlocked the door to the bathroom, and a handful of kids rushed past me toward the urinals. I jogged through the station, boarding the train for the return trip to Cologne.

Thirty minutes later, I was walking toward the hotel and said, "Granger here. Anybody listening?"

"Yeah, we got you," Ryan said.

"Anything on Furukawa?"

"Zero," Zach answered. "I ran the name through all the databases; got nothing back."

"Well, I guess we have tomorrow to look forward to. Leecy and Val, ready for the ten o'clock meeting?"

"Ready," Val said.

"Roger that," Leecy replied.

"I just want to take this opportunity," Ryan began, "to once more, and for the record, register my complaints about this mission formally, and with witnesses present."

"Dully noted," Wakefield said. "That's enough, Ryan."

"As long as you're aware of my strenuous objection to the operational line up and planning, and that I think, though she's shown improvement over the past sixteen months, Leecy Granger is still green and the wrong choice for this assignment."

"Okay, that's enough!" Wakefield said. "Need I remind you it's your colossal screw up that almost killed Ron and gave Russia all the reason they needed to invade the Ukraine? Let's not forget about that. And while I'm on the subject, I just received an update. Putin is sending in forces. NATO spotters report unmarked, green army vehicles with heavy tarpaulin covers, towing howitzers, crossing into Eastern Ukraine today. I could argue that's on you, Agent Ryan. So, unless there's anything anyone wishes to add, let me close by saying from this point forward all objections will be submitted in writing and in triplicate."

Silence.

"Ron," Val said. "I'm waiting for you in room two-thirty-seven at the Marriott. The hotel is a couple of blocks north of the train station."

"Roger," I said, and then without thinking asked, "Where's Zach?"

"I'm bunked with Ryan," Zach answered. "Why do you ask?"

Feeling a little embarrassed, I covered nicely, saying, "Just curious who ended up with the short straw."

"Ron, that's uncalled for," Wakefield said. "Tomorrow morning, my suite, briefing at oh-seven hundred. Everyone is to be present and accounted for. That's an order. Ron, I'll expect a thorough accounting of today's events."

MERCENARIES FOR HIRE

"Focus, people," Wakefield said. "Now that we know all the players, it's important everyone be up to speed. I know it's early and everyone's tired, but if we can just run through it one more time so I know you have it, that would be great."

"Hodges, Ryan, and I rotate surveillance on CCP every fifteen minutes," Franks said.

"I'm monitoring communications," Zach said, "and searching for a way to overcome the jamming signal."

"When we're finished at CCP," Val said, "we make our way to the cable car ride at Rhine Park for debriefing."

"And remember, under no circumstances do any of you use lethal force. We're out on a limb, here, and everything we do is under a microscope."

"Ten-four," I said.

"Roger that," Leecy added.

"Got it," Valerie chimed in.

Checking the time on her watch, Wakefield said, "It's a long walk; best get moving."

As we left the hotel, walking south through the train station, I saw the sign for Starbucks and asked, "Coffee, anyone?"

"Sure," Val said. "I'd rather be late than punctual."

"Why's that?" Leecy asked as we entered the coffee shop.

"Good question," Val said. "I don't like appearing too eager when I'm undercover, and I like rocking the boat whenever I'm operating on the target's turf. I want them off their game, so to speak."

"You want them to be pissed at you?"

"If that's what you want to call it, sure."

With drinks in hand, we found an empty table in the most remote corner of the café. Signaling the girls to turn off their earpieces, I waited for the lady seated on the couch opposite our table to finish the last of her muffin and leave before I shared what was on my mind.

"We need to discuss something before this mission goes any further," I said.

"What's that?" Leecy asked.

"Look," I said, pausing, sipping my coffee. "It's your career, and your life, and you should pursue them both the way you want. You've never given your mother or me any reason to doubt your decision-making abilities. You're intelligent beyond my ability to comprehend, motivated, and determined. I don't want to stick my nose in your business, and have fought the urge to do just that for as long as I can."

"And what?" Leecy asked. "You're sticking your nose in my business somehow?"

"That's exactly what I'm going to do."

"Hello, walking contradiction," Leecy said. "Who are you, and what have you done with my father?"

"That's my problem, see, I'm allowing that part of me, the dad part, to creep into the operational side of me."

"Really? That's news to me. Since when?"

"Don't be silly," Val said, sitting across the table from Leecy. "He's fought that internal battle since we started working with you."

"You're joking," Leecy said. "I haven't noticed him being overly protective or anything remotely like that. He's been Ron Granger. You know, tough guy and all that stuff."

"Yeah, well don't ever confuse what he does for a living with who he is. Besides, he unloads all those gooey daddy emotions on me, and until recently that's been enough. But I think the concerns are mounting, and he needs to, no, *we* need to get them off our collective chest. Cut us both a little slack. Neither he nor I want to interfere if we don't have to. We feel we have to."

"Hold on. So this is coming from both of you now? You both have concerns?" Leecy asked, looking between Valerie and me. "Well, let's hear it. Let's lay all the Granger cards on the table this time."

I squirmed in my seat then asked, "Tell me about you and Zach?"

Leaning away from me and against the glass wall, Leecy looked across the table at her mother as she answered.

"There's nothing to tell. We're friends. That's all."

"That's all? Really?" I asked.

"Yes, Dad, that's all, and why are you choosing now to talk about this? I know I said lay all the cards on the table, but I didn't think personal stuff was in play. Shouldn't we be talking about the mission at hand?"

Nodding my head, I said, "Yes, of course we should, and we will, but you have to admit we're not the normal sit around the dinner table talk about our day type of family, are we?"

"No, I suppose we're as opposite of that as we can be."

"And it's not every day I almost get blown up, and well, that near-death experience, though I've had one's similar to it in the past, was my first as a father. And you and Zach have been on my mind, and I wanted to know if there was anything between you two."

"That's why you asked where he was last night? You thought he was in my room?"

"No, I didn't think that," I said, embarrassed having not considered the full repercussions of having asked that question last night. I managed to stammer out, "Look, I know you're a...you're right. I'm sorry."

"It's okay," she said, patting my arm, letting me off the hook, "but Zach and I are just friends. Nothing else is going on with him, okay? Maybe one day, but not now."

"Okay. Thank you, and I'm sorry for that. I don't know why I get so tongue tied with you and your mother when in any number of dangerous situations; I'm in perfect control. I'm sorry I brought it up. Whatever you and Zach are or aren't to each other is not important. What is important is I...just know...I want you to be happy."

"Easy, big fella," Leecy said, continuing to pat my arm. "All this from a little explosion? Wow, don't worry about it, Dad, it's okay. I'm not upset, but," she paused, looking across at Valerie then back at me, and continued, "you said concerns, plural. Tell me what's really on your mind, 'cause it's not my love life."

"Like your father said, I, too, battle keeping 'Mom' out of operational issues, but there's one thing I can't remain silent about."

"What's that?"

"The rule against the use of lethal force."

"So this is what you two have been building toward? Me breaking the rules?"

"Yes. I mean, no, I don't want you to break the rules," I said, leaning closer to her, "but I need you to go into CCP prepared to do whatever you have to do to ensure you come back out alive."

"I agree," Leecy said. "But if I disobey a direct order and use deadly force, it's game over, Leecy and game over for the Grangers."

"Maybe so," Val responded, "but you'll be alive."

"You forgot to add, and out of work, and my career with the CIA is over. Is that what you want?"

"No; absolutely not. We just want you to be safe and prepared to handle anything, not cautious and reluctant."

"But deadly force? I don't think Wakefield's joking around about that one. You heard her; we're way out on a limb here and under a microscope. I break the number one rule, and I don't think I'll get a second chance."

"Even Ryan gets second chance after second chance," I countered.

"Ryan just runs his mouth, that is, until recently," Leecy said, pushing back. "Sure, it borders on insubordination, but when he stops talking there are no dead bodies at his feet."

"It's your call," Val said. "We just wanted to make sure we voiced our opinion. We know you'll use your best judgment."

"I will," Leecy said, assuring us.

***

We ate, drank, and talked about everything but the job, and for the first time in almost two years, behaved like the family I remembered us being before the events of that summer. Realizing how much I'd missed the normalcy, I wondered if we'd made a mistake embarking on this career as freelancers and joining our daughter's A.D.D.T. unit.

Pushing the doubt away, I checked my watch and saw it was just after 10 a.m. I knew they'd be coming for us soon. Surveying the crowded train station, I noticed Furukawa sitting on a bench, watching us.

"Time to flip the switch," I said. "We'll be in play any minute. Remember, I'm Peter Heely."

"Yeah, I know, but how do you know it's on?" Leecy asked.

"The man who followed me last night is watching us. Check your nine o'clock. See the bald man dressed like one of the Blues Brothers?"

"Yeah, I see him."

"If he's there, his friends can't be far away. Are you ready?"

"Ready."

"Good, 'cause here they come."

Looking through the glass wall over Leecy's shoulder, I watched Hector and Lee approach the Starbucks from across the square. They entered quietly, opening their suit coats and displaying their guns briefly before waving us over.

"As a one-time courtesy," Hector said, following us out of the Starbucks and across the square to a waiting Mercedes sedan, "I'll allow this one misstep, but from now on, be where you're supposed to be, and be on time."

"That's very kind of you," I responded, opening the rear door for Valerie and Leecy, "but until I'm paid to be somewhere," I paused, taking a seat. "I'll do as I please."

"Who are your friends?" Big Guy asked, making his presence known behind the wheel.

"Didn't we cover this yesterday?" I said. "No names, remember?"

He was looking at Leecy like she was the appetizer and Val the main course.

"Whatever." Then, looking Val over, "You've got real pretty friends."

"So, what's on the agenda today?" I asked in an effort to change the subject.

"You know. You three are; that's what," Lee said, sliding to the middle of the front seat and staring at Leecy. "Laird's waiting to meet the new people you said you'd be bringing to the office, and when he sees them he'll be very pleased. He's got a thing for the young ones. Ever seen his masseuses?"

"You're both disgusting," Leecy said.

"You have no idea," Big Guy said, laughing, "but you might find out. You never know. You and I might become best friends."

"Okay," Hector said, squeezing in the front seat next to Lee, "that's enough. You two turn around and face front. There's a time and place for that and this isn't either."

The Mercedes cruised through the streets of Cologne, coming to a stop in front of the offices of CCP.

"Same place as yesterday," Hector said, stepping out of the car and opening the rear door for Valerie. "Tia and Laird are waiting. Taka will escort you."

Opening my own door, I climbed out of the back seat and leaned inside the open front driver's side window.

"I've decided if someone has to die today, it's going to be you, Big Guy."

As I entered the open door of thirty-three Portalsgasse I heard him yelling, "Fuck you!" as he drove away, but I was too busy noticing the electronic locking mechanism on the door to care. The lock looked like one of the new hotel room locks that utilize RFI chips embedded in the keycards. The ones you don't insert, but just touch to unlock the door.

"Please, will you follow me?" Taka said. He was waiting for us inside the lobby.

Leading us through the downstairs time capsule of an office and opening the rear door, he showed us to the spiral staircase. We climbed the stairs without him, entering Laird's private suite.

"Ah, Mr. Heely," Laird said by way of a greeting. He was lying on his stomach on the elevated table in the center of the room. "So good of you to come, but you're late. I don't like being kept waiting; I've a schedule to maintain."

"It's not like we had a choice," I responded. "Your goons saw to that."

He was in the final stages of a massage session under the hot light of the chandelier. I knew it was hot, because both Laird and the young lady were covered in perspiration.

Leecy, nudging my elbow, nodded in the direction of the far end of the room. Following her gaze, I saw Tia Reins standing in the shadows near a small bed. I hadn't noticed the bed yesterday. That corner of the room had been poorly lit, almost invisible, but not today.

I could see Tia was wearing the same dark suit she'd worn the day before. I wondered why no change of clothes. She didn't strike me as the type to repeat outfits. Maybe the suit was some kind of uniform. I logged the information and would think about it later.

With the light from the chandelier stretching to all four corners of the room, I looked away from Tia, inspecting the space. I realized Laird's suite was a perfect rectangle, with the elevated table at its center. The wall of glass blocks bisected the room at about three-fourths of its length, shielding the bath area from view. The small bed, where Tia stood, was nestled in the far right hand corner, its headboard against the glass block wall. The swaths of red floor-to-ceiling fabric, covering three of the four walls, made the room look like a staged production set and not a real living space.

Laird was sliding into the red robe with the help of his masseuse when he noticed me looking around.

"Do you know what curiosity did to the cat, Mr. Heely?"

"Yes," I answered as the young female masseuse walked past the three of us and exited the room. "I know what curiosity did to the cat, but I'm no less curious about your life here. Tell me something, do you ever leave this room?"

"Curiosity is a good thing, but be warned, I have limits and you three are right up against them. To answer your question, yes. On occasion, I've been known to leave here and walk downstairs to be reminded of the past, but I haven't done that in many years. I have everything I need here but, more importantly, I have nothing I don't need."

"Is that a riddle?"

"No, it's a statement of fact, and it's a way of life. Simplicity, I discovered after my wife's untimely death, is the pathway to clarity, focus, and eventually, peace of mind."

"Your wife? The tragedy. I forgot... I'm sorry."

"No need to apologize. That was a long time ago. She passed, but not before giving me a daughter to remind me of her."

"At least you have each other."

He was smiling and walking down the stairs when he replied, "Kindness from a mercenary is unexpected, and I appreciate the sentiment. You see," he said, eyeing Leecy and Val, "I lost my lovely bride and unborn son in a tragic car accident."

"That's horrible," Leecy said.

"Yes, yes it was, and perhaps next time you three are scheduled to meet with me you can show an equal amount of kindness by being punctual. I'd hate to have to make an example of one of you, but I will if you ever keep me waiting again."

"My apologies," I said. "That won't happen again."

"Let's hope not, for your sake."

"If you don't mind my asking, what's the reason for the massages and the hot lamp above the table?"

Laird, standing in front of Valerie, looked her up and down before answering.

"The chandelier is not a heat lamp; it's made entirely of Japanese chakra crystals warmed by the rays of the sun via a skylight. The crystals have tremendous healing power over me," he said, reaching out his hand to greet Valerie. "But enough about me. Who do we have here? I'm Laird."

"Pleasure to meet you," Val said. "I work with Heely."

"Oh, that's right. I forgot. Heely did mention you ladies wouldn't be using your names. I'd so hoped he was not serious, but I see he was. That won't do, I'm afraid. No, that won't work for me at all. Tia?"

"Look... Laird, is it?" Val asked.

"Yes."

"Peter said the deal was contingent on you meeting us. Well, consider that done. I don't do names, and neither does she," Val concluded, nodding toward Leecy.

"Hmm," Laird said thoughtfully. "And this is the team?" he asked as Tia sidled up behind him. "I must verify you're who you claim to be or we can't do business. Tia, here, needs to take your fingerprints."

"They're the best in the world at what they do," I said. "You can trust me on that."

"I trust no one but my daughter, Mr. Heely. My life is on the line, here. We've been infiltrated, and I need certain assurances to feel safe. One of those assurances is that I need to know whom I employ. I can't run the risk of hiring one of my enemies' thugs. You must understand that. Now, either these two ladies submit to fingerprinting, or I'll force them to submit."

"That would be a horrible mistake," I warned.

"This one," Laird said, disregarding my warning and gesturing at Leecy with his chin. He snapped his fingers, "She'll go first, and you know what? As an added bonus, I'll teach her the meaning of punctuality while I'm at it."

Hearing the door opening behind me, I turned to see Big Guy entering the room.

"I need her prints," Laird said, pointing a long pale finger at Leecy. "Make that happen. I don't care how it's done. Bring me her fingers if that's what it takes. Then you can do with her as you like." He paused as if a thought just occurred to him, then continued. "I want these mercenaries taught a lesson. When you've finished with the girl, kill her. Then the other two will know who they're dealing with. After which, I doubt I'll have a problem with them being obedient, submissive, and timely. Yes! That'll do nicely," he bellowed, walking toward his platform.

Big Guy wrapped his beefy arms around Leecy, pinning hers to her side, and rested his chin on her left shoulder near her ear.

"Not a problem, Boss. I'll have her prints in no time." And then to Leecy, "Don't worry; I'll be gentle with you. I want to take my time."

Leecy kicked her left leg up and back, sending the toe of

her boot smashing into his left eye. The big guy stumbled backward, covering his face and his screams with his hands. Leecy, free from his grip, sent a spinning heel kick crashing into his right knee.

The sound of Big Guy's medial collateral ligament exploding under the impact of the blow was audible to everyone in the room. Falling to the floor, he landed on his side with one hand reaching for his knee and the other covering his bleeding eye. Leecy rushed forward, grabbing a fist full of his hair and pulling his head back, exposing his neck. She crushed his trachea with one punch. She let go of his hair and his head bounced once off the hardwood floor like a deflated ball.

It happened so fast no one had time to intervene. The man was dying on the floor before Tia could draw her sword. She was yelling for Leecy to stop, but Valerie, faster with her Glock 17, was pointing it in Tia's face without taking her eyes of her daughter.

"Gun beats sword," Val said. "Not another step."

"Enough!" Laird bellowed. "Just stop! Everyone stop."

"She puts the sword away," Val countered, "or I'll put two bullets in her head."

"There'll be none of that," Laird ordered. "Tia, it's over. Put the sword away, and Madame, please lower your weapon."

"No fingerprinting and no names, that's how we operate," she said, draping an arm around the neck of her daughter.

"If that's how you wish to proceed, I can make an exception this time. It's fine with me. Names aren't germane to the process, anyway," he said, walking up the stairs to his table, visually shaken and muttering. "So young to be so deadly, and with no weapon. Well, none other than her body, that is." Then talking louder, he added, "I must say, you made me pay for my arrogance. I won't make that mistake again, I can assure you."

"And I can assure you if anyone touches me I don't want touching me," Leecy said, "they'll suffer a similar fate."

"That, young lady, I do not doubt," he said, still shaking as he climbed the last stair to his perch. "Now," he said, taking a deep, calming breath before sitting down on the edge of the table, "let us commence with the business at hand."

"That's what we're here for," Val said. "But you keep sword lady away from me, deal?"

"Not a problem. Oh, that reminds me," he said, turning to Tia, who was standing by the small bed again. "Dear, we need to upgrade our security measures; she has a gun. And call the boys up here to remove the body."

Tia nodded, then picked up an iPad that was lying on the bed next to her and began typing.

"You see," he continued, turning his attention back to us, "we don't get any visitors here. As a matter of fact, the last time anyone other than my usual staff entered this building was so long ago I can't even recall who it was." The door opened, and Laird paused as Hector and Lee struggled to remove the body of the big guy. Laird picked up the conversation where he'd left off as the door closed behind me. "Before that, we were just a simple company with no reason for security measures. But you don't care about that, do you? No, I didn't think so. Let's get to business, shall we?"

"The sooner the better," I said. "This room gives me the creeps."

Looking wounded by my statement, he said, "I'm sorry to hear that. This room, as I've said, brings me peace of mind. Anyway, on to the matter at hand, right now I need you to do something for me."

"Something?" I asked. "What kind of something?"

"I need you three to find out who planted the device we discovered yesterday. Then, once you've found them and discovered for whom they're working, I want you to kill them all."

"Murder? For planting a device?"

Scoffing at me, he asked, "And what do you call what the young lady just did, if not murder?"

"I call it self-defense," Leecy answered. "What do you call telling someone to do with me as they wish?"

"I call it a mistake, but I was only hoping to scare you into being compliant with my orders."

"We could've just agreed to disagree and gone our separate ways. Don't make me the bad guy because you told that giant he could have his way with me, and I stopped that from happening."

"Point taken."

"Look, Laird, we don't kill indiscriminately," Val said. "But we'll find the people responsible, and then you can send the rest of your goons to deal with them as you like."

"That won't do," he said. "That won't do at all. I thought people like you were morally compromised and would do just about anything for money."

"People like us? You mean mercenaries?"

"Yes, you know that's what I meant."

"I suppose there's some truth to that. My moral compass can be made to point in a different direction for eighty pounds of US currency."

"Eighty pounds? That's what..." he said, closing his eyes and running the numbers in his head, "four million dollars? That's ridiculous. How about you do what I require or I kill all of you?" he countered. "Is that a good enough reason for you three?"

Laughing, Leecy answered him. "No, it's not a good enough reason. And it's an empty threat. You should be the one worried about dying. We can kill you and the girl over there right now. We walk out of here and just disappear. Agree to pay us what we ask, or we'll be on our way."

"What's the real number?" he asked. "Four million is too much."

"Two million, US," I said.

"That's still a ridiculous sum. I can have it done for half that amount."

"Then call the people that work cheap and pay them half. If you want us for the job, it's two million. Take it or leave it. You've got exactly sixty seconds to decide and then we're gone."

"You're a tough negotiator, Mr. Heely. No real give and take to be had here."

"You can just call me Heely. Thirty seconds."

There was a hint of laughter before he waved his hands.

"Okay, okay. You win. Round one goes to you. Enjoy the moment; it won't happen again." He lay on his back under the light emanating from the crystals. "How long will you require to complete the job?"

"In anticipation of your asking me to do this for you, I started the ball rolling last night. We'll be wrapping this up in forty-eight hours or less."

"Really? That's very good news. I'll tell you what I'll do. If you make it thirty-six hours, I'll kick in another half a million-dollar bonus. How's that sound?"

"Sounds like easy money," Leecy answered.

"How do you want it done?" Val asked. "Discreetly? Or do you want to send a message?"

"Privately. Quietly. Don't draw attention to it. Just make them disappear. But I'll require proof."

"What sort of proof?" Val asked.

"Oh, nothing too complicated, just a picture of you three with the corpses."

"You're joking," I said. "If we do that, you'll have proof we killed a man, or men, and we'll be beholden to you forever. I don't like that."

"No, you misunderstand me. I don't want to keep the pictures for any future use or blackmail. Tia will explain how it works. She's developed a computer program that'll erase any proof you share with me. But I'm afraid without the proof, there's no deal. What do you say?"

"Then there's no deal," Leecy said.

"I beg your pardon?" he said, sitting up on the table. "I agreed to your terms. You can't agree to my one stipulation?"

"Sorry, you misunderstand me. I'm still negotiating terms."

"Proceed, young lady."

"I'll produce a picture, a Polaroid, and then I'll burn it. We don't do smart phones, computers, or email. Too risky."

"Okay, that's fine with me."

"But wait, there's more. I don't come back here once I leave. There's only one exit from this room, and you've got those goons lurking about. No, when the job's done, we meet in public. I understand you don't go outside, but you can send Tia to the meeting. Agreed?"

"I don't like it. That's not how I do things. But just for curiosity's sake, where would you like to conduct business if not here, young lady?"

"I've got a couple of places in mind, but nothing definite right now. We'll let you know when and where. Maybe Peter will drop by to tell you. Regardless, when we figure out the particulars, just send Tia with the money and we'll provide the proof. Take it or leave it."

"I'll take it, but don't just run away after it's done, cash in hand," he said, lying back on the table and opening his robe. "I may have other business that requires your attention. Now, if there's nothing else, you're dismissed."

***

We were making our way down the spiral staircase after leaving Laird's room when we heard from above us, "Don't go that way."

I turned to see Tia beckoning us back up the stairs, and Leecy asked, "You want us to follow you? What, do we look stupid?"

Shaking her head, Tia said, "It's not like that. I just want to talk."

Climbing the stairs, we followed Tia behind the red curtains into a computer room.

"What's this place?" I asked.

Ignoring me and smiling at Leecy, Tia said, "You're quick. I like that. And smart. I like that even more. I can see now how valuable you and your teammates can be to my organization."

"Your organization?" Leecy asked. "I thought CCP was your father's business."

"CCP is defunct. My father hasn't worked in twenty years or more. Don't concern yourself with him. I, however," she continued, waving her hand at the computers and workers in the room, "can offer you a permanent position with my growing organization. This position is highly lucrative, and will allow you three to stop living job to job for a change."

"Sounds too good to be true," Leecy said. "And we know what that means."

"Smart girl. Sure, it pays to be cautious," Tia purred, "but hear me out before you rush to judgment."

"Well? We're listening."

"All you have to do for me is not find the people who planted the device."

"I'm sorry," Valerie began, walking toward one of the metal cages, "did I just wake up and miss something? I was under the impression you worked for dear old Dad. You don't? And what is this place? What organization? And the cherry on top of this shit sundae is you're asking us to walk away from a two million dollar payday. Like I said, sorry, but lady, that's one too many unanswered questions."

"Fair enough. Let me begin again. I don't work for my father; I work for myself, and if all goes well, soon I'll head a much bigger organization. What you see before you is just a hobby when you compare it to what I've been offered. And now, I'm offering you a job. Do you want it or not?"

"Slow down," I said. "We don't even know what you do or what the job is yet. What do you do exactly?"

"I'm a computer hacker, and a very good one."

"I bet all you hackers say that. We're not computer people. We have no way to know if you're legit or not. Why should we believe you?"

"Fair enough, Mr. Heely. Come over here," she said, walking past Valerie. She picked up an iPad from a small desk in the center of the room, then with the wave of a keycard she opened a cage. "Keep your eyes on that monitor," she added, pointing at a flat screen mounted on a pole inside the cage. She was typing on her iPad. "I'm slaving this screen to my iPad," she explained. "Keep watching the monitor."

The JP Morgan Chase emblem appeared on the screen for a second before being replaced, albeit briefly, with a picture of the CEO, and then numbers filled the screen.

"Okay, so you hacked JP Morgan Chase," I said. "You're a hacker. So what?"

"Oh, Peter," Leecy said. "Do you know what you're looking at?"

"No, I don't."

"But that's impossible," Leecy said, continuing to stare at the screen. "JP Morgan Chase only reported the theft of email accounts. But that's not emails. Those are account numbers, amounts, and access codes for every client handled personally by the CEO."

"That's correct," Tia said. "And for now, JP Morgan Chase's computer security has successfully blocked my attempt to liquidate those accounts, but what they don't know is that I'm still in the system. In two days' time, I'll have enough computing power at my disposal to bypass their new security measures and drain the accounts you see listed here, along with every single JP Morgan Chase holding."

"But that's impossible," Leecy said.

"If you believe that, then keep an eye on the news coming out of America, and I guarantee in three days, JP Morgan Chase will be begging your President for another bailout."

"Amazing," Val said, "truly amazing. And terrifying. What else have you done? Are you behind the Target attack, too?"

Smiling a toothy grin, Tia said, "Yes, of course I am. I'm behind all the attacks being reported in the US, including Sony."

"If that's true, then you're really good, because the Secret Service and the FBI are chasing their tails blaming Chinese hackers."

"Yes, I know. It's what I want them to think."

"And investigating who planted the device in your system somehow interferes with what you're doing?" Leecy asked.

"Yes, that's correct. My partner insists on complete anonymity. I can't afford to have you three poking around, but as I've said, I would employ you to work for me, instead."

"Sorry," I said, "but we made a deal with Daddy."

"Deals are made to be broken, Peter," Tia said. "Mercenaries have no loyalty; they work for the highest bidder."

"So, what? You're making a counter offer?"

"I'll have a significant counter offer for you, but I'll need time to put the funds together, and that might take me forty-eight hours. I want you to know the offer I'll be prepared to make at that time comes with a job description and a future. But for your more immediate needs, I can most certainly match Father's offer, in cash, and pay you up front. Call it a signing bonus."

"Why?"

Tia looked hard at the three of us, like she was deciding how much to tell us before answering.

"I've told you more than I should already. Peter, here, has proven to be knowledgeable about details of my business I thought were secret, and I'm willing to pay you three to prevent you from learning anything more. Does that answer the question to your satisfaction?"

"No, but it's an answer."

"One more thing," Val asked, walking toward Tia. "Where are you getting the money? Stealing it from dear old Dad, or this partner you mentioned?"

Stepping forward to meet Valerie toe to toe, Tia answered. "No, I'm not stealing from Father, but that's all you need to know. What do you care where the money comes from as long as you get paid?"

"Okay, message received," Leecy said, separating the two women. "We'll take our money and be on our way."

"Hold on," Tia said, startled. "I never said I had the money on me. I'll have to get it together, and that will take some doing. Give me till seven o'clock tonight?"

"Okay, but at seven oh-one, we start looking for the people that planted the device."

"Fair enough. Meet me outside the northern entrance of the train station at seven o'clock. I'll have the money, and I'll even throw in two black duffle bags free of charge. Will that work for you?"

"Sure, that works."

Satisfied, Tia looked at me as if for the first time, and said, "I didn't notice the bruises on your face when we were upstairs. Get into a little scrape, did we?"

"Nothing I couldn't handle."

"Oh, of that I'm sure," she responded before turning to lead us out of the computer room.

Walking behind her, I could see the tip of the scabbard beneath the hem of her suit jacket. Looking at Val, walking beside me, she nodded her head as she noticed it too.

"So, I assume you'll be leaving the sword at home for our little get together later?" Val asked.

Tia stopped walking at the elevator door and before pressing the button, turned to face Valerie, who was several inches taller and more than just a few pounds heavier.

"I carry the Katana at the request of my father to honor the memory of my late mother," she answered. "She was Japanese. Father's a great admirer of all things Japanese, especially the Samurai culture of early modern Japan. I'll have my sword on my person, and I'm certain you'll have your Glock 17, and the young miss will have her Sig Sauer P320. The only one of us that's unarmed now, and will be unarmed later, is Heely. I must admit, I'm curious about that."

Val inched closer to the much smaller woman, saying, "Nothing to be curious about. He doesn't carry because we do."

Tia's laugh was light and lilting and short-lived. She pressed the button, calling the elevator to the second floor lobby.

"You have quite the crew here, Heely. Here's hoping they live long enough to spend all that money. Now, my men, what's left of them, are waiting in the lobby to show you out of the building. See you three tonight."

THE CABLE CAR

The cab ride took about five minutes and no one spoke. Paying the cabbie, we walked toward the park entrance and the debriefing we didn't want to give. As we approached the ticket window, I saw Hodges reading a newspaper just inside the gate. Zach and Franks were seated on a park bench. Franks was eating a pretzel while Zach was busy on his computer.

Moving forward in the queue, I caught sight of Ryan walking toward the public restrooms. I saw Tammy waiting near the line for the cable car ride, and knew she'd jump in line just ahead of us on approach. We'd soon be trapped inside the car with her, telling her what happened.

The long line to purchase park tickets was moving slowly, giving me time to consider everything that had happened, and I made a decision. Turning to face Leecy and Val, I touched my ear, killing my communication with the rest of the team, and waited for Val and Leecy to do the same.

"I'm sorry, Leecy. I should've kept my mouth shut, and none of this would've happened."

"Me, too, kiddo," Val agreed. "I wish I could take it all back. I feel like we pushed you into it."

"Stop being ridiculous," Leecy said. "You really think I was leaving that room with the Neanderthal? No way that was going to happen. That freak got what he deserved."

"Maybe so, but when we get in the cable car with Tammy, you two follow my lead, okay?"

"What're you up to, Dad?" Leecy asked.

"Just promise me you'll follow my lead?"

"Okay, I promise."

"Sure thing," Val said.

Buying three round-trip tickets, I joined the queue for the ride directly behind Valerie and Leecy, with Wakefield entering the line ahead of us as we approached. I took a deep breath, preparing myself for the dressing down. Having suffered through them in the past, I knew what was about to happen and I knew it wouldn't be pleasant. While we waited in the line, I surveyed the area, making sure we hadn't picked up a tail. Spotting no one suspicious, I tried to relax, but failed miserably at it.

The young man taking tickets asked Wakefield, "How many in your party?"

She responded, "Four of us, round-trip."

Handing over my three tickets, we stepped forward into the cable car. I sat beside Wakefield, facing Leecy and Valerie, and nodded at the teenager as he closed the door. No one spoke till we were off the ground, high above the park.

Wakefield, gesturing for us to power down our earpieces, waited before speaking first.

"How'd it go? Any progress on determining if Tia is the hacker?"

I looked out the window, gathering my thoughts, and

then turned slowly, looking at Tammy.

"Definitive proof. She told us she was behind the cyber attacks, and then demonstrated her skill. You can tell Interpol they can back off Jenny."

"Good, so we can take her down, and put this one in the win column."

"We will, but not just yet."

"Why not?"

"There's more to it than just the hacks Tia blamed on Jenny."

"Well, I'm waiting. Let's have it."

"We don't have anything concrete," Val said, "only what Tia's told us, which, now that I'm thinking about it, isn't very much."

"Yeah," Leecy agreed. "She's hiding something. She's got a partner. She said she was going to be the head of a much larger operation. Maybe she's working an angle? We need more time."

Wakefield shook her head.

"Time is up tomorrow morning. Unless we have hard, irrefutable evidence that Tia is connected to something bigger than the hacks in the US, Jenny and Tia both go down. Although, I must admit, I have a great deal of respect for the Granger intuition, but that alone isn't going to cut it with either Langley or our friend Robert Leeds at Interpol. I need proof."

"Then we need more time," I said.

"We're out of time. If I had any time to give, I would hand it over, but without something substantial to motivate me into making that call, I'm sorry."

"Okay," Leecy said, "just hear us out, then."

"You've got till the end of the ride."

"First of all, the device that was found yesterday, the one Tia was so livid about," Leecy said, "today is no big deal to her. In fact, she offered us two million dollars to look the other way, because she doesn't want us interfering with whatever she's involved with. Question is, what's happened to Tia in less than twenty-four hours to bring about her change of heart?"

"She dismantled the device," Wakefield countered. "She's had a day to think about it and realizes it's no longer a concern."

"I'd buy that if not for the two million dollar inducement not to pursue who planted it."

"I concede. Point made. Score one for the Grangers. What else?"

"Tia showed us her computer room," Val began. "If I'm right, the computers Tia's running are the ones she got from Jenny, and she's staffed the place with dozens of top-level hackers. She showed us her hack on JP Morgan Chase."

"You've seen this proof?"

"Yes. It's definitive."

"Can someone like Zach access her system?"

"I doubt it. Well, maybe if he was in the building."

"Maybe we could make that happen when we arrest her tomorrow. If there's proof on the system, it's worth looking into, and if we find it, Jenny would be in the clear. Okay, that's worth a try. I can find the time for that. Score another one for the Grangers. What else?"

"We're supposed to meet Tia," I said, "at the train station at seven o'clock to pick up our payment for doing nothing about the device."

"The payoff. That's normal. I don't see a problem," Wakefield said. "Do you?"

"Paying us off doesn't make any sense to me," Leecy answered, "and because that act alone is so odd, then I have to question her motives."

"Yes, exactly," Val agreed. "It's just a feeling, but I think she's setting us up."

"She is setting us up," I said. "But for what?"

"Don't you dare say she's trying to kill you," Wakefield said. "That doesn't track."

"Sure it does," I said. "Now follow me on this. She's angry about the device and accuses me of planting it. Threatens me with the sword. The next day she's not angry. She's willing to pay us serious money, too good to be true money, to look the other way? Come on. She wants us gone. Her daddy wants us around. She's going to try to take us out."

"But why, Ron? It doesn't track. It just doesn't."

"It does if you consider this. I think her new partner planted the device to keep tabs on her. She confronted the partner about the device and made a deal. Now he's her benefactor. It's the terms of that deal she doesn't want anyone finding out about."

"When did she have time to do that?"

"Did we have eyes on her after I left yesterday?"

"No, I didn't think that was necessary."

"There you go. We don't know what she's been doing, but I do know one thing."

"What?"

"Whatever she was doing kept her busy so long she didn't have time to change her clothes before ten this morning. Have Zach hack the CCTVs at the train station and the airport. Tia went somewhere. We find out where she went, maybe we find out who she was with. Who knows? Maybe we even find out who this partner is."

"It explains her odd behavior," Leecy added.

"It's still a stretch," Wakefield insisted. "Any thoughts on who might have planted the device?"

"I have a thought," I said.

"Before you share your thought, is this going to make me cringe?"

"If you thought what I just guessed was a reach," I said, smiling, "you'll think what I'm about to say is just pure fantasy."

"Jesus Christ. I'd forgotten what it's like working with you. Go ahead. Let's hear it."

"March of this year, Russia annexes the Ukraine's Crimea region, justifying the action in part by saying they're protecting their Black Sea Fleet after the overthrow of Kiev's Pro Russian President by protestors, and to support the rebels."

"He has a history lesson for me," Wakefield said. "Ron, the ride's at the halfway point. Hurry this along."

"Fast forward to October. The cease-fire is in place and holding. Everything in the region is quiet. Then the multiagency taskforce, of which the CIA is a member, gets word about an article that'll be published in USA Today about Putin having an army of computer hackers. What happens next? Even before the article shows up in the paper, reports start coming out of the Ukraine that the Russians are supplying the rebels. Then we hear rumors that Moscow is at the head of the pipeline of arms into Eastern Ukraine. The cease-fire is almost broken. NATO is fielding reports of Russian troops amassing along the Ukrainian border. Russia is denying each report, countering with reports of pro-Nationalist Ukrainian forces active in the Sevastopol area."

"Yes, yes, enough. We get it. It's mass confusion,"

Wakefield said.

"Exactly," I said. "It's mass confusion. And all eyes are focused on the Ukraine."

"What are you implying?" Wakefield asked. "Everything happening in the Ukraine is one big distraction?"

"Not everything," Val answered. "Putin got what he wanted when he wrestled control of the Black Sea Fleet away from the new western-leaning Nationalist Ukrainian government. He couldn't give a damn about anything else. The rest is all smoke and mirrors."

"Distracting us from what?" Wakefield asked.

"From the army of hackers he has under his control," Leecy answered.

"You've got three minutes. Spit it out."

"Take everything we've discussed as one connected event, not separate events, but all as part of a plan: Tia, the device, the events in the Ukraine, and the article alleging the army of hackers. It starts to come together."

"I'm not seeing it."

"The world worries over the Ukraine and all the while, Putin's making ready his army of hackers. Jenny told me Russians were trying to buy the MI5 components from her before she turned them over to Tia. Maybe when the Russians failed to acquire the computers, they tracked the sale to Tia's location, planted the device, and learned about Tia and what she does. Now, what I do know is that she's made a deal, and what if that deal is to be a part of the rumored army of Russian hackers? She said she'd soon have more computing power. It fits."

"The ride is over. Let's continue this outside."

The car stopped, and the attendant pulled the door open. "Thank you," Val said, and we followed her out of the car.

Wakefield was walking toward the exit in silence, absorbing all the information, then asked, "Is she really that good at what she does?"

"We've seen her in action," Leecy said. "She showed us her work and, like Dad said, even boasted that in less than forty-eight hours, she'd be in a position to do more harm."

"That's right," Val said, agreeing with Leecy. "I almost forgot. She did say that."

"It all adds up," I said. "She's got enough computing power to complete the hack and bring down a big banking firm. All the pieces will be in place in forty-eight hours. And by then, she could be the head of the Russian hacker army. Question is, what do you want to do about it?"

"I'll have to call this in," Wakefield said. "Till then, I want you three to be at the meeting at the train station. I'll post Ryan, Hodges, and Franks nearby, and we'll take Tia down when she tries to leave. Once she's in custody, we'll breech CCP and confiscate her equipment. I'll inform Langley of our plan, and should have the go ahead well in advance of tonight's meeting with Tia."

"You don't want to know who she's working with on this thing, or at least, what's going to change in the next forty-eight hours?" I asked. "I think that's a pretty big piece of the puzzle, don't you?"

"All I can do is inform the higher ups and see how they want to proceed, but I can tell you now, I doubt they'll grant us any more latitude, considering the hypothesis you've just shared with me. We were already out on a limb when we left Jenny to pursue this hacking thing in Cologne. They made it clear to me they want this wrapped up nice and neat. What you're suggesting is anything but that."

"What happened to finishing things?" I asked.

"Ron, not now, all right? Let me make the call. That's it, end of discussion. Anything else to add?"

"Nothing important," Leecy said, "other than Laird and his hired help have an interesting way of getting people to do what they want them to do."

"Bad experience?" Wakefield asked.

"Nothing I couldn't handle," Leecy answered.

"What does that mean, Leecy?"

"There was an incident, but nothing to worry about. Laird's people cleaned it up."

"*What?*" Wakefield fumed. "Hold on." She placed a hand on my chest to stop me from walking past her. "What did you do, Ron?"

"It was him or me," I said, catching Leecy's eye and shaking my head slightly, signaling for her to let me take the fall, "I did what I had to do."

"I warned you, Ron," she said, walking away a few steps before turning back to face me. "Damn it. I can't believe this. I'll be lucky to be manning a desk in Reykjavik, considering Ryan blew up a building on a Russian Naval base and now you've gone and killed someone. Don't you realize the trouble we're in?"

"Well," Leecy blurted out, "the next time a two hundred fifty-pound man that looks like the Hulk has his arms wrapped around you and is told he can do with you as he likes before he kills you, you can handle it your way! I handled this one my way."

"What? What are you saying? You did it? You killed a man? Is that what I'm to understand? Do you think taking the blame for your father is the best career choice you can make right now?"

"He was trying to take the blame for me," Leecy corrected her boss. "I'm telling you, I did it, not my dad."

"Listen to me," Wakefield said, so calmly that it sent chills down my spine, "no more killing. We're to apprehend the targets and bring them back to the US for questioning and sentencing. Those are my orders, thus they're your orders, and they come from the top. Leecy, when the mission is over, and quite possibly before it's over, you'll be notified of any sanctions against you. Until such time as I receive those sanctions, consider yourself on disciplinary suspension."

"And tonight?" Leecy asked.

"You're expected. Can't have you as a no show; it might make Tia suspicious."

"Roger that, but..."

Tammy, smiling that smile of hers and crowding Leecy's personal space, said, "Not another word. I mean it. Don't utter another syllable. You three report to the hotel ASAP. That's an order, and I expect you to follow it."

Looking at my daughter, I couldn't remember a time I was more proud of her. Then I saw Ryan cresting the hill behind her. He was running toward us holding something.

"Communication down or something?" he asked, stopping next to Tammy. "I thought you guys were coming back online once you left the ride. What gives? We're not receiving any of your transmissions." He handed her the SAT phone he was carrying. "Langley's trying to reach you."

"Interesting," Tammy said, turning and taking the phone from Ryan. She grabbed him by the arm as she did so, pulling him alongside as she walked away. "We powered up when we left the cable car. I tell you what, go find Zach and have him run diagnostics on our earpieces," she ordered. "Then have him, Franks, and Hodges report to my suite. I need to prep all of you for a seven o'clock at the train station."

"I'm primary, I hope."

"We'll cover that in the meeting. For now, round everyone up and let's get out of here. We don't have a lot of time." She looked at her watch. "Just five hours till the meet." Releasing her grip on his arm, Ryan ran ahead. Tammy stopped walking. Turning around, she looked at the three of us as she began to speak into the SAT phone.

"Go for Wakefield."

***

We were assembled in the hotel room, staring at the TV screen displaying an overhead view of the Cologne train station. Pointing at the satellite view, Tammy began.

"Franks, I want you positioned inside the north entrance, but just inside the entrance with a clear view of the run up to the station. Make certain you can see all the way to the roundabout and Hodges' position."

"Roger that, boss," Franks said.

"Hodges," Tammy said, pointing at the screen, "I want you here, positioned on the northeast corner of the roundabout looking toward the entrance of the station. From here, you'll have a clear line of sight along the exterior of the building and of all the approaching vehicles."

"Will do."

"Ryan."

"Yes, boss."

"Your position is the most critical. I want you here," she said, indicating the elevated platform inside the train station.

"What? You want me inside the train station? Why so far from the action?"

"Look," she said, pointing at the screen just left of the northern entrance. "This is the cab and bus designated area. The buses block our line of sight on the ground. That's why I need you to make your way to the platform overlooking that area. If the Grangers venture toward the bus loading and unloading area, you'll have a bird's eye view. Got it?"

"Why not just have me take up position in the bus area, then?"

"Because you won't be able to see anything. You'll be trapped inside a maze of buses."

"Okay, fine, but I want to..."

Wakefield cut him off, saying over the ringing of her SAT phone, "All complaints in writing and in triplicate."

After a few minutes of listening to Tammy say 'yes sir' and 'no sir,' she ended the call.

"We've been ordered to take Tia down tonight. A CIA computer forensics team will be on the ground before midnight with Interpol Station Chief Leeds. Once they're in place and ready to go, we'll coordinate with them, making the arrest and helping with removal of any and all hardware in use inside CCP. Got it?"

"And Jenny?" I asked.

"She's in the clear, but back on the CIA radar. We'll be keeping tabs on her activities once again. Both agencies are looking for a reason to take her down."

"And what about whatever it is Tia's into, and who she's working with?"

"The consensus coming out of Langley is by bringing down Tia and her operation here in Cologne, we stop whatever else is in the works. Tia's the lynch pin holding the entire scheme together. We stop her, everything you suggested might happen, Ron, never gets started. It all ends. Game over."

"That's a mistake. We should follow this to its source."

"Not going to happen, so let it go. Now, back to the mission tonight. Ron," Tammy said, pointing at the screen, "I want you three and Ryan arriving at the location for the meeting from inside the train station. This accomplishes two things. First, if Tia's watching, she doesn't see where you three came from, and second, it gets Ryan inside the station and on the platform area with ease."

"Agreed," I said.

"I don't want you three engaging the target any longer than it takes to get the money and walk away. Don't give her a reason to suspect anything. Understand? While all that's going on, I'll be coordinating with the inbound team and formulating a plan of action for the takedown."

"We understand," Val said.

"Any questions?" Tammy asked, looking around the room. "None? Good, that's the way I like it. In addition to monitoring the communications, Zach will be following up on a hunch Granger has. He'll be looking for Tia at the train station and the airport last night."

"Why?" Ryan asked.

"Ron," Zach began, "thinks Tia went somewhere last night, and I'm going to confirm or deny it."

"Telling us what, exactly?"

"The thought is, if we know where she went, we find out who she met with."

"Well good luck wasting your time looking for that needle in a hay stack."

"Be that as it may," Tammy said, "I'll be monitoring here with Zach, calling the shots and awaiting your safe return. Franks, you and Hodges drop the Grangers and Ryan at the closest station, then get into position. And as always, remember your mobiles and, if things go sideways, your emergency protocols."

"Yes, boss," Franks said.

"Let's go," Tammy said over her ringing SAT phone. "You've got your assignments."

CHAPTER
SEVEN

THE TRAIN STATION

The train pulled into Cologne's central station, and I heard, "Franks, here. All clear, and no sign of the target or the Grangers," in my ear.

"Hodges in position. I have a visual on Franks inside the station. So far, so good."

"We're here," I said, exiting the train, following Leecy and Val down the stairs to the main concourse. "Making our way to the northern entrance."

Descending the stairs from the arrival platform, I could feel the energy of the crowd as if the station itself was alive. Reaching the bottom of the stairs, we waded into the river of bodies passing in front of us. The surge of people moving south through the station engulfed us, separating and pushing us in the wrong direction, forcing me to fight against the tide of stampeding bodies and the smell of body odor and cigarette smoke. I felt like a lone salmon swimming upstream.

Remaining calm at first, saying "excuse me" and "pardon," easing my way through the crowd, I realized the energy of the pack fed on politeness, and would soon be feasting on my trampled carcass. I pushed my way past several business travelers unwilling to yield the right of way, and said, "Follow me." I looked back, expecting to see Leecy, but instead, saw no one I recognized.

I froze in the middle of the tight hall, and the sea of bodies parted and flowed around me undeterred. Searching the crowd, I looked for Leecy and Valerie. Seeing neither of them anywhere, I joined the surge of people moving south, hoping they had just been swept away by the current. Reaching the southern exit of the train station, I walked into the plaza, turning and looking toward the entrance. They were nowhere in sight.

"Leecy, Val, report your location."

No response.

"Anyone with eyes on Leecy or Val?" I asked.

"No," echoed in my ear.

"What's wrong?" Wakefield asked.

"Rush hour crowd separated us. I've lost them."

"No you haven't," Leecy said. "We got knocked around a bit, and when no one was responding to our transmissions, realized our earpieces had been inadvertently turned off somehow. Probably from all the jostling we took. But we're fine. We're inside the station next to the ticketing kiosk."

"On my way," I said.

"Good," Franks said, "'cause I've got eyes on Tia. She's approaching on foot from the north."

"Grangers passing your three o'clock now," Hodges advised.

"I've got them, too," Franks said. "They're just inside the entrance, moving toward Tia. Should have contact in ten seconds."

"I can't see anything," Ryan added. "I'm moving for

better sight lines."

"All hold," Wakefield said. "Don't move."

"We have contact," Hodges informed.

"I don't see any money," Leecy said by way of greeting. "So, I guess we go to work for your daddy, now."

Smiling at us, Tia responded. "I can't carry forty pounds of cash. That's almost half my body weight."

"So where's the money?"

"Easy," Tia said, smiling. "It's closer than you think. Follow me."

"Tia's walking away to her left," Hodges said. "Grangers are following her."

"Looks like she's headed for the bus parking," Franks added.

"Roger that," Hodges said. "That's exactly where she's headed, but I'll lose her in fifteen seconds behind a wall of buses."

"Ryan," Wakefield said, "she's all yours. Call the game."

"Yeah, I, uh, don't have them yet."

"They should be directly under you by now," Hodges said.

"Yeah, yeah, I've got them. They're at the bus park."

"What else?" Wakefield asked.

"Umm, I, uh, don't..."

"Damn it, Ryan. You moved, didn't you?"

"I was trying to get a better sight line, and I..."

Interrupting Ryan, Wakefield said, "Franks, do you have eyes on them?"

"Hold one. Moving for a better view. Yeah, I see them. They're standing near the buses. It looks like they're talking, but I'm not picking up anything on my earpiece."

"Me, either," Wakefield said. "Zach, what's happening?"

"I'm picking up the same jamming signal I picked up at CCP. She must be carrying a portable RFI jammer."

"Damn it. Get moving, Franks. I need eyes on the Grangers."

"I'm almost in position, boss," Franks said. "I'm running between the buses where I saw..."

Then silence.

"Ryan, Hodges, get in there. We've lost Franks' transmission," Wakefield ordered. "Get in there. Franks, do you read me, Franks? Ron? Valerie? Leecy, do you read me?"

Silence.

"Granger," Wakefield said. "Come in. Report."

Silence.

"Hodges," Wakefield said. "Ryan, come in." Looking at Zach, she asked, "What's happened to our communications?"

"She's jammed everything now," Zach answered.

"But how? Damn it." Wakefield paced back and forth inside the hotel suite. "Call Hodges on his mobile. Put it on speaker."

"Hodges here."

"Franks?" Wakefield asked.

"Dead."

"Tia? Grangers?"

"Caught sight of a black Mercedes speeding away as I arrived on scene. I think she was inside. She's gone. A white cargo van was speeding away ahead of the sedan. I think it's safe to assume the Grangers were inside the van. What do you want me to do about Franks?"

"Protocols, Hodges. Clean the scene, and report back here ASAP, and bring Ryan. Zach," she said, ending the call with Hodges, "I need you in the police system, and as soon as they post the information about the dead American, I need you to work your magic, got me?"

"I'm on it now, boss," Zach said. "I'm also searching CCTV cameras in the area for any clue as to where the sedan and the van are going."

"Great. Good thinking," Wakefield said, answering the ringing mobile phone. "Yes."

"We're just going to leave Franks in the street like this?" Hodges asked.

"Listen to me, Hodges," Wakefield said, leaning forward, a palm pressed down on the tabletop. "I don't like it any more than you do, but it's SOP. Follow the procedures, and get back here. Where in the hell is Ryan?"

"Jumped in a cab. He's chasing the Mercedes."

Disconnecting the call with Hodges, Wakefield said, "Get me Ryan."

"I'm here," Ryan said, his voice erupting in her ear.

"How's that possible?" Wakefield asked, looking at Zach. "You said we were jammed."

"The effective range of one of those portable jammers is less than a fifty-foot radius. Ryan must be outside that effective range. If the device was off, I'd be receiving the tracking signal from the Grangers, and I'm not receiving anything."

Then, turning her attention to Agent Ryan, she asked, "What are you doing?"

"I'm in pursuit of Tia. She killed Franks."

"What's your plan?"

"To follow and apprehend her."

"In a cab?"

"Well, I..."

"Yeah, I know, you didn't think that through. Your little plan involves a civilian witness. Turn around immediately and report back here. That's an order. Do it now."

"But she could lead me to wherever she's taking the Grangers."

"And she could just as easily lead you on a wild goose chase. Return here immediately. Final order. Follow it or..."

"Or *what!*" he raged. "You'll fire me? You need me more than ever, now. You're four men down."

"Agent James Ryan Taw," Wakefield began calmly, "it's my duty to inform you this transmission is being recorded and will be entered into evidence against you at your dismissal hearing, along with other similarly recorded acts of insubordination, if you do not follow my order to return here immediately."

"Ten-four, I'm en route to your location, abandoning my pursuit of the person that killed Agent William Bubba Franks."

Staring out the window, Wakefield said, "Zach, anything on those CCTV cameras in the area? Any sign of anything that might help us? Maybe we'll get lucky and can ID the vehicle transporting the Grangers. But I suspect Tia probably jammed those camera signals, too, since she was prepared to cut off our communications."

Typing quickly, he said, "That's an accurate assumption, but," he paused and pointed at the TV screen, "she made one mistake. Check this out."

"What am I looking at?"

"Camera view from the ATM machine of the bank located across the street from the bus loading and unloading zone."

"What am I seeing?"

"That's," Zach said, looking up at the TV screen, "Ron Granger being loaded into the rear of a van by two men that fit the descriptions Ron gave us of Hector and Lee, and," he paused to enlarge the image, "that's the license plate."

"How did those idiots get the jump on Ron? That's just impossible. We're missing something here, or those MMA guys are more highly skilled than we thought. Or maybe..."

"Or what?" he asked. "What're you thinking?"

"As we were leaving the park, I received word the CIA databases had been breached. I wonder..."

"You're thinking Tia hacked the CIA?"

"That would be one explanation for the sudden turn of events."

"Sure it would, but you're forgetting one thing."

"What's that?" She asked.

"Even if the CIA database was breached, it's just a storage facility housing hundreds of servers and too many terabytes of data to imagine. No way she finds out anything about the Grangers or us. The search would take days."

"Okay, so if not that, then what caused her to change her mind about Peter Heely and his team? And how the hell did they get the jump on Ron and Val? Do you think those two MMA goons planned this?"

"No," Zach said, "it's not the MMA guys. I think we're right about those two." He paused and typed furiously. "I've blown up the image. If you look where my cursor is on the screen, you'll see a bald head in the reflection of the rearview mirror."

"Furukawa?" Tammy asked.

"Yes, Furukawa. He's the great unknown, and he has to be the mastermind behind what just happened."

"All of it?" Wakefield asked. "Including killing Franks, or just the takedown of the Grangers?"

"Just the takedown. I think killing Franks was Tia acting on impulse. Maybe he startled her when he ran into the situation like he did."

"That's certainly plausible," Tammy said, looking in the direction of the door opening as Hodges entered the suite.

"Here are his personal items. Isn't much," he said, carefully placing the mobile phone, earpiece, and Indian head penny Franks always carried for good luck on the table near the door.

"Bag it and tag it, Hodges," Wakefield instructed. "We'll be resting in shifts till we find the Grangers. You're taking the first shift. Thirty minutes to get washed up and eat. It's going to be a long night. Report back here at 2030 hours. Dismissed."

Bagging and tagging Frank's personal belongings, Hodges placed the bag on the table next to Zach's computer. Turning toward the sound of the opening door, he saw Ryan. "Where were you?" he asked.

Ignoring Hodges' question, Ryan brushed past him. Hodges grabbed Ryan's left arm, spun him around and punched him in the face, knocking him to the floor. Wakefield and Zach rushed to separate the two men, but not before Hodges kicked Ryan in the side.

"You killed him! You were out of position!"

"Fuck you, Hodges! It's not my fault. Wakefield sent him in there!"

Pushing Hodges toward the door of the suite, Wakefield said, "Go on. Get cleaned up and rest. Take an hour. I'll see you at nine. That's twenty-one hundred, sharp. Now go. Let me handle Ryan."

Closing the door, Wakefield turned to face a now-standing Ryan.

"I'll get to you in a moment. Right now, we need to focus on finding the Grangers. Any thoughts?"

"CCTV cameras in the area?" Ryan asked.

"Only image we've found is the one on the screen," Zach said, pointing to the TV mounted on the wall of the suite.

"She came prepared, didn't she?" Ryan asked, rubbing his jaw with his hand.

Ignoring his question, Wakefield said, "Zach ran the plates. The van was reported stolen today. So whatever she came prepared to do, she prepared it today and in a hurry."

"So, we've got nothing?" Ryan asked.

"Zach's compiling a top ten list of the most likely locations she'd use to house and question the Grangers. We doubt she'd bring them back to the offices of CCP."

"We'd know where she was bringing them if you had let me follow her."

Smiling, Tammy said, "Yes...about that, or more precisely, about you. I think now is as good a time as any. Account for your actions tonight."

"Is this a formal review?"

"Yes, it is, and may I add it's long overdue. Zach will video the session and act as witness."

Ryan, seeing Zach aiming his iPhone at his face, smiled, rubbed his jaw, and said, "So this is it, then? I'm finished at the Agency?"

"I can't answer that. You know how the process works and how long it takes, but even though you haven't done yourself any favors these past few days, the mission isn't over yet. You still have an opportunity to add something positive to your file."

"Really? And just how do I do that?"

"Finish strong, Agent Ryan. If you stop complaining and defying orders, and help wrap this thing up with Tia in a nice little bow, and get the Grangers back in one piece, I'll make note of your actions in your file."

"That'll help?"

"It certainly won't hurt. So you want to get to work finding the Grangers, or what?"

"Yeah bring me up to speed."

"What'd you find?" Wakefield asked, turning her attention to Zach.

"I searched all known CCP holdings and identified two possibilities."

"That's it?"

"Yes, that's it. Though the company is heavily invested, it doesn't have many brick and mortar holdings other than the office space in the city. A hangar at the airfield and the plane inside, that's it."

"A plane?"

"It's a nineties relic that hasn't been in service for twenty years. I wouldn't worry much about the plane."

"Okay," Wakefield said, turning to face Ryan, "you'll stake out the CCP office and, using your mobile, notify me of any activity. I'll head to the airport and check out the hangar and the plane. If they're there, I'll call for all three of you. If not, I'll wait for the arrival of the CIA team and Agent Leeds. Text me the location of the hangar, Zach, and then you keep digging. There's got to be more. If you find anything else, put Hodges on it immediately."

"Roger that," Zach said.

As Ryan left the hotel room, he asked, "You sure you want to go the airport alone? It could be the place, and if it is, you'll have to hold the fort till we can get there to help you."

Hailing a cab, Wakefield said, "See, that's exactly the kind of thing I've been talking about for over two years now. I'm not going to engage them by myself or 'hold the fort,' as you call it. If they're inside the hangar, I'll wait for you, Zach, and Hodges to back me up. Now, I can drop you near the CCP building if you like; it's on the way to the airport."

"No thanks, it's a short walk from here."

"Remember," she said, opening the door to the cab, "mobile phones. She's using a jamming device."

"Yeah, I got it."

Watching the cab drive away, he started walking south toward the train station till the cab was out of sight, and then turned around, running back toward the hotel.

"Zach," Ryan said, entering the suite and startling the kid.

"What the hell?" Zach responded. "You're supposed to be on a stakeout. What are you doing here?"

"Yeah, well, she changed her mind and asked me to help you with your search."

"Really? Why didn't she call my mobile and tell me herself."

"Because I was standing right next to her when she changed her mind, and she told me to come up here and tell you."

"All right," Zach said. "You can use Wakefield's laptop to begin searching for CCP holdings. She was using it before you two left, so I know it's still hacked into the German business filings database."

"Okay, what now? Keyword search?"

"Yeah, and don't worry if you don't know any German. I've got a translation program running in the background. All you have to do is type, and the program takes care of the rest."

"Easy enough."

Minimizing the open windows on Wakefield's computer, Ryan began searching for his disciplinary file. Finding it was easier than he'd imagined. A file with the heading "Mission Brief" was open beneath the windows he'd minimized.

Reading the contents of the file, he realized not only was he in more trouble than Tammy had led him to believe, but Leecy Granger had killed a man. He wondered briefly if there was a way to use this new information on the prodigy to his advantage, but quickly moved on. He continued reading, finding all of his actions, both good and bad, accounted for and listed in chronological order, including his latest breach of protocol, which Wakefield linked directly to the death of Franks. He quickly changed that entry.

"Hey," Ryan asked, "any word on Franks?"

Looking up from his computer, Zach answered, "Yes, the body was discovered shortly after you guys left the train station. The police have issued APBs for the two men and the woman seen fleeing the scene. The descriptions witnesses gave the police match you, Hodges, and Tia perfectly."

Reading his own file, Ryan knew that was spot on, because the information was included in the disciplinary report.

"Oh, that's not good."

"Which part? The part that Franks is dead and now officially known as Bill Kirby from Kansas City, Missouri, or that you're wanted for questioning in connection to the crime?"

"Yeah, you're forgetting I know the protocols, too.

You'd be required to change any description the police have of an agent. So I know you're messing with me."

"I was, but Tia isn't part of our team so I left her description as is."

Smiling at Zach's comment, Ryan began changing the negative entries in his file. He'd adjusted about half the entries when Hodges entered the suite.

"What the hell are you doing here?" Hodges asked. "I just spoke to the boss, and you're supposed to be on stakeout."

Scrolling to the end of the document, leaving the cursor exactly where he'd found it, he hit save. He quickly reopened the search window and typed "CCP holdings" in the address bar.

"Yeah, I know," Ryan said, standing and closing the laptop. "She thought I might be able to help, but honestly it looks like a dead end." He walked toward the door. "The old boy has his fingers in many pies, but nothing made of brick and mortar."

"The old boy?" Hodges asked.

"Yeah," Ryan said, reaching for the doorknob. "You know. Heinrich Laird."

"You weren't much help," Zach said, watching Ryan open the door. "You put in ten minutes at most."

"Hodges can help you. I'm headed to CCP. I'll call you when I'm in position."

The two men watched Ryan leave the room and Hodges said, "Heinrich Laird my ass. I'm willing to bet my paycheck he wasn't searching for anything to do with Heinrich Laird."

"You're right, he wasn't," Zach said. "He was searching for CCP holdings."

Pulling out the chair Ryan had been seated in, Hodges

said, "No, I mean he wasn't helping you."

Looking up from his computer screen, Zach asked, "What was he doing, then?"

"Oh, I don't know. But I do know Ryan, and he only helps himself. He wouldn't waste his time with a computer unless it benefited him in some way." Smirking, he repeated, "Searching for Heinrich Laird, my ass."

Zach stopped typing and looked at Hodges for a long moment before saying, "That's exactly what we should be doing."

"What?"

Typing again, Zach answered. "Searching Heinrich Laird, not CCP."

CHAPTER

EIGHT

THE INTERROGATION

"Remove the tape from their mouths," Tia said.

Furukawa did as instructed, ripping the tape off of our mouths.

"Christ, that hurt," I said, shaking my head from side to side. "Care to tell me what this is all about?"

"Damn, that stings," Leecy added. "What the hell, lady? First, we're tazed and now what? You're going to torture us?"

"Hey," Val said, "I think you need to be aware of something. You need to review the CCP Human Resources manual, 'cause I'm pretty sure you're violating every code in the book."

"Shut up," Tia said. "That's enough." Walking toward me, she added, "I'll do the talking from now on. And the first thing I want to talk about is you, Peter Heely."

"What about me?"

"I'll tell you what I now know to be true."

"Well, as you can see, I'm not going anywhere so take your time."

"Always with the jokes. We'll see who's laughing soon

enough."

"Sure," I said, "let's hear the truth as you know it. But first, tell me just how much crazy should I factor in."

Smiling and ignoring my comment, she said, "You, Peter Heely, are with the CIA."

"Really, since when? 'Cause last time I checked, I'm Peter Heely, mercenary for hire."

She began circling me slowly. "Peter Heely is what men in your line of work call a cover identity."

"My line of work? I'm a mercenary for hire. We've been over this. What are you talking about, anyway? Where's this coming from? Don't you remember? You ran my fingerprints. You know who I am. I'm Peter Heely."

Grabbing a fist full of hair and pulling back on my head, forcing me to look at her, she said, "Stop lying to me, or I'll lose my temper and kill you like I killed your man at the train station."

Looking at her upside down, I said, "First off, threatening to kill the person you want to make talk is counterproductive. If the prisoner thinks there's no chance of walking away, what reason does he have to be cooperative? See, it's mistakes like the one you just made that make working with amateurs futile. And now you tell me you killed someone at the train station? Why? Because you thought he worked with me? You met my team, and I'm the only man on the team. Sorry, lady, but you killed a bystander. You murdered a tourist or a local, not anyone I know. Where's this line of questioning coming from, anyway? Why do you think I work with the CIA?"

"Stop lying," she seethed, letting go of my hair and slapping the back of my head before spinning me around in the chair to face her.

Facing in the opposite direction, I could see Leecy's

face. She was now on my left. I winked at her, trying to assure her everything would be okay as Tia continued.

"Did you search them, Mr. Furukawa?" Tia asked, walking toward Leecy.

"Yes."

"And what did you find?"

"The women were carrying guns, but we knew they'd be armed. We expected to find weapons. Heely isn't carrying a weapon. All three had some cash, but not much. No IDs."

"That's all? What about the earpieces? You said if they were CIA, they'd have earpieces to communicate with their teammates. That's why I brought the RFI jammer from the office with me. You're telling me you got this wrong?"

"No; they could've ditched the earpieces. They're CIA no question. Your report says so."

"Hold on," Leecy said interrupting, "you're basing all this. The tazer attack and the kidnapping on the presence of some kind of earpiece?"

"Shut up," Tia barked slapping her hard across the face. "No one is talking to you."

"Even so," Leecy said undeterred, "you're making a huge mistake. That report, whatever it is, doesn't have anything to do with me. I'm not with the CIA, and neither is she," Leecy added, nodding her head in Val's direction.

Drawing her sword and spinning counterclockwise, Tia stopped the blade inches short of cutting into Leecy's throat.

"I had no intention of harming you or the other woman, but speak again, and I will end you."

"You're really not very bright, are you?" I asked, looking Leecy in the eye. I could see the fear washing across her face. Cutting her eyes in my direction, I hardened my gaze, hoping she would follow suit and remember to never let the enemy see fear.

Tia pressed the sword into the nape of Leecy's neck, and blood trickled from the wound, running down the length of the sword, "You dare to insult me with my blade cutting into the flesh of your partner? You're the one who's not very bright."

"Insult you? No, I'm just pointing out the obvious. You'll probably kill all of us. Of that, I have no doubt. Sadly, that will be a waste of great mercenaries, but I'm not going down without a fight. I hired her and the other woman out of Turkey a year ago. I don't know them. Don't care to know them. All I cared about at the time was they're really good at their jobs. That's something you should care about, too."

Tia dropped the sword from Leecy's neck and walked away, dragging the tip of the blade across the concrete floor. She circled the three of us and asked, "So what you're trying to tell me is that their safety is of no concern to you? Is that right?"

"It's kind of a code with people like us. We're in this business to make money, not friends."

"Okay, so be it. Let's see if you care so little about your own self-preservation."

"Are you moving on to the main event so soon?"

"Oh yes, Mr. Heely. It's time to employ some of your own agency's tactics."

"The CIA?"

"Yes, your government released a CIA torture report for all the world to read, and now Mr. Furukawa is going to use your agency's methods on you."

"Sounds ominous, but like I always say, if you're going to do something, give it all you got."

"Still with the jokes? Even now? Knowing what's about to happen to you?"

"Sure. Why not? I mean, what the hell difference does it make? But there is one thing: before you start working on me with scary toys, tell me about the other report you have. Tell me about the report that says I'm CIA, and give me a chance to refute it. At the very least, check and see who you really killed today. If you did that and nothing else, you'd see I'm right. You killed a tourist. You should really check it out. You're wrong about that man being my backup, just like you're wrong about me."

Spinning my chair around again to face her and Furukawa, she said, "You're stalling. Last chance. Who are you, who are you working for, and who are these women?"

"Why don't you run their prints like you did mine and find out for yourself?"

Tia leaned forward, her hands on my knees, and said, "I'm not hacked into AFIS out here. You do know what AFIS is, don't you?"

"Automated Fingerprint Identification Method," I answered. "Yes, I am aware of what it is. People like me and my team work very hard to stay out of databases like that."

"Okay, then, I'll tell you what," she paused long enough to straddle my legs and sit on my lap. "After Mr. Furukawa finishes with you and you've screamed, cried, and begged him to stop, I'll keep you alive; I promise I will. And I'll bring you back to the office with the women and let you watch as I run their prints, and then when I know who they really are, you can watch them die first. Okay?"

"There's one problem with that plan," Val said.

"What's that?" Tia asked, still perched on my lap.

"Weren't you listening? He just told you people like us work hard to stay out of databases. My prints and the kid's here aren't in any database. We've never been printed. Ever. You won't find anything on us. So, I guess that leaves you with two choices."

"And what's that?" Tia asked, looking into my eyes and stroking my hair.

"Let the two of us go," Val said. "We'll forget all about this. It'll be like it never happened."

"Ridiculous. I'm not letting any of you go till I get the truth."

"Okay," Val said, smiling and shaking her head. "Then you better kill me right now, 'cause if you leave an ounce of life in me, I'll use it to find you wherever you go. You'll be looking over your shoulder for the rest of your life."

Tia grabbed the sides of my head in her hands, forcing me to look her in the eyes. Ignoring Valerie, she said, "Tough talk from your woman. Let's see how tough they are when I'm finished with you. Personally, I think they'll be singing a different tune."

"What happened to us?" I asked. "Hmmm? Where'd we get off track? I helped you find the device, didn't I? We came to a mutually beneficial agreement, then it all fell apart. What happened?"

"Let's just say I had a meeting yesterday that will make me very rich and very powerful. The deal I made is much bigger than anything you could offer me." Standing suddenly, she spun on her toes, walking toward the wooden crate on the floor at Furukawa's feet. Laughing, she looked at Furukawa and asked, "Are you ready?"

Furukawa removed a set of jumper cables from the crate with one hand and a car battery with the other.

"We'll start slow, okay?" Furukawa said, walking toward me. "I don't want to kill you by accident."

Watching him connect one end of the jumper cables to the battery, I tried to prepare myself for what was going to happen next, but I knew that was impossible. Touching the positive cable clamp and negative together, Mr. Furukawa held them up a few feet from my face, the sparks erupting.

"Last chance to admit who you really are," Tia said.

"I'm Peter Heely. I helped you discover you were being spied on. Someone's trying to turn you against me. Why is that? Ask yourself who benefits the most if me and my team are out of the picture."

Mr. Furukawa motioned to Lee and Hector. Lee walked forward, removing a knife from his pocket and cutting away the duct tape from around my chest. Splitting my sweater and undershirt down the middle and pulling the cut halves away, he exposed my bandaged torso.

Seeing the bandage, Tia walked toward me and said, "Hold on a second. What's this?"

"It's nothing," I answered.

She pushed her hands inside the cut halves of my clothing, pressing her palms against my sides, getting the reaction she was looking for when I winced. She smiled.

"Looks like we don't need the battery after all. Our man, here, has a soft spot we can exploit. Get him out of the chair and..." She looked around the room and pointed overhead, "hang him by his wrists from the engine hoist and remove the bandages. I want him dangling with his toes barely touching the floor."

"Physical torture is very unreliable," Val said. "I've never been a big fan of it. No, I prefer a more cerebral approach. I've been known to use a little psychological torture now and again."

"Interesting," Tia said, walking toward Valerie. "I was going to make you two watch as I made your boss tell me what I want to know, but you did threaten me, and now you've given me a better idea."

"Psychological torture takes planning," Val said. "What could you possibly do to us on the spur of the moment?"

Spinning Val's chair around to face the rear of the dark building, Tia leaned close to her ear.

"Did you notice the rectangular holes cut in the floor?"

"Sure. I think they were once used to work on the trucks that came in for service."

"Very good; that's correct. And did you know this place belongs to my father?"

"I assumed."

"Yes, of course you did. You see, at one time it was a very successful shipping operation. My father owned a fleet of big trucks that hauled merchandise all over Europe, but that was a long time ago; back when I was a child. I was a very curious young girl. Much like you are, I imagine," she said to Leecy. "When my mother brought me here to see Father in his shipping office, I would sneak away to play and explore the property. One day, I discovered the doors to this place had been left open, and I came inside. I saw the openings in the floor beneath the big trucks, and I couldn't help myself; I just had to see what was down in those holes."

"Dangerous place for playtime," Val said.

"That's true; it is a dangerous place. It's also like a maze. You know, thinking back, it was a wonderful place to play. However, judging from the snarling sound and smell emanating from the pit tonight, I'd say it's become more like a labyrinth now. Something is living down there."

Seeing that Hector and Lee were busy with me, she continued.

"Mr. Furukawa, if you don't mind bringing the ladies down into the pit while we wait for Mr. Heely to be lifted into position, I'd be very grateful."

Dropping the jumper cables into the crate, he looked up and asked, "Are you serious?"

"Yes, and I want you to tie them securely to the end of the stair railing at the bottom of the stairs."

"Yes. Right away, Miss Reins."

Tia watched Furukawa grab a flashlight and a gun from the box on the floor before cutting away the tape holding Valerie in the chair. With her hands still bound with duct tape, he led her down the stairs at gunpoint.

The sound of metal grinding on metal got Tia's attention. She looked toward the noise, seeing both Lee and Hector pulling on the chain, lifting me from my sitting position with the old manually operated engine block hoist. Furukawa returned, cutting Leecy free from the chair and escorting her down into the pit.

Shining the light on the two women, Tia could see them standing with their backs against the vertical post at the end of the stair rail, their hands secured to the post behind them. The oily black paw prints of the animals inhabiting the pit covered the metal stairs. Tia completed her inspection of Furukawa's handiwork from a safe distance.

"No need for me to come down there. The knots look good from here. Come on; you've got more work to do."

Turning away from the pit to see me dangling just as she instructed, Tia admired my bruised physique, now suspended, shirtless and bandage-free.

"Tell me you're CIA, and I'll let you down and end this quickly."

"I can't admit to that," I said through gritted teeth. "I'm Peter Heely."

Laughing, she asked, "Oh, Peter, you're determined to make this very painful, aren't you?"

"You're wearing the same outfit you wore yesterday, and I could smell the sex still on your skin when you sat on my lap. Let me guess. This mystery partner of yours promised you the world, then screwed your brains out, and now you're in love."

I could barely see Hector, Lee, and Tia standing on the edge of the darkness. Furukawa, walking toward me, touched the ends of the cables together, sending sparks arching toward the ceiling. He smiled, moving the cables over my chest, and I screamed.

"Tell me I'm wrong, Tia," I yelled as soon as Furukawa backed away from me. "I think your new boyfriend planted that information about me being CIA. He probably even rigged up a dummy CIA site, and your people think they hacked the real thing. He planted that device. He was in your system, so it's possible. Is he part of the reported army of Russian hackers Putin employs?"

I'd struck a nerve. I could see the change of expression on her face even in the semi-darkness, despite her best efforts to hide it.

"Even if everything you said is true," she said, "it doesn't matter. Goodbye, Mr. Peter Heely. I won't see you again after tonight. I have a plane to catch, and a new life to begin. Furukawa, I want you and the boys to take your time with him, then kill them all and dump their bodies inside three empty oil drums. There are plenty of them lying around the property. Or just drop them down in the pit and let the animals eat them." She turned and walked into the darkness, adding. "I'll drive myself back to the office."

"What? You're leaving before the fun starts?"

"I have preparations to make and a plane to catch. I'm satisfied you're CIA. I don't need to hear anymore."

"No, you're not satisfied; that's why you're leaving. You want to hurry back to the office and check the legitimacy of the hack your people claim to have made. No one hacks the CIA, lady. No one. This is a set up; that's all it is. Your new lover wants you isolated so he can control you. When you see it's all fake, you'll know I'm right, but it'll be too late."

"Too late for you, but not for me."

"You really believe these bozos you've hired are capable of killing a man like me?"

Walking slowly toward me, she said, "Here's what I know. You're CIA. My bozos captured not only a man like you, but your teammates as well. You're hanging by your wrists and your women are food for wild animals. I'll be airborne by midnight, and you'll be dead."

Laughing as much as the pain would allow me to, I said, "Best stick around and make certain the job is done right, 'cause if these boys make one mistake, I'll be coming for you and the money you promised me. You're making an enemy of the wrong guy."

"Miss Reins," I heard Lee calling in the distance. The sound of his cowboy boots running across the floor toward the exit echoed off the walls. "He's right."

"Right? Right about what?"

"The man you killed. I checked. I pulled up the local news on my iPhone, and the police say the man you killed outside the station was just an American tourist. A man named Bill Kirby. He was from Kansas City."

"Impossible," she said. "I heard the voices screaming in his ear. Like he had an earpiece."

"No, you didn't. You didn't hear any voices in his ear," I said to the darkness. "You heard the voices of the people around you screaming as you killed that man. I bet the police are looking for you."

"No one saw me. I made certain of that."

"I'm sorry, Miss Reins," Lee said, "but he's correct again. Your description is listed on an all points bulletin the police have released. They're looking for you. They even have a description of the car."

"Damn it," she said. I heard the clicking sound of retreating footsteps followed by the sound of a car door opening and closing. An engine revved to life.

NINE

THE SEARCH AND ESCAPE

"Hello Zach," Wakefield said into her cell, "I'm at the airport walking toward the private hangars south of the Fixed Base Operator office."

"Great. I've got news, also. I've found where they've taken the Grangers."

"That's great. Send Hodges to the location immediately."

"He's en route as we speak. No need to check the hangar now, I guess."

"Maybe so, but I'm going to take a look anyway. I mean, I'm here."

"Yeah, that makes sense. Just be safe and all."

"There's something else I want you to do for me."

"What's that?"

"They're several private planes here. I'm going to text you the tail numbers, and I want you to run down the owners for me."

"All due respect, but why waste time with that? I'm already working on the Tia thing. You know Granger's hunch? She didn't take a train. I'm scanning airport CCTV now."

"Christ, is Ryan rubbing off on you? Now I need to explain myself?"

"Absolutely not. I'm sorry. I was just curious as to your thinking on the tail numbers is all I meant."

Pausing to regain her composure, she ignored him, shining her flashlight through the window of the pedestrian door of the hangar. "I'm at the hangar and it's locked up nice and tight," she said. "No sign of anyone inside or of anyone having been here recently."

"That's good, then; we can be confident Hodges is on the right track."

"Yeah, tell me about that. How'd you find the place?"

"Oh," Zach said, typing on his computer keyboard. "Well, it was actually something Hodges said about something Ryan said that got me thinking."

Walking away from the metal building, toward the row of six private planes, Wakefield paused.

"What are you talking about? Back up and start from the beginning."

"Okay, sure. Well, let me think. Where to begin? All right, after you left the hotel with Ryan, I was working on the search for CCP holdings that might..."

"Yeah I got that part. Jump forward to what Ryan said and when he said it."

"Sure. After Ryan came back to the hotel to help with the search..."

"He did what?" Wakefield asked.

"Ryan came back after you two left, saying you told him to help me with the search I was doing. Hodges showed up, Ryan left, and Hodges said..."

"Forget that," Wakefield said. "I need you to tell me

exactly what Ryan did when he came back to the hotel."

"He sat down at your computer and helped me search."

"My computer? Is that right? Ryan used my computer?"

"Yes. I'm sorry, but he said you told him to help me, and it was the only other computer in the room."

"Don't give it a second thought, Zach. There's nothing for you to worry about, okay?"

"Okay, but what about Ryan?"

"If he calls in, don't mention a word of this conversation to him. Do you understand? It's very important that you don't say a word."

"Roger that."

"Good. Now, I'm sending you six tail numbers. I need you to get to work on them for me. I'll be here at the airport waiting on the arrival of the Interpol agent and CIA team. If you need me, call me. If Ryan contacts you, let me know. I'm calling Hodges now."

Walking toward the FBO building, Wakefield dialed Hodges' mobile number. As she entered the building, the phone began to ring. She made her way past the small lobby desk and around the corner, entering the ladies room. Pushing the door open, she heard Hodges say, "Hodges here."

"What's your twenty?"

"I'm five miles north of the city with another ten to drive."

"Destination?" she asked, checking the stalls.

"Abandoned shipping company once operated by Laird on the outskirts of the city."

"How certain are you the Grangers are there?" she asked, leaning against the sink basin of the empty bathroom.

"One hundred percent certain. It's the only physical

building owned by Laird other than the CCP building. I'll find them; I know it."

"Do you want me to send Ryan to back you up?"

"No, no need for that. I can handle it. Did Zach tell you Ryan was on your computer?"

"Yes, he did."

"Well?"

"It's handled. Don't worry about it. I need you to focus on the task at hand. This mission is blowing up in our faces, and we need to get it back under control and in a hurry."

"Roger that."

"All right, keep me posted and let me know as soon as you have the Grangers."

"Ten-four."

Ending the call, she pocketed the cell phone in exchange for her SAT phone and called in the update Langley was expecting. She knew they'd have heard about the dead American tourist in Cologne and recognized the local police report for what it really was. She'd have a lot to answer for. Dialing the number, she breathed deeply as the phone rang.

"East Bay Telecom," a young lady answered. "How may I direct your call?"

"Wakefield, Tammy Daniel. Agent 72733002."

"Hold, please."

The baritone voice of her boss was intimidating enough. Adding to that his six foot two inch ex-navy SEAL frame and, well, she didn't like the position she was in, even if it was from the safety of another continent.

"You've got ninety seconds to explain," he said.

"We underestimated the threat, making a few miscalculations in our tactical approach, which resulted in the death of one of my agents and the capture of three others. We've located the captured agents and are currently acting to secure their return."

"Name of the deceased? I need to notify next of kin and prepare a cover story."

"William Bubba Franks."

"And those agents captured?"

"The Grangers. Leecy, Valerie, and Ron Granger."

"Hold on a second, Agent Wakefield. Are you telling me Ron Granger allowed someone to get the drop on him?"

"Not just him, but all of us, sir. No one saw it coming."

"I'll be damned."

"We're thinking the database breech your office notified me of may have aided our targets in outflanking us. The main target of this operation is suspected to be a world-class hacker."

"Let me get this straight, Agent." His voice dropped an octave, causing the phone in her hand to vibrate. "First, there's the explosion in Sevastopol, and now the death of an agent and the kidnapping of three more. And you're trying to cover your ass by blaming the mission failure on the attempted computer hack? Look, I don't need to tell you this doesn't bode well for you or your team. I hope you have more of an explanation than that."

"All due respect, Sir, but the hack is a viable explanation given the skill set of the target."

"Yes it is," he agreed, his voice retreating to its normal tone, "but there's a problem with that theory."

"What's the problem?"

"Our IT people are reporting the hack was a multi-pronged attack. It involved a dozen or more breeches to our system all running concurrently. IT has even given the method a nickname. They're calling it 'Medusa.'"

"That sounds ominous, but what's the problem?"

"It is ominous. In an effort to stave off the damage, the IT folks tell me they sent back some sort of a scrubbing virus to the hackers, attaching it to Medusa—which, I'm told, is essentially a very sophisticated computer algorithm—in hopes of erasing any pilfered data. If your target is behind it, and we believe she is, she's much more dangerous than we first believed her to be."

"Still not hearing the problem, Sir. What data did she extract from the system?"

"That's the beauty, if you will allow me, and the problem with what she's done. The folks in the IT department don't yet know the extent of the damage. I'm told it will take days to discover what she was after, but thankfully, they've been able to lock her out of the system. They think. Jesus, this is bad."

"What? We don't know what information got out? Look, I...*we*...don't have days; we have hours. I've got agents in harm's way."

"We're running it down. That's the best I can do for now."

"And if this breech leads to the deaths of my agents?"

"Follow your protocols. That's all any of us can do now."

"Jesus, it sounds like we're giving up."

"Just being pragmatic," he said, his voice more stern as he changed the subject. "Look, our two best computer forensic people are en route, and Interpol will be joining the takedown tonight. Our top priority, or should I say *your* top priority, is Tia Reins and her equipment and software. Do you understand?"

"I understand."

"I'll be eagerly awaiting your post-mission report. I'll

expect it before noon tomorrow."

"I understand."

"Are you hearing me, Agent?"

"Yes, I hear you, and I'll submit the full report as always when the mission is over."

"Very well, Agent Wakefield, but do yourself and me a favor and no more mistakes. Keep this hacking incident under wraps for now. We don't want it getting out to the public and undermining the confidence of our agents in the field, okay?"

"Roger that, Sir."

With the connection severed, she pocketed the SAT phone and made her way to the lobby to do the only thing she could do, which was wait. Checking her watch, she saw it was a quarter till ten. Feeling powerless, she retrieved her mobile and called Ryan for an update.

"Ryan, here."

"Status?"

"All clear. No sign of life inside the building and no movement on the outside."

"Zach's found the Grangers. Hodges is on task."

"I better get moving. He'll need backup."

"No, stay put. I need eyes on that building. I need to know the second you see any activity at all. Do you copy?"

"Roger that. Staying put, and babysitting a building."

"Wakefield out," she said, ending the call. She wondered if her problem child of an agent would stay put, then she got an idea. Looking around the small lobby, making certain she was alone, she called Zach.

"Zach, here."

"Can you access any CCTV cameras near the CCP building? Or how about the camera Granger reported seeing mounted on the building itself?"

"Can't do the camera on the building because Tia's system is too difficult to access. Well, I could, but it would take way too long."

"Zach, I need you to focus," Wakefield said.

"Sorry," he said, typing again. "Okay. What do we have? We've got traffic cameras located on the eastern corner, but I'm only getting half the building and no shot of the front door. Wait a tick. What's this?"

"What? What'd you find?"

"The bank next door to the CCP building is watching its entrance from across the street, and that camera view is picking up the entrance to the CCP building."

"Perfect," Wakefield said. "Start recording now. And tell me what you know about the rear of the CCP building."

"That's useless to us. It's a courtyard. No vehicle access at all, and since all the other buildings on that block back up to the courtyard, it's not private. I don't think Tia would risk using it."

"I agree. Stay on that camera view of the entrance and alert me the moment you see any activity, and I mean anything. Even if it's a pizza delivery boy, you got me?"

"Roger that."

Dialing another number, she said, "Hi, it's Wakefield."

"Pleasure hearing from you," Robert Jeffery Leeds said, "but I should be seeing you very soon."

"That's why I'm calling you. I wanted to know your ETA."

"Once your boys from Langley arrive here in Brussels, which should be any time now, we're a two-hour flight away."

Glancing at her watch, she said, "Looks like you guys will be maintaining the schedule if you're in the air in the next fifteen minutes. That's perfect. Great, then. Okay, I'll see you at eleven."

"Yes, and I've just received a text that your boys have landed. All according to plan."

"Great. See you in a couple of hours. Bye."

"Yes, hold on. Don't dash off just yet."

"Why? Is there something else?"

"I know what I'm about to say is highly irregular, but may I be so bold as to suggest if all goes well, you join me for tea after we conclude our business?"

"Are you asking me out on a date after the mission?" Wakefield asked, looking around to see if anyone was listening. Remembering she was alone, she relaxed and added, "I can't do that."

"Why? Are you married?"

"No."

"Involved with someone?"

"No, not currently," she said, allowing a smile to creep across her face.

"It's settled, then. You'll join me for tea after we bring this operation home, won't you?"

"Sure," she said, "but I have reports to file and..."

"So do I," he said, interrupting her. "What say I call you on your mobile when I've completed my paperwork and we make some concrete plans?"

"Okay."

"Now, I have to run. Your boys are taxiing to a stop. Wheels up shortly. See you soon."

"Bye," she said, ending the call, only to have the phone vibrate in her hand immediately.

"Wakefield, here."

"I've got a car arriving at CCP," Zach said.

***

"Now what?" Hector asked.

"Now whatever we want," Lee answered. He walked toward me and asked, "You're not CIA, are you?"

"Why are you wasting our time questioning him?" Hector asked. "Grab a flashlight and let's bring the women topside and have some fun."

"Yeah, we'll get to that in a minute. Those ladies aren't going anywhere. But right now, I have questions for this guy," Lee said, walking toward the crate and stuffing his phone in his pocket. He grabbed the gun and shoved it down the front of his pants with the handle hanging out over his waistband. Then he picked up the flashlight and shone it in my face. "Well?"

"No," I answered. "I'm not, nor have I ever been, CIA."

"And what's the preparations she had to make. What's that about?"

"I'll answer all your questions, but I've been hanging here for a long time. Can you let me down, first?"

Spinning clockwise on the heel of his left boot, Lee sent a kick crashing into my right side.

"No, you answer my questions or the next kick is full strength into your injured ribs."

I was spinning in circles from the force of the blow, and said, "That wasn't full strength? Jesus, man, that's the kick I saw you knock Ronaldo Hoya out of the ring with a few years back."

"So you're a fan?"

"Sure, I'm a fan," I said, spinning to a stop. I looked at the tape around my wrist, hoping to see some tearing. I did.

"Look, I don't want to beat on you, so just answer my questions."

"To hell with this," Hector said. "It's a waste of time. I'm getting the ladies."

"Hector!" Lee said. "Don't do that. Just wait. Give me a minute. If I'm right, you're going to want to hear what Heely has to say."

"Whatever, man, but I get first crack with the young one when you're finished with Heely."

"We'll see," Lee said, taking charge of the situation and looking at Furukawa standing near the crate a few feet behind him. "You're part of this, too, remember, but I think we'll need to renegotiate the terms we agreed to in the van, seeing as how I'm getting my hands dirty and all."

"Sure," Furukawa said. "No problem. I see you're onto something. Please continue."

"You're onto something, all right," I said. "But you can forget your agreement. I assume it's about splitting the two million dollars Tia offered you to kill us."

"Why should we forget about that?" Hector asked, suddenly interested.

"Lee knows. He's onto your boss and her little plan to run off with this mystery partner of hers and take her two million dollars with her."

"You don't know that," Lee argued. "We're supposed to meet her when we finish with you and your women. She said she'd pay us tonight and take us with her. She said our future depended on killing you."

"Come on, man," I said. "I thought you were paying attention earlier. She left you here. She's preparing for a trip; one that doesn't include any of you. She's not bringing security guys with her to the new gig. You two are not only unemployed, but also broke. She's taking that two million dollars with her."

"Look, I was contracted to kill Heely, not partner up with the guy," Hector pushed in. "Let's have some fun with the ladies, then do our jobs and collect our money before it's too late. Something big is living down there, and if we wait much longer, there won't be anything left of those ladies to have fun with."

"Yeah, I agree," Lee said, watching me. "Let's stick to the agreement we have with Tia. But which one of us is going down there to get the girls? That growling sounded like a wolf or something."

"That's not a wolf," I said.

Turning his light toward Hector, Lee froze. His light was shining on Leecy. She was standing next to Hector, holding the flat edge of a tire iron to his throat.

"That's impossible."

"Take it easy, fellas," Leecy said.

"That's right, boys," Val added, standing on the other side of Hector, between him and Furukawa, and holding a tire iron of her own. "Don't get excited and do something stupid."

"But I tied you up," Furukawa said, inching away from Valerie toward the edge of darkness on my right.

"Not very well," Leecy said. "You need to work on your square knots. I'll tell you what: you come down in that pit with me and I'll demonstrate on you while I tie you to the stairs."

"No, I don't think I'll be joining you down there," he said before bolting away, running toward the rear of the building.

Leecy ran forward a few feet, but Lee drew his gun. The sound of breaking glass echoed through the building.

"He's jumped out a rear window," Lee said.

"How do you know that?" Hector asked.

"He told me about three offices along the back wall

with windows to the outside."

"Coward," Hector said.

"Not a coward," Val disagreed. "He got out before he got himself killed."

Waving the gun in her direction, Lee said, "Drop the weapon and come stand next to your friend here where I can see you. And you," he gestured at Leecy with the gun, "drop that tire iron."

Val did as he instructed and stood next to Leecy. Looking at me, she asked, "You hanging in there?"

"That's about all I'm doing."

"Not much longer now."

"Good, I'm getting tired."

"Shut up," Hector said, walking toward me and punching me in my bruised rib cage, sending me swinging and spinning wildly away from him. I screamed, but only loud enough and long enough to cover the sound of the tearing duct tape. Hector walked away, leaving me swinging slowly back and forth, and continued talking to Lee. "Since the coward ran away, looks like we get all the money and the women."

Grabbing Leecy by the arm and pressing the gun into her check, Lee said, "I'm taking this one. You can have the other one."

Pulling down hard on the tape that was holding my wrists together, screaming with pain and lifting my legs, I kicked Lee in the face. The force of the blow sent me swinging and spinning away from him as he crashed into Hector.

Swinging back toward the falling pair, reaching the bottom of the arc, where the greatest amount of downward force was being applied, the tape gave way. Free of the chain, I was flying into the two men. The gun fell to the floor and slid across the concrete till it landed on the floor inside the pit, firing off one round.

Picking up the tire iron she'd dropped, Leecy sent the metal bar smashing into the back of Lee's head and said, "No one touches me, or did you forget what happened to your big friend?"

Val kicked Hector in the face, following it quickly with the same spinning sidekick she'd taught Leecy. The heel of her boot crashed into his head, knocking him unconscious.

"Well done, ladies," I said, lying on the filthy floor, exhausted.

"Way to hang in there for so..." Leecy started to say, but was interrupted by the sound of the van's engine turning over. Unable to stop him, all we could do was watch Furukawa drive away.

"Well, there goes our ride," I said, staggering to my feet.

"Jesus, Ron," Val said, pulling one of the rolling chairs over and helping me sit. "How bad is it?"

"You need to ask?"

"Your ribs are broken, now, no question. We've got to get you to a doctor. You might have a punctured lung. Take a deep breath for me."

I did as my wife instructed.

"No. No lung punctures. Leecy, grab that flashlight and see if you can find any bandages."

"On it," she said, grabbing the light lying on the floor next to Hector and began searching both men and the immediate area. "Lee's phone was broken in the fall. It's useless now. Hector only had some cash on him. I've got your bandages. Good thing they didn't cut them off of you like your clothes. We can use them."

"Now I need you to strip off Lee's shirt," I said. "He's the bigger of the two. Then use their belts to bind their hands together behind their backs."

"Mom, I need some help with that last request."

"Okay, but first you help me wrap Ron's ribcage. We'll deal with those two in a minute."

With my ribcage wrapped up tight, and wearing Lee's shirt and sweater, I said, "Leecy, unhook the chain from the wall and walk that hoist closer to the bodies."

"That thing moves?" she asked.

"Yes, it's a trolley engine block hoist. It's designed to serve two sides of the building or two inline pits. Shine your light up there and you'll see there are three of them mounted in the rafters. I've been staring up at them for over an hour."

"Oh yeah, I see. So you think it'll move?"

"Only one way to find out."

With both Val and Leecy pulling on the chain, the trolley slowly moved into position over the two unconscious men.

"Okay," Leecy said, breathing heavily, "now what?"

"Pull the chain I was suspended from down to the floor."

"Okay."

The chain moved more freely than the hoist had, because Hector and Lee had broken it free from the rust that was hampering its movement.

"Ron," Val said between breaths, "why are we doing this?"

Ignoring her question, I said, "Now sit those two up back to back and wrap the chain around them. Make it as secure as you can."

"What the hell?" Lee asked, coming around.

"Yeah," Hector said. "What the hell is going on?"

"I told you two the first day we met not to make this relationship adversarial," I said. "Do you remember that conversation?"

"Yes, I do," Lee said. "But we were just following orders. Besides, Furukawa's the one that shocked you with the battery and the jumper cables, not us."

"Yes, that is true, but he's not here and you two are. The question is, do you want to help me get you your money, or do you want me to leave you here? You two talk it over. I'll be back."

Standing and leaning heavily on Valerie and Leecy, we walked toward the exit and the fresh night air. Once outside, I stood under my own power and breathed in as deeply as the pain would allow.

"Now what about this report Tia claims to have?" Val asked.

"Do you think she really hacked the CIA?" Leecy asked.

"I don't know," I said, rubbing my wrist, "and it really doesn't matter. All we can do is try to convince her otherwise."

"Disinformation campaign?" Leecy asked.

"Yes, exactly," I said. "I laid the foundation while she had me trussed up, and even though I saw her start to doubt herself, we've got more work to do."

"That's if we can get close to her again," Val said.

"We can, and we will," I said.

"How?" Leecy asked. "We're out here in the middle of nowhere without a ride."

"Yeah, that's a problem," I said, looking around the moonlit shipping yard. "Nothing here's been used in decades. We'll just have to wait on the cavalry, I guess."

"Leecy," Val began, "I want you to follow this road back

to the main highway and find somewhere to wait that's out of sight. Someone from our team will be coming for us. When help arrives, prep whoever it is to play the role of a passerby you flagged down for help. We don't want Hector and Lee getting suspicious. We need them to help us get close to Tia."

"Roger that," she said, turning and running away from us in the moonlight.

"Ron," Val said, "we've got to get those two muscle heads on our side. You ready?"

"Yes, and I think Lee's ready to join us. Hector, not so much."

"That's fine. I know what to do. Come on, and just follow my lead."

"Boys, boys," Val said, walking into the rectangle of light and pulling a chair close to the bound men before having a seat. "Have you reached a decision?"

"Of course, we want to get paid," Lee said.

"But that doesn't mean I want to help you," Hector said.

"That's too bad," Valerie said. "I guess we'll be seeing you."

"You can't leave us here," Hector said.

"Sure we can," I said. "Weren't you going to rape the women and then kill all three of us a few minutes ago?"

"That was just talk," Lee said. "We were just trying to scare you, that's all."

"You two," Valerie said, rolling forward in her chair, "are as dumb as you look, you know that?"

"Come on, lady," Hector said. "Don't leave me here."

"You want to leave, then you have to help me."

"How can I help you?"

"We want to get even with Tia for trying to kill us," I answered. "I know you guys were just following orders. I, too, follow orders, but what she did tonight crossed the line, and that doesn't sit right with me."

"That's right, man. We just follow orders," Lee agreed. "She's calling the shots not us. Hey, count me in. I'll help you."

"Hold up," Hector said. "First, let's talk money. If I agree to get you inside CCP, then I'm double-crossing Tia, and if I'm going to do that, then I need getaway-type money."

"Are you really in a position to negotiate?" Val asked.

"The way I see it, I die if you leave me here and I die if I cross Tia without having enough cash to run very far away. You want my help, pay me for it."

"How much money is getaway money, Hector?" I asked.

"Me and Lee split half the take, you and your team split the other half."

"I don't know. Doesn't seem fair. I mean, if I leave you and break into CCP, I can keep all the money."

Laughing, he said, "You do that, Mr. Heely, and she'll see you coming and disappear. You forget you're dealing with a very paranoid woman."

"And just how would she disappear?"

"No, no, no," Hector said, shaking his head from side to side and smiling. "No more answers till we have an agreement on the money and you let us go."

"And give me back my shirt," Lee said. "I'm freezing."

Standing and walking toward the exit behind Val, I said, "Don't go anywhere, boys. We'll be right back."

The hum of the engine grew louder the closer we got to the exit, and there in the darkness, I spotted the outline of the van we'd been using since landing in Cologne. Standing next to it, I saw Leecy talking to the undeniable shape of Hodges.

"Glad to see you," I said, extending my hand.

"You, too, all of you. I guess you heard about Franks?"

"Yes," Val said. "We're sorry. We had no idea she…"

"No," he said, raising a hand. "I don't blame you guys. It's the job. It can happen to any of us at any time. I thought we'd lost you three tonight, too, but I'm glad you're okay."

Placing a hand on his shoulder, I asked, "What's been happening since we lost contact?"

We listened as he brought us up to speed with the team's movements and positions, then we followed suit, telling him all that we'd been through.

"Jesus," he said, rubbing his face. "And to think all this could've been avoided if Ryan had just stayed in position."

"Yeah," I said, "that's crossed my mind a time or two."

"Me, too," Leecy said.

"I'd be lying if I said otherwise," Val offered. "But we can't change what's happened."

"No we can't," Hodges said. "So now what?"

"We'll be bringing Hector and Lee along," I began, "but we need to keep the conversation in front of them to a minimum and make certain we stick to our covers. When we reach the airport, we'll leave the two men with you unless you need Leecy, and meet with Wakefield and the other inbound agents. Then we'll figure out what's going to happen next."

"Okay, sounds good. I can handle them by myself," Hodges agreed. "Do you want me to back the van up inside there or wait here?"

"You and the kid stay right here and check in with the

boss," Val said. "Wait inside the van. We'll be right back."

***

"What's that?" Wakefield asked. "Say again."

"I've got movement in front of the CCP building," Zach repeated. "A big sedan. A lady is getting out and entering the building."

"Are you recording?" she asked, her phone vibrating against her ear, indicating another call was incoming.

"Yes."

"Good. Stay on it, and let me know the moment you see any other movement," she said, ending the call and accepting the new one, expecting it to be Agent Ryan. She said, "Yes, Ryan?"

"No, it's Hodges here, and I've got good news. The Grangers are all present and accounted for, and only slightly worse for wear."

"Brilliant."

"We'll be heading to your location soon."

"Why here?"

"I'll let the Grangers explain when we arrive."

"Oh no, it's one of those, is it?"

"Yes, it is. They're on the scent of something, and you know how they are once that starts."

"Yes, I know all too well, but this time it may be out of our hands."

"Is that right?" he said, looking at Leecy in the rearview mirror. "They won't like that."

"They may not have a choice."

"Well, that's why they pay you the big bucks, Boss. You can handle them. See you in half an hour or more. And you can break the news."

"Great," she said, rubbing her eyes with her fingers. "Regardless, I'm glad they're okay."

"That the boss?" Leecy asked.

"Yes; she's glad you three are okay."

"But not that we're coming to see her?"

"No, I don't think she is."

"Can't say I blame her. This mission's been one bad turn after another. I'm sure she just wants it to be over."

"Yes, I'm sure she does. I know I do."

***

"Okay," I said, unwrapping the chains, "you've got yourselves a deal. One million dollars to split between the two of you for helping us get to Tia."

"Fantastic," Lee said, taking his sweater from me, leaving me wearing his long sleeve t-shirt, "but how do we get back to town?"

"Yeah," Hector agreed, replacing his belt. "I'm not walking fifteen miles in these shoes."

"No one's walking anywhere," Val said. "The young lady flagged down a passerby, and he agreed to give us a lift to the airport where we can rent a car."

"That's awesome," Lee said. "Let's get the hell out of here."

"Hold on," Hector said, grabbing my arm, "let's get something straight before we go anywhere."

"What's that?" I asked, grabbing his fingers as he tightened his grip on my arm.

"You try and double-cross me, and I'll kill you, Old

Man."

I tore his fingers away from my arm.

"That'll be harder than you think."

Grabbing my shoulder with his free hand, he started driving his knee toward my ribs, screaming.

"Fuck you, CIA!"

Releasing my grip on his fingers and blocking the fast-rising knee with both forearms, I decided in an instant to send a message by quickly ending Hector. Swinging my left forearm up under his jutting jaw, I snapped his head back, then stepped forward and slammed a right cross into his exposed trachea. He was dead before his back hit the concrete floor.

I stood over Hector, looking at Lee.

"That's a million, all for you now, or you can take your place beside him. What's it going to be?"

Holding his hands up, he said, "Hey man, I was with you from the beginning. I never believed you were CIA. I just want my money."

"So you won't be giving us any trouble?"

"None. Zero. For a cool million, you'll have my total cooperation."

"Well," Val said, "if we're done playing around, can we get out of here? Our good Samaritan isn't going to wait all night."

"One question for Lee before we go," I said.

"What, man?"

"Hector mentioned Tia would disappear if we broke into CCP. How would she do that?"

"Oh, yeah," Lee answered. "She has an escape door that leads to the courtyard. It's hidden at the back of the building, concealed by a white trellis."

"And how does she gain access to the door from inside

the building?"

"The door is hidden behind the curtains at the bottom of the stairs leading to Laird's room."

"Can the door be opened from the outside?"

"After you unlock it from the inside."

"Thank you, Lee," I said. "Now we can go."

Climbing in the van, Leecy introduced Lee to the man he would only know as Hodges, the passerby, and then she asked, "Where's Hector?"

"He decided to stay," Val said. "Let's get going." Closing the front passenger side door and taking her seat, she added, "Thank you so much, Mr. Hodges. I hope we're not putting you out. Did you call your family and explain to them you'll be late?"

Driving through the shipping yard, Hodges said, "Talked to the wife or, as I call her, the boss. She's expecting me to be a little late, but just glad you folks are all in one piece after your accident. She's glad I'm here to help. She's a big believer in karma."

"And you don't mind driving us to the airport?"

"Like I said, I'm happy to help. Just sit back and relax; we'll be there in thirty minutes or so."

CHAPTER

TEN

RETALIATION

"Mr. Hodges," Val said, "do you mind our troubling you for a little while longer while we check on the availability of a rental car?"

"Happy to wait."

"This may take a few minutes. Are you sure you don't mind?"

"Take all the time you need. Don't give it another thought. I don't see many Americans, and it's been nice talking to you. I'm happy to wait for as long as you need."

Climbing down out of the van, Val said, "Thanks so much."

"Lee," I said, opening the sliding door, "stay here with our new friend. We'll be back as soon as we can."

"Yeah, man. Sure, no problem. It's warm in here."

Walking toward the airport, I asked, "Laying it on a bit thick, aren't we?"

"No." Then Val smiled and added, "Well, maybe a little."

"Where are we going?" Leecy asked. "I know we're not renting a car."

"No, we're not," I said. "We're headed toward the FBO, or fixed base operator section, of the airport. It's a separate section of the airport grounds where the private planes can refuel and hangar as needed. That's where Wakefield will be."

"I knew that," Leecy said, "but I thought FBO was strictly an American thing."

"It was, but it's catching on overseas," I answered. "This way. Come on; we don't have a lot of time, it's after eleven."

Pushing through the doors leading to the FBO offices, we jogged across the open tarmac toward the small glass and steel building a hundred yards away. A small private jet was landing in the distance, and I wondered if it was the CIA team Wakefield said would be joining us. Reaching the building, I could see Agent Wakefield through the glass doors. She was alone and seated on the couch, sipping coffee from a disposable coffee cup.

"Wakefield," I said, entering the lobby, "we need to talk."

Turning her head in our direction, Wakefield did a spit take at the sight of us spraying the floor with coffee, "My God," she said, "what in the hell happened to you three?"

"Long story," Val said, "but right now we need to talk about Tia."

"What's that on your clothes and faces?"

"Decades-old motor oil and grease," Leecy said. "Bonus is, it smells worse than it looks."

The pungent aromas replacing the warm fresh air of the small waiting room finally reached her nose.

"Christ, that's awful, but only half as bad as you look. Ron, you're pale and sweating like a pig. What gives?"

"Slow down," I said, raising my hands, "just pump the

brakes on all this worry. I'm solid. What we need to worry about is Tia. It's worse than we first thought."

"How so?" She asked, reaching into her jacket pocket and retrieving her vibrating mobile phone.

"There's no more questioning the silent partner's influence over her. This person has enough cachet to convince her she's in total control of the operation they were conducting together. She said as much herself. We need to pursue this thing."

Looking at her phone, Wakefield spoke to us while reading a text.

"Yes, I know what you want to do, but the fact remains that we follow orders, and your feelings about this operation don't change a thing." She waved her phone at us and added, "CIA computer boys and Agent Leeds of Interpol have landed. Game's over. We take Tia and her people down, confiscate her gear as instructed, and we'll be out of here by midnight."

"Did you hear what Ron said?" Valerie asked. "This thing, whatever it is, is bigger than just her, now."

"End of discussion," Wakefield said, walking toward the door of the FBO. "We have our orders."

"Would it change your mind to know Tia claims to have hacked the CIA? She tried to kill us because she discovered Peter Heely was a name in the CIA database."

With one hand on the door, she stopped and looked at us in the reflection of the glass.

"Impossible. Now drop it, and follow me."

Walking toward the taxiing silver Gulfstream 5, growing more determined to make my case, I decided I wasn't going to give up so easily.

After collecting our old friend Robert Leeds and the two-person CIA computer forensic team, we were walking toward the main airport when I made my play.

"Agent Leeds," I said, "there's new information you need to be made aware of."

"Can't this wait till we've left the very public airfield?"

"No, sir," I answered. "It can't."

He looked around, spreading his arms wide before checking the time on his Rolex.

"Well we're out here on the tarmac, and I doubt anyone is listening. I'll give you five minutes. Please proceed." He placed his hands in his pants pockets.

I tried not to make eye contact with Wakefield because I knew she was fuming with anger over my act of insubordination.

"As you may or may not be aware, we were taken prisoner by the target earlier this evening and held for several hours."

Shuffling his stance, clasping his hands behind his back, he said, "That explains it, then."

"Explains what?" Leecy asked.

"You're...well, I wasn't going to say anything, but it explains the dreadful smell and attire."

"Yeah, well, fieldwork's not all tuxedos and cocktail dresses," Leecy snapped. "That crap only happens in James Bond movies. What we've been dealing with is real life."

"Please continue, Mr. Granger," Leeds said, smiling that megawatt smile of his.

"While we were being held," I said, "Tia revealed she's about to improve her standing in the organization she's a part of. She also claims to have hacked the CIA and discovered my cover identity in the process."

Shuffling his stance again, unclasping his hands and rubbing his chin, he said, "I must admit I was curious as to how you, of all people, came to be a prisoner. So, she got the drop on you because of the information derived from the hack."

"Hold on a second," Wakefield said over her vibrating mobile phone, "there's no evidence of any hack on the CIA or any of its various databases."

"Then how do you explain her knowledge of the name Peter Heely?" Agent Leeds asked, turning to face Wakefield.

"Excuse me," she said, placing the phone to her ear.

"They're any number of explanations," I said, answering for Tammy. I realized that her defensive posture meant there might be some truth to Tia's claim of hacking the CIA. "The one explanation I worked very hard to get Tia to believe was that her new partner planted the info by dummying up a CIA website for Tia and her hackers to access."

With his eyes on Tammy, he asked me, "Do you think Tia bought it?"

"Yes. Well, almost. Enough to justify pushing her harder on the subject, and maybe getting the name of her partner in the process."

"That's risky," he said, turning to face me.

"Sure it is," Val said. "But we've risked everything getting this far. Give us a chance at bringing this home for you."

"You really believe you can pull a fast one on her?"

"Tia's paranoid," Leecy said. "I don't think it'll take much of a push. From what Ron's told us she's halfway there."

"I can give you half an hour with her, but not a minute longer," he said, looking at his watch again. "I have a schedule I must keep. People to answer to."

"Believe me, I know, and thirty minutes is more than

enough time," I said. "But there is one other thing you should be aware of."

"Sorry about that," Wakefield said, ending the call. "One of my other agents reporting in. He's got eyes on the CCP building. What's this other thing you're talking about, Ron?"

"It's nothing. Really, it isn't. It's just we can't walk in the front door of CCP without spooking Tia."

"Tell me you've found a way in, or this entire conversation's been a colossal waste of time," Agent Leeds said.

"I've got a plan, but it involves one of Tia's henchman and a payoff." Sensing push back coming, I quickly added, "The money isn't a problem. Tia has it, and the guy we're going to use to access the building knows where it is."

"Then, why do I sense a major 'but' coming my way?"

"Because we need to let the guy go, or make him think we're letting him go, for this plan to work."

"Ron," Wakefield said, "I'm calling an end to this right now. We don't have the manpower to tail this guy."

"We don't want you to tail the guy," Val said. "Just let him walk out of the building and pick him up a few blocks away."

"I say again, we don't have the manpower for that. The guy could go in any number of directions."

"Jesus," Leecy said, "just have Zach meet us and tell him to bring his microdots. You'll be able to track the bag of money wherever it goes."

"Okay," Wakefield said, "and when he ditches the bag, then what? And now that I'm thinking about it, how do you know this guy will even cooperate with you?"

"First, he won't ditch a bag containing a million dollars,

and to answer your second question, we know he'll cooperate because he's in the van with Hodges right now, waiting for us."

"And when, exactly, were you three planning on telling me all of this?"

"We tried to tell you in the FBO lobby, but you shut us down."

Agent Robert Jeffery Leeds' laughter filled the void that followed our arguing with Wakefield and said, "Okay, okay, you have your thirty minutes. You Americans are nothing if not entertaining, but," he slowly regained his composure, "also effective. Come on, let's get on with it. Wakefield, you ride with me."

"Yeah," I said, "don't drive off just yet, 'cause you'll need to make room for Hodges, too."

"Really, and why is that?"

"We're going to need to stage a little carjacking to sell this thing to Tia's boy."

Walking toward the main airport, he quipped, "Pulling out all the stops to sell the charade, are we?"

"Yeah, something like that," I said, bracing against the cold. "Tammy, you guys can take up position west of CCP on the corner nearest the bank. Have Zach meet our van under the walkway next to the museum. Tell him to bring the bag and the microdots."

"Anything else?" she asked. "Like maybe a jacket?"

"No, don't want one."

"Suit yourself. I'll let Ryan know we're in play and bring him up to speed. I don't want him panicking when he sees you three on scene."

"Just make sure he holds his position," I said. "I don't need him running off half-cocked on this."

"Neither do I."

***

Arriving at the rendezvous point beneath the walkway connecting the museum and the Cathedral, Lee asked, "Why are we stopping here?"

"What?" I asked. "Did you really think we're walking in the CCP building to see sword lady unarmed?"

"I didn't really think about it. After what you did to poor Mr. Hodges back at the airport, not to mention Hector, I didn't think you needed any weapons."

"Well, we do," Leecy said. "We're meeting a contact here to make a quick purchase and then we'll be on our way. Just sit tight and think about all that money you'll be counting soon."

"Yeah, whatever. Just hurry up. The sooner we get where we're going, the sooner I can get out of town. I mean that's the deal, right? I get the door open, see you three get inside, and then I get to bolt with the money."

"That's exactly what we're thinking," Val agreed.

"Good. I was hoping you wouldn't make me stick around."

"Flashing headlights," I said. "That's our contact. Let's go. Lee?"

"Yeah, man, what's up?"

"We're leaving you unguarded while we meet with this guy," I said, opening the driver's side door. "If you run, not only will you not get paid, but in addition to your pockets being empty you'll be hunted by the three of us."

"I'm the least of your concerns, my man," he said, stretching out across the rear bench seat.

Walking toward the car that flashed its headlights, I

said, "Zach, that you?"

Opening the door of the smart electric car, he said, "I know. Don't say it. The hotel lets guests use it as a courtesy."

"Some perk," Leecy said. "It looks good on you."

I don't know why that comment struck me as odd, but it did. Looking between the two of them, Leecy playfully punching Zach in the arm, I had to push my daddy thoughts aside.

"Did you bring the bag?"

"Yep," he said, catching a whiff of us. "What's that smell?"

"Long story," I answered. Unzipping the bag, I handed Leecy a Sig Saur and Val a Glock. "Microdots?"

"Oh," he said, reaching into his jacket pocket. "I almost forgot. Here." He offered each us an earpiece and a microdot.

"But I thought she could jam our earpieces," Leecy said, looking at the two objects in the palm of her hand. "And why three microdots? We only need one."

"I've been making a workaround. The earpieces have been reengineered to function over my cell phone frequency. I just used the Bluetooth feature on the phone to pair with the earpieces, and by using three way..."

"Zach," I said, interrupting him. "Sorry, buddy, but we don't care about the how."

"I care, Zach," Leecy said, touching his shoulder.

"Thanks, I know you do, but Granger's right. I get carried away sometimes. You'll be patched in and able to hear everything that's said. Now, as far as the microdots are concerned, they've always been an unreliable technology, so I'm just covering our collective asses by using three."

"Good, then," I said, walking away. "See you when it's

done."

Climbing inside the van, Lee asked, "You guys all geared up and ready to go, now?"

"Yeah," I said, "we're ready. You'll be a rich man in about ten minutes."

I parked the van one block south of the CCP building. Leecy, Val, Lee, and I began walking north toward Portalsgasse. I could hear the sounds of music playing and the voices of the dwindling crowds in the shopping district two blocks west. The smell of stale beer and cigarettes had replaced the aroma of fried dough and French fries I remembered from the day before.

We walked by the van I knew held Wakefield, Leeds, Zach, and the two CIA computer forensics teammates. "Lee," I said, "the three of us will hold in front of the bank. I don't want to be spotted by the camera mounted on the CCP building. Someone might be watching."

"Yeah, man, I get it," Lee said. "But you see that car? That's Tia's car. What if she's in the lobby when I go inside?"

"That's why you're here. Run interference, and know we'll be right behind you," Leecy assured him. "You can always tell her you're there for your money. Where's the money being kept, anyway?"

"Yeah, I can do that. The last place I saw the money was in the downstairs office."

"Great. That's our first stop," Leecy continued, focusing Lee's mind on the money. "Let's get you paid and get you the hell out of there as quickly as we can."

We watched as Lee waved his keycard in front of the

door sensor. Entering the building, I said, "Move in five, four, three..."

But Lee opening the door and calling to us cut me off. "Come on. No one's here."

We joined Lee in the lobby and followed him through the doors leading to the downstairs office. Val said, "That wasn't part of the plan."

Walking through Laird's mini history museum toward the office manager's door, Lee responded. "Yeah, I know, but we're in. That's what you wanted."

"Let's just get the money and get you out of here," I said, brushing past him and opening the door to the office. Seeing the two black duffel bags on the desktop, I said, "Great, they're exactly where you said they'd be." I unzipped one of the bags, thrusting my hand inside like I was checking the contents. I dropped a microdot. "And the money is inside," I confirmed.

Pushing past Lee to unzip the other bag, following my example, Leecy said, "This one looks good, too, and you know what that means, don't you, Lee?"

"No. What're you talking about?" Lee asked.

Slapping him on the back, affixing her microdot to the fabric of his wool sweater, Val said, "It's all yours. All two million."

He walked toward the desk, looking inside both bags before zipping them closed and lifting them over his shoulders. "That's awesome. Thank you so much. It's been a pleasure doing business with you."

We followed him out of the office toward the lobby, opening the front door for him, and watched him leave the building. I asked, "Zach? You there?"

"Reading you loud and clear."

"Money bags just left the building."

"We've got the signals," Wakefield said. "Hodges is on it."

"Now," I said, turning to face Leecy and Val, "let's find Tia."

***

Typing feverishly on the wireless keyboard, Tia paused, reading the results of her labor, and said, "So that's who I was sleeping with."

Removing her cell phone from her pocket she called Taka and said, "Where are you? Have you loaded the MI5 components?"

"I'm doing that now, Miss Reins."

"I'm leaving soon. Make sure I don't leave without them."

She leaned back in the chair before pushing off the tabletop to stand, and walked forward toward the mostly empty computer cages. She briefly flashed on her father. He would be asleep now. She wondered what he'd do when he woke up tomorrow and found himself alone, but laughed away the concern, saying to no one, "He'll just check his balance sheet like always, and call his masseuse. He'll never even know I'm gone."

"Oh, sure he will," I said. "After all, you're Daddy's little girl assassin, aren't you?"

Spinning around and drawing her sword in one swift motion, she was running in our direction, covering the thirty meters of floor between us in a furious rage.

"Impossible!"

Aiming her Glock, Val said, "Stop, or I'll shoot."

Tia was six feet away when the shot rang out. It echoed

loudly off the concrete floor and ceiling, knocking the sword from Tia's hand and sending her sprawling across the floor on her back. The bullet, having ricocheted off the hilt of Tia's sword, exploded the iPad into hundreds of pieces.

"She said stop," Leecy barked, holstering her gun and running toward the downed Tia. She kicked the sword away. "What, you got a death wish all of a sudden?"

"I heard what she said," Tia seethed, cradling her injured right hand in her left. "But why'd you shoot me in my hand?" Then, smelling Leecy, she added, "You stink."

"Yeah, well you put me down in that hole, so it's your fault I smell like raccoon piss and shit." Grabbing Tia's left arm and helping her to her feet, she added, "Don't worry; we're not going to kill you right away. We've got some questions for you."

"Can I at least have something to wrap my hand with?" Tia asked.

"Come on," Leecy answered, "I thought you were tough. It's just a little flesh wound. The iPad took more of a hit than you."

"Yeah, but I'm bleeding."

"Wrap it up in your shirt. That's as good as it's going to get."

Tia stopped walking and bent down, retrieving a piece of paper from the floor and placing it over the wound in her hand. She asked, "How'd you three escape?"

Picking the overturned desk chair up off the floor, and righting the small desk that once held the now shattered iPad, I said, "Here, sit down." I pointed at the busted iPad. "I hope nothing too important was saved on that thing."

Tia shrugged, looking over her shoulder in my direction, and said, "You'll never know. I've got nothing else to say, so just get to it. Kill me."

"I don't think so," Val said. "That's not what you had planned for us."

I heard Wakefield coming in loud and clear over Zach's new earpiece. She announced that Hodges had picked up Lee and the money. The two men were waiting in the van I'd driven from the airport.

"You should know Hector and Lee are dead," I said. "You'll be joining them in the afterlife, but not before I learn the name of the man you met yesterday."

Pressing the piece of paper into the fleshy part of her hand between the thumb and forefinger, she looked at me and said, "Go to hell."

I walked toward the broken pieces of the iPad, bending down and selecting the largest piece. I handed it to Val. "You of all people should know that everyone talks."

"We want to know the name of the man you're working with," Leecy said.

"I don't know his name. He never told me who he was."

Val sat down on Tia's lap. She pinned Tia's hands beneath her thighs one at a time, and then grabbed hold of her hair with one hand while she pressed the piece of broken iPad into the skin below her left eye. "We need a name or I'm going to pop your eyeball out of your head like a cork out of a bottle," she said. "Do you feel the pressure building at the base of your eyeball?"

"Yes, yes," Tia said. She tried to turn her head, but Valerie's grip was too strong.

"All it takes is sixteen pounds of pressure to dislodge your eye from its socket, and I'm about halfway there. Who are you working with? Is losing your sight really worth keeping his name a secret?"

Tia tried closing her eyes, but with her head pulled back, all she managed to do was look right into Valerie's unflinching gaze. Tears filled Tia's eyes and began spilling down her cheeks.

"Next thing to happen is your eyeball pops out, hanging on your cheek like a grape. Then I'll slice through the connective tissue and feed it to you," Val said.

"His name is Ilion!" Tia screamed through her tears. "Just stop, okay! Just stop!"

Valerie stood up.

"Ilion. Tell us all about him. Start with how you met."

"I should've listened to you, all of you," Tia said, blinking rapidly and rubbing her face. "I should've especially listened to you, Peter. You tried to tell me when we were back in the garage." She paused to wipe away another tear. "You're much better at this torture thing than I am, or even than Mr. Furukawa claims to be."

"Ilion?" I asked. "How'd you meet?"

She looked at the three of us like she was seeing us for the first time.

"Where is Mr. Furukawa? Did you kill him, too?"

"No," Leecy answered. "He ran away before we got the chance."

"Peter called it," Tia said. "Everything he said was true. Ilion is the guy that had the device planted, and the man I met with yesterday. He's rich and..." She paused, looking sideways and blushing, "well, he's just too good to be true. But that doesn't mean we can't all go work for him, now. It's not too late. I mean, that is, if you can get past the part where I tried to kill you."

"Yeah," Leecy said, leaning against the small desk, "that might be a tough ask. What else can you tell us? Where'd you meet him? Here in Cologne somewhere?"

"No, he flew me to Geneva. We met in his hotel suite and then he flew me back early this morning. His plane is waiting to bring me to him tonight."

***

"Zach," Wakefield said. "Looks like Granger was right. What'd you get on those tail numbers I asked you to run down for me?"

"Oh yeah, I almost forgot. Five of them were registered to Cologne businesses."

"And the sixth one."

"That one's ownership is buried under a list of subsidiaries a mile long."

"I need to know who owns that one particularly."

"I'm on it. But right now," pointing at his computer screen, "we've got movement again in front of the CCP building."

"Is that Ryan?" Wakefield asked.

"It appears so. Looks like he's abandoned his position."

"Ryan?" Wakefield asked. "What are you doing?"

"I'm just moving in for a closer look."

"Hold position."

"All do respect, but I'm doing my job," he said as Wakefield watched him on the laptop screen check the trunk of the sedan parked in the street. "Computers. Looks like she's planning on taking the MI5 components with her."

"Okay," Wakefield said. "Just return to your previous position and hold."

"Wait, I think the guy's coming back," Ryan said.

Wakefield watched as Ryan hid behind the sedan and the man opened the rear passenger door placing a square object on the rear seat before walking toward the building. Then, she saw Ryan pursuing the man and said, "Stop what you're doing, and return to your position and hold."

Ryan was last seen entering the building before the door closed without responding.

"Move out," Wakefield said. "Hodges stay in the van with the prisoner. Zach, Leeds follow me and I want the computer nerds bringing up the rear."

***

"Geneva?" I asked. "Why Geneva?"

"Look, I don't know. All I know is that's where he was and so that's where I went." She held her wounded hand up. "This thing is killing me. Can I have something for the pain?"

"Yeah," I heard the voice behind me and in my ear simultaneously. Turning toward the sound, I saw Ryan walking into the room aiming a Taser at Tia. "You can have something for the pain," he said, and fired.

"What the hell, Ryan?" Wakefield said, rushing into the room behind him. "How many times did I tell you to hold? What've you done?"

"I've just prevented Tia and her man from escaping with the highly valuable computer components we wanted to secure. You can thank me later."

"That's not the only thing we were after, Ryan," Wakefield said.

"All's not lost," Agent Leeds said. "You three still have

time if you want to try and salvage something out of this mess."

"There's not enough time in the world to fix this," Wakefield said. She walked toward Zach, saying. "Come with me. There's something I need you to do for me." She stopped "I'll be downstairs in the lobby," she said to us. "If you come up with a brilliant idea, let me know."

"Look, I'm sorry," Ryan said, "but I didn't want the guy driving away, that's all."

"If that was all," Leecy said, "then why come up here and tase Tia?"

"'Cause I thought the guy came up here. Did you see him?"

"No. Seems to me you lost the guy you claimed to be such a threat."

"Trust me; he's in the building. We'll find him. But the real reason I came up here was to protect the target from you three. I know you don't carry Tasers, and I didn't want you to injure her with one of your fancy interrogation techniques."

"But weren't you listening?" Leecy asked, pointing at her ear. "We weren't torturing her."

"My cell phone was fading in and out," he said, shaking his head. "The last thing I heard was her screaming, so I made a judgment call."

"Yeah," Leecy said, walking away from him, "you love making those, don't you."

"Listen, kid," Ryan said, "don't talk to me..."

"Enough!" Agent Leeds bellowed, silencing Ryan. "I've heard enough bickering. This is my operation now, and you'll conduct yourselves with a modicum of respect for each other and the task at hand. Now, Interpol has charged me with finding out where this computer hacking buck stops. If this ends with Tia, then so be it, but from what I've heard, she's found a partner. What's his name? Ilion? Is that right?"

"Yes," I said.

Leeds unbuttoned his suit coat and walked toward the tased body of Tia Reins. "Ryan, you search the building for the missing man."

"There's a hidden exit downstairs," I offered. "I'll show you where it is."

"Fine. Go ahead, you two. And while they sort that out," Leeds continued, "we need to figure out a way to turn this cock-up in our favor. Any ideas?"

"Yes," Val said. "I've got one."

ELEVEN

ARREST

Waking up on the black leather couch in the downstairs mangers office, Tia saw the three of us staring back at her. She tried pushing her hair out of her face, only to realize her hands were cuffed behind her back.

"What happened? How'd I get down here?"

"They made us carry you down," I answered, sitting on the desktop. My hands were cuffed in front of me where Tia could see them.

"They?" she asked, leaning forward on the couch, trying to find a more comfortable position. "'They' who?"

"Interpol," Leecy answered, seated on Tia's right.

"What?" Tia asked, looking at Leecy and seeing that she, too, was cuffed.

"You heard her," Valerie answered, causing Tia to look to her left. She saw Val's hands cuffed in front of her, but also tethered to shackles on her ankles.

"What did you do to deserve that?"

"I shot one of the Interpol agents."

"Are you crazy?"

"No, I don't think I'm crazy. I just didn't want to be

arrested."

"Now what?"

"Don't know exactly," I said. "They dumped us in here and locked the door, but I think they're confiscating your equipment."

Smiling and laughing, she shook her head. "Perfect, that's just perfect," she said.

"I know, right?" Leecy asked. "And we were getting somewhere, too."

"What do you mean?" Tia asked.

"Nothing, really. I mean it doesn't matter now."

"Well don't go silent on us," Tia said. "Might as well share since we're not going anywhere."

"No, I mean it finally felt like we were actually beginning to trust one another."

"Even for you?" she said, looking at me. "After all the...well, you know."

"Not really. Not yet, but I did think you were finally being honest. I have to admit, I was warming to the idea of working with this Ilion."

"Yeah?" she asked. "Too bad that ship has sailed. Or rather, that plane has flown."

"Looks that way," Val said.

"Hey, like you said," I began, "we're not going anywhere, ever. So, why not tell us what we just missed out on?"

"You know what," Tia said, "seeing as my life, our lives, are now over, I guess it doesn't matter if I tell you guys the truth. You see, I wasn't being honest upstairs. I was holding back. I know exactly who Ilion is and what he's doing."

"Tell us," Leecy said.

"Why? So you can make yourself a sweetheart deal and

not me? No way."

"Fair enough," I said, "'cause that's the only reason I want to know. But can't you tell us most of what you know, saving the juiciest bits for yourself? Maybe that way we can all cut deals."

"I see," she said. "Everyone has a piece of the pie, kind of thing."

"Won't work," Val said.

"Why not?" Tia asked.

"I heard the Interpol agents talking. They're only interested in you, Tia. They're turning the three of us over to the locals after they take you away, which I'm guessing is going to happen anytime now. No one will be offering the three of us any deal. It won't matter what we know or what they think we know. Interpol is only after you."

"What're they going to do with me?"

"Can't answer that. Never had any dealings with Interpol. So tell us, what did Ilion want from you?"

"Well, it's like this. He wanted me to come to work for him and bring my hacking algorithm, and the MI5 components I purchased a year ago. But I would have to leave my security team at home."

"Interesting," Leecy said. "And what is it you were going to be doing for Ilion?"

"That's immaterial."

"Why?"

"Because I haven't told you who Ilion is."

"Well? Go ahead. Who is he?"

"Ilion Volodarsky is the Deputy Chairman of the Government of the Russian Federation."

"No way," Leecy said. "You and a guy like that? I don't believe it."

"Why would I lie?"

"I'm not calling you a liar; it's just hard to believe, is all."

"If I'm lying, I'll remove my own eyeball, okay?"

"Don't do that," Leecy said. "I believe you."

"Yeah," I said, "if you say you're partners with a high-ranking member of the Russian government and flew on his private jet, then you did."

"Don't do that. Don't patronize me. You know what? I can prove it." She stood and walked toward me. "Reach inside my left front pants pocket. There's a card in there that will prove to you I'm not lying."

Reaching inside her pocket, I found the card. Reading it, I said, "This proves nothing." I dropped the card on the table. "It's a phone number and an address, nothing more."

"Yes, yes, I know that," Tia said, pacing in the small room. "If you hadn't destroyed my iPad, I could show you the picture I found of Ilion and Vladimir Putin posing in front of the plane I flew to Geneva. And the...never mind," she said, retaking her seat. "I know it's true. I'm done talking."

***

"Ryan," Wakefield said, walking away from the group clustered around Zach's laptop, listening and watching the scene unfold with Tia, "you come with me."

"Where're we going?" Ryan asked.

They exited the building, turning right on the sidewalk and walking toward the first of the two vans parked on the corner. "Hold here. I'll be right back," Wakefield said over her shoulder, and walked toward the second van. She gestured for Hodges to roll down the window and said, "Secure the prisoner and the vehicle. I want you to join

Ryan and me inside the other van."

"Roger that, boss," Hodges said.

Opening the sliding door of the first van, Wakefield said, "Climb in Ryan, and have a seat. We need to talk."

"Sure thing. What do you want to talk about?"

She closed the door behind her and reached around the front passenger seat to pick up her laptop before sitting down on the opposite end of the bench seat from Ryan.

"Correction. I'm going to talk, and you're going to listen," she answered.

"That sounds serious."

"And that's the last thing I want to hear come out of your mouth until I ask you for a response," Wakefield said. "Do you understand?"

"Yes, I understand."

"The information the Grangers are trying to elicit from the target would already be in Agent Leeds' hands if not for one thing. Do you know what that one thing is?"

"No."

"It's you," she said. The front passenger door opened and Hodges climbed in and sat down.

"Prisoner safe and secure?" she asked Hodges.

"Safe and secure."

"Good. Thank you," she said, then turned her attention back to Ryan. "You mucked it all up by disobeying a direct order, and tonight was far from your first time displaying such behavior."

"But as I explained..."

"No talking, Agent Ryan. Agent Hodges, if Agent Ryan speaks again, I want you to assist me in binding and gagging him."

"My pleasure."

"Ryan," Wakefield said, opening her laptop and making

a few keystrokes, "I've compiled a detailed list, enumerating each and every one of your acts of insubordination, and was prepared to email that document to my boss at Langley along with my recommendation for your immediate termination."

"May I speak?" Ryan asked.

"No, you may not. As I just said, I was prepared to do just that, but now I'm forced to do something that, in all my years of service, I have never done before. Agent James Ryan Taw, you are under arrest."

"On what charge? I demand to know what I'm being charged with!"

"Fair enough," Wakefield said. "Did you access my computer earlier this evening?"

"No, I did not."

"You didn't return to the hotel suite after I left you and access my computer? Before you answer, I feel I must remind you there are witnesses."

"First of all, yes, I did return to the suite, and I did access your computer because I thought I could help search for the Grangers. And if by witnesses you mean Hodges and Zach, what did they see? I'll tell you what they saw. Zach saw me sit down across from him and open your laptop, but he didn't see me type anything, and I can prove it. I never entered anything into his complicated search engine; just check the file logs. And Hodges never saw me type anything on the computer either. By the time he arrived, I was standing to leave the room."

"Hodges and Zach weren't the only witnesses," Wakefield said, spinning the laptop around so he could see the screen.

"What's that?" Ryan asked.

"That's a video of you accessing my computer."

Staring at the screen in disbelief, he asked, "But how is that possible?"

"It's a little security device Zach installed on my laptop last year after the incident in Malaysia. Remember when I walked in on you using my computer?"

"Yes," he said, looking up at Wakefield. "But I was just..."

"Enough with the excuses, Ryan," Wakefield said, cutting him off. "The security program requires anyone using my laptop to enter a four-digit code or be filmed by the camera embedded in the laptop. Simple, clean, efficient. And one other thing I forgot to mention: the program Zach created also records every keystroke made by the person illegally using my government-issued computer."

"But..."

"No, no buts. No excuses. No double-talking your way clear of this. You're under arrest. Hodges, place soon-to-be former Agent Ryan in cuffs, remove him from this vehicle, and place him in the van with the other prisoner. I want you to stand guard until we are ready to transport them back to Langley with Tia Reins."

"Roger that."

***

"Whatever," I said to Tia. "Talk, don't talk, I don't care anymore. It's all a load of shit. Every word you utter is false. You've concocted some fantasy world. That's what you've done."

"That's what it's starting to sound like to me, too," Val agreed.

"Don't listen to them, Tia," Leecy said. "I believe you. Even if Ilion does sound too good to be true, I believe you."

"Thanks for that," Tia said. "But it doesn't really matter. We're at the end of it."

"Maybe that's why I want to believe you. We've reached the end, and I want something to take with me, wherever they send me, that I can hold on to."

"God, is that what I've done to myself?" Tia said, looking at Leecy. "Am I so pathetic and desperate that I've made this whole thing up in my head?"

"No. Well, maybe some parts, but so what? Forget about what he thinks," Leecy said, jerking her head in my direction, "and tell me what you and Ilion were going to do if you had joined him."

"You won't believe me."

"Try me."

Leaning back against the couch and closing her eyes, she said, "He wanted to put me in charge of Putin's army of hackers."

"Get out. For real?"

"Yes, he told me he wanted me to use my algorithm to focus on the Fortune 100 companies in the US like Google and Apple."

"Can you do that? I mean can you hack into places like that?"

"Theoretically, any computer system can be hacked, given enough computing power. So with my skills, plus the MI5 computers and his army of hackers, he'd have the perfect weapon. Nothing would be off limits."

"You're serious?"

Ignoring Leecy's question to relive a moment from the night spent in Ilion's arms, she said, "He promised me we'd fill Russia's coffers with the money drained from the 'too big to fail' western companies. That one day he'd rule the new Russian empire, and I'd be by his side when he did."

"Tia?" Leecy asked, trying to snap her back to reality. "Tia, can you hear me?"

Shaking off the memory, Tia looked at Leecy and said, "What?"

Before Leecy could respond, the door to the small room opened. Agent Robert Leeds entered and said, "We haven't been properly introduced, mainly because you were unconscious when I arrived earlier." He removed his credentials and extended them for Tia to read. "My name is Robert Jeffery Leeds. I'm with Interpol. I'll be taking you into custody, and you'll be charged with several computer crimes, too many to list at the moment, but we'll have time for a formal reading of the charges soon enough. As for right now, I need you to come with me, Miss Reins."

Tia stood without a word, leaving the room escorted by the dapper Interpol agent, who closed the door behind him.

"Can someone get me out of these cuffs?" I asked the mobile phone lying on the desk behind me.

The door opened again and Zach entered, then froze, covering his nose. "Whose bright idea was it to lock you three in an enclosed, unventilated space? My God it stinks in here."

"Is that really what you want to have said, Zach?" Leecy asked him.

"No, I'm sorry. Come on, let me get you guys out of those cuffs so you can..."

"What? So we can what?" Leecy asked, rubbing her wrist.

"Well, you know," he said, unlocking Val's cuffs and shackles, "bathe."

"That's it," Leecy said, walking toward the door, "I'm going to have to hurt you now."

"What's going on between you two?" I asked, rubbing

my freed wrist. I immediately regretted that thought escaping my head and tried to change the subject. I picked up the card on the desk and said, "Zach, this may prove to be valuable. Best hold on to it."

"Dad!" Leecy said, turning around to face me from the other side of the doorway. "What do you think's going on between us?"

Looking at Valerie for help but finding none, I said, "You know what? Forget it. It's none of my business. Sorry I said anything."

"That's right," Leecy said. "Come on Zach, give me ride to the hotel in that cute little electric car of yours."

"I can't," he said, accepting the card from me. Leecy fixed him with a stare. "But it's not for the reason you think. It's got nothing to do with how bad you smell. Wakefield wants me to ride with Hodges. I'm to help with transporting the prisoners to the airport and loading them on the CIA flight back to Langley."

"All right," Leecy said, smiling, "give me the keys to the smart car, 'cause you won't need it. I'm going straight to the hotel to take a three-hour bath. Where'd you leave the car?"

Handing her the keys to the car as he brushed past to leave the room, he said, "Make a left out the front door then another left at the corner, and you'll see it. Just drop the keys at the front desk for me. I'll call you when I return from the airport."

"Don't bother calling, I'll be asleep," Leecy said, following Zach.

"Hold on a second, kiddo," Val said. "That little thing is big enough for two. I'm coming with you."

"What about me?" I asked, watching them walk toward the lobby.

"Looks like you're walking."

"But wait," Zach said. "I almost forgot; there's more."

With one hand on the door leading to the lobby, Leecy asked, "Can't it wait till morning? We've done the job. Tia's admitted to exactly what Ron thought she was involved in. She's in custody. What else is there?"

"Wakefield wants you three to report to her suite at zero seven hundred to complete your post mission reports. That's all."

***

"Hodges," Agent Leeds asked, closing the van door on a handcuffed Tia Reins, "can you handle three prisoners?"

"Sure, no problem, but I think Wakefield wanted Zach to ride shotgun."

"Yes, I know, but I've spoken with her and asked that he be allowed to assist the Computer Forensic Team with their work. He's going to be a while yet, and I'd like to have those three airborne as soon as possible."

Checking the time, Hodges said, "It's only eleven-thirty, and it's just a fifteen-minute ride to the airport. I'd like to wait for Zach if that's all right with you?"

"Sure," Leeds replied, confirming the time on his Rolex. "I tell you what let's do, being we're short on manpower. You know how it is, we can't have the undercover agents being seen and all."

"Yeah, I get that."

"Give me a hand transferring the computer components from the Mercedes to the space behind the rear seat of the van while you wait for Zach."

"Sure, that should kill some time."

"I think there's twenty pieces or so," Agent Leeds said, walking around the corner toward the Mercedes. "The two of us should be able to handle moving all of them."

Grabbing one of the stainless steel boxes, Hodges asked, "And if Zach's not finished by the time we're done here?"

Returning to the van, Leeds said, "If you're concerned about safety, I'll ride along with you."

Walking toward the rear door and opening it, Hodges said, "No. No need for you to do that. There's really nothing to this. It's just prisoner transport. All I have to do is get them locked and loaded on the plane, and then sit back and enjoy the ride back to the States. I think I can handle it."

"Very well, then," Leeds said, stacking the components in the rear of the van before returning to the sedan for another load. "The pilots of the plane I arrived in this evening have been notified, and they're expecting you and three prisoners. They're armed CIA agents. They'll assist you securing the prisoners, which the plane is equipped to handle, so it's not like you're all alone on this."

"And my team? What about them?"

"They'll remain here with me in Cologne, I'm afraid. We'll be posting mission reports. We've got to debrief the Grangers, as you know, and they have to account for their actions. It's a lengthy process, but one that must be done while the events are fresh in their minds. After that, I imagine they'll either return to the States or you'll join them for your next assignment." Pausing at the trunk of the sedan, he asked. "Is everything all right, Agent Hodges? You seem to be a bit out of sorts."

Hodges shook his head, removing more components from the trunk of the sedan and stacking them in his arms like firewood. "I'm fine. It's just been...well, you know, we lost a man. It's been tough. I just wanted to know what was happening, that's all."

As they rounded the corner, they spotted a man lingering near the rear of the van they were loading, Hodges, arms laden with the MI5 devices, starting running and shouting, "Get away from that vehicle!"

The unidentified man ran away, disappearing in the darkness between the gaps of the adjoining buildings before Hodges could catch up to him.

"Who was that?" Leeds asked. "I thought we'd accounted for everyone."

"No, sir," Hodges said. "We never found the man Ryan said he followed into the building. We looked. We even checked the secret doorway, but we didn't find him."

"Well, there's nothing that can be done about him now. We've a schedule to keep." He deposited the components he was carrying into the van. "And that's the last of it," he said. "Now be on your way, Hodges. We wasted all the time we're allowed."

"Let my boss know I've gone, will you?" he said. He climbed inside the van, closed the door, turned the engine over and rolled the window down.

"Will do," Leeds said, looking toward the other van parked a few meters from his position. "If I'm not mistaken, she's on the line with the boys in Langley. I'll let her know you've gone as soon as she's free. Oh, I almost forgot. I've sent you a text with the contact numbers for the agents on the plane. Let them know when you arrive and they'll give you hand."

"Thanks," Hodges said, pulling away from the curb.

***

Exiting the elevator and walking toward the room I was sharing with my wife, I thought about checking on Leecy, but only paused momentarily outside her door before continuing to the end of the hall.

Reaching up behind the wall-mounted air conditioning unit, I retrieved my room key. I heard the blow dryer running as I entered the room and began stripping off my filthy clothes, piling them on the floor in the hall outside our door.

"I'm back," I announced.

Turning off the hair dryer, Val asked, "What took you so long?"

"Tired, I guess," I answered, stepping in the shower and turning on the water. "What're we going to do for clothes? I left my dirty ones outside in the hall."

"No need to worry about that."

Washing my hair, I asked, "Why?"

"Benefits of traveling with an American Express Black Card holder, I suppose. Wakefield called the valet number on the card and the shopping is being taken care of for us. Tammy said by the time we wake up in the morning, we'd have new clothes."

"Great," I said, smelling my skin. "How many washings did it take you to get rid of the smell?"

"Hold on."

I rinsed the shampoo out of my hair for a second time. Feeling something nudging me on the arm, I opened my eyes to see a bottle of V8 juice and asked, "What's that for?"

"We don't have any straight tomato juice in the mini bar, and room service is closed for the night. Use these. It helps cut the odor."

After the shower, I was drying off when the door opened. Val was wearing one of the hotel robes and extending the other to me. "I've thrown our clothes away in the bins located in the stairwell. You'll have to make do with this."

Running the towel over my heavily bruised left side, I said, "No thanks. Those things never fit me right. The arms are always too short and it's always too tight in the shoulders."

"So what, then? You're just going to walk around naked?"

Draping the towel over the shower rod, I answered, "I'm walking from here to the bed naked, then I'm going to sleep. Tammy will have us filling out reports and being debriefed all day tomorrow." Squeezing past, I added, "I'm exhausted."

I pulled back the covers and eased my bruised body down on the mattress. "Please turn off the lights," I said.

Dropping her robe on the floor next to my side of the bed, she responded, "Well, if you're not wearing a robe then I'm not wearing one, either."

"The lights?"

"Not yet," she said, sliding between the sheets and kissing me softly, "I want to check your ribs first."

"That isn't my ribs."

She kissed me again. "I know."

***

"Zach?" Wakefield called from the entrance to the third floor server room. "Where are you?"

He popped out from behind a row of servers, startling her. "Almost done downloading all the data," he said. I just need another couple of minutes."

"Great. Get that info uploaded to Langley; they're expecting it."

"Already begun transmission. It's a huge file. They'll be

combing through it for months."

"About that. I've been on the SAT phone giving my unofficial report, and I need to inform you that you've been promoted and reassigned. As of this moment, you're Special Agent In Charge of the Computer Forensics Division. You'll remain here in Cologne with the other two agents for as long as needed to pack up and ship all this stuff to a storage facility in the US."

"I'm off the squad?" he asked, pausing his typing long enough to turn and look at her.

Placing a hand on his shoulder, she said, "There is no more squad. The A.D.D.T. operation has run its course, I'm afraid. We've all been offered reassignment. Or in some cases, termination."

He was typing again, then stopped. "The Grangers?" he asked, without looking away from his computer screen.

"Yes, and Ryan."

"But why?"

"Ryan," Tammy began, dropping her hand from his shoulder. "Jesus, what a mess. His firing should come as no surprise. It's obvious, really, and the only way for him to avoid jail time. As far as Valerie and Ron are concerned, they were freelance operators. They were only hired to be part of the A.D.D.T. unit."

"And Leecy?"

"She's being handled a little differently. She'll be given the option to accept a new posting with sanctions in her permanent record, of course, or she can choose to leave."

"So, you haven't told her yet?"

"No, I just learned about all this myself, and I imagine they've all gone to sleep, don't you?"

Zach typed briefly before powering down his laptop and

disconnecting it from the server.

"Job's done here. Langley will be receiving data for a few days." He looked at Wakefield. "Do I have the option of refusing my new assignment?"

"You'd want to do that?"

"Possibly. I don't know. But I don't like being shipped around like a parcel from one department to another without so much as a 'hey what do you think about doing this for us' coming my way."

"Zach, don't be ridiculous. That's not how the CIA operates. You're given assignments. That's it."

"And what's your new post?"

"Zach, what's wrong with you? You've never acted like this before. You know I can't tell you my posting. That's classified."

He shook his head and rubbed his eyes with his free hand. "Nothing's wrong with me," he said. "Sorry, I'm just tired and need some sleep. Walk me out?"

"Yeah, sure. Come on. I'll give you a ride back to the hotel."

Walking out of the building, they were greeted by Agent Leeds. "I hear we're all wrapped—for tonight, anyway—and that my stay here has been extended. At least until the team arrives to haul away all the servers on the third floor."

"So, you drew the short straw?" Wakefield asked.

"Something like that, I suppose." He looked at Zach. "I understand congratulations are in order, young man."

"What for?"

"You've been promoted and reassigned. Isn't that right?" Leeds asked, looking at Tammy. Then, realizing he'd overstepped, offered, "My apologies for speaking out of turn, Tammy." Climbing the stairs to the CCP offices, he changed the subject. "Now, I've been charged with the unenviable task of informing the father."

"That's right," Wakefield said. "I forgot all about him. What's going to happen to him?"

"Nothing. There's no evidence of his involvement in any of his daughter's dealings. I imagine, once we're gone, he'll live out his days here."

"Good luck with that," she said. "See you later?"

"Can't think of a reason why not," he said before entering the building.

"Why does he know about my promotion?" Zach asked after the door closed completely.

"Forgive me," Wakefield said. "He was on the most recent call with our superiors, and it came up. That's all."

"Whatever," he said, opening the door to the van. "It's a small twenty-person division working out of a warehouse in Alexandria. It's not a big deal. Can we just go to the hotel? I don't want to talk about this anymore."

"Yeah," she agreed, climbing behind the wheel. "Let's go. We could both use some rest."

CHAPTER
TWELVE

RUDE AWAKENING

"Hurry up, Ron," Val called, exiting the elevator ahead of me. "We're late. They started ten minutes ago."

"Yes, I'm aware of that," I said, following Valerie out of the elevator, pulling at the neck of my new wool sweater. I felt like a kid at Christmas having received a gift I should be thankful for but secretly despised. The new clothes had been delivered promptly at 0600 this morning. I was grateful, but the sweater was too small for me. I felt like I was choking.

Zach opened the door after a few gentle knocks at Wakefield's suite.

"Good morning. Coffee is on the table, and all your personal effects are there, as well. I charged all your phones last night. Tammy's talking to Leecy in the other room."

"Thanks," I said, while pocketing my passport, wallet, and mobile phone. I noticed the dark circles under Zach's eyes and the absence of Ryan. "What time did you finally get to bed? And where's very Special Agent Ryan?"

Zack closed the door and sat down on the couch, facing his open laptop.

"I guess it was after two, and I don't know where Ryan is."

"Well," Val said, "this is the homestretch, right? Almost at the finish line."

"I suppose it is," he said, without looking up from feverishly typing on his keyboard.

I was about to ask him a question when the double doors opened behind us, and I turned to see Tammy and Leecy.

"Sorry for being late this morning."

"Don't be," Tammy responded, pouring a cup of coffee. "I needed to spend some time with Leecy, so it's fine." Looking Val and me over as she sipped black coffee, she added, "I see your clothes fit."

"Just," I said, pulling at the neck of the sweater again.

"Where's Hodges?" Val asked, sitting down at the circular table.

Tammy looked at her watch. "He's landing in the States right about now, or should be soon enough."

"So the wrap-up went well?" I asked.

"That's been delegated to Agent Leeds, and not what we need to discuss. No, we need to talk about the future."

"You don't want to debrief us first?"

"No, I want to get this other part over with. Then we can dive headlong into the paperwork."

Val took sip of her coffee.

"Why do I sense bad news?"

Looking down at the tabletop, smiling that grin of hers, Tammy shook her head.

"I think I'll miss your incredible ability to read a situation most, Valerie."

"I see."

"Yes. First thing is, the A.D.D.T. units are being

disbanded. Most of us have already received our reassignments, but Val, you and Ron will be dismissed."

"This takes effect immediately?" I asked.

"Yes. As you know, there's no severance for freelancers. You'll be issued travel vouchers to return to the States and you'll be paid what you're owed. I can get that money to you in cash, or Zach can wire transfer it to your US accounts."

"Wire the money."

"Fine," Wakefield said. "Zach if you will, please."

"What about the rest of you? What happens to you now?" Val asked looking at Leecy.

"I'm not allowed to talk about the posting I've been offered," Leecy said, "but I can say if I were to accept the post I also have to agree to the sanctions that come with it. You know, because of the use of lethal force."

"Sure," I said. "When do you have to make the decision?"

Leecy walked toward the window.

"I already did. I'm not staying on with the CIA."

In the corner of my left eye, I saw Zach's head snap to attention and his hands freeze above his keyboard, and I knew. I'd been right all along about him and Leecy. The truth was on full display and written across his face in bold type. I could see the struggle as they tried not to stare at each other.

"And Zach," I said, "what about you?"

"Oh, I, uh, am considering a promotion I've been offered, but I don't know. I need time to weigh all my options."

"I guess that leaves Ryan. Where is he, by the way?"

"Okay," Tammy said, ignoring my question, "Ron and Zach, let's move into the other room. Ladies, the forms you need are over on the sidebar. I think you know what to do while Zach and I video Ron's post-mission interview. It's going to be a long day, so let's get started."

Pushing off the couch, I was following Zach through the double doors when a knock on the door of the suite sent a shockwave through the room. Tammy wasn't expecting anyone, not even Ryan, and I knew she always registered in hotels as a foreign dignitary, citing her religious beliefs to prevent hotel staff from entering her room. With everyone present and accounted for, who was at the door?

"Zach," Tammy said, "see who it is."

Zach opened the door after checking the peephole, and Brit Interpol agent Leeds entered the room. His face was ashen gray, and his eyes bloodshot and his formerly tailored appearance was now wrinkled and disheveled.

"Robert, are you all right?" Tammy asked. "What's happened?"

"They've vanished."

"Who? Come in. Sit down," she said, taking him by the hand and leading him to a chair. "Would you like something to drink?"

"No," he said, pulling away from her. He placed his hands on his hips and paced back and forth. "I need you to listen to me." He paused and wiped his hand over his mouth before returning it to his hip. "Last night, after you and Zach drove away, I went to see Laird and explain to him what was happening to his daughter."

"Yes, I remember."

"Well that turned into quite the ordeal. He called lawyers and the local police. It was just a mess, and took me forever to clear it all up. I just finished. I was going to my room to have a bit of a rest when I realized I'd never heard from Hodges or the pilots. So I started calling. No answers.

Then, I phoned the airport and they told me the plane I was calling about was still on the tarmac. I thought about calling my boss, and yours," he added, nodding at Tammy, "but decided against it and came here instead."

"When's the last time you saw Hodges, and where?" Leecy asked.

"We were moving the MI5 hardware into the van. I guess that was after eleven last night."

"Zach," Wakefield said.

"Already there. I'm pulling up the recordings I made from the bank's security camera feed we were tapped into last night," he said, typing. "I didn't shut it down till after I was finished in the server room. Here it is. Let me rewind to the correct time, and okay." Grabbing the TV remote with his left hand and typing with his right, he powered on the TV. "It's coming up right now."

"Yes," Leeds said. "There we are walking toward the van. See? We're carrying the gear."

"Who's that?" I asked. "Pause it, and back up a couple of frames. Can you enlarge that image?"

"Sure," Zach said.

"That's Taka. Tia's assistant. What's he doing there?"

"Don't know," Leeds answered, "but we didn't pursue him given the manpower issues and schedule we were being asked to keep."

"That's understandable, but where'd he go?" Wakefield asked.

"Don't know. He disappeared around the corner or something."

"I showed Hodges the escape door," I said, "but when I did, it was locked. Ryan looked for Taka inside the building, but he couldn't have been hiding anywhere. He used the door after we left. I think that's obvious."

"If we assume Taka was in and out of the building," Val explained, "then it's safe to assume he had a reason to risk being discovered, right?"

"Okay," Leeds chimed in, "but still not following you."

"Yeah, I see that. Zach?"

"Checking all outbound communications for the building's hard lines. No emails were sent, but one phone call was placed. The number called is 492.219.0000. It's a local number. Running it down."

"Leecy," Wakefield said, opening her computer and entering her security code, "jump on my laptop and start tracing the van's movements. Zach's got a link saved on the home screen that will put you directly into the city's CCTV system."

"On it."

"The phone number is a dead end," Zach said. "It dumps into a Beijing voicemail service that's completely untraceable."

"I've got the van," Leecy announced. She looked at Zach. "You want to take over?"

"Sure," he answered, trading seats with Leecy. "I'll put it up on the TV. These CCTV video archive records are recorded over every twenty-four hours so we should be able to track Hodges' every move."

"Let's look for him near the airport first," Wakefield said. "If we don't see the van there, then we know he never made it that far and can eliminate it."

"Sure thing, boss, just give me a second, here."

"There he is," Leeds said, pointing at the van Hodges was last seen driving. "But what's he doing? He's driving past the exit. Can you follow him?"

"Nope, that's the last of the cameras on that stretch of highway."

"Zoom in on the van, and replay that part right before he merges right," I instructed.

"See the blinker?" Leecy asked, gesturing at the replay. "It stays on long after he merges right, like he's signaling he's going to exit."

"Maybe he forgot to turn the damn thing off," Leeds said. "He did miss the exit."

"He'd never leave a blinker running like that," Leecy said.

"That's true. I agree. But there's nothing on that exit," Zach said.

"What'd you mean?"

"I mean if Hodges takes the next exit there's nowhere for him to go. It's unfinished, not paved. There's a dirt road that will eventually circle back to the airport, buts it's nowhere near completion."

"Can you jump ahead, say, five minutes?" Val asked. "See if the van comes back toward the airport?"

"No problem," Zach answered. He skipped ahead five minutes, then ten. Just before the fifteen-minute mark, we saw the van enter the highway, driving toward the airport.

"Now where is he going?" Leeds asked. "Driving in that direction there's no construction, so he should take the second exit for the airport, but he's taking the first. That leads to the maintenance entrance."

"That's odd," Wakefield said. "Why would he do that?"

"A better question is what was he doing for the fifteen minutes we didn't see him?" Val asked.

"Agreed," I said. "There's a real good chance Hodges isn't even driving the van anymore."

"Don't say that, Ron," Wakefield said, pulling on her

jacket. "I don't even want to think about that right now."

"Here's another question," Leecy said. "Why was Hodges alone with three prisoners?"

"My call," Wakefield said, walking toward the door of the suite. "Last night, we took Ryan into custody. And with Franks having been killed, we were short-staffed. The forensic guys from Langley were overwhelmed, and instead of sending Zach with Hodges I pulled him off transport duty, putting him to work helping the computer guys."

"Hold on," I said. "Ryan's been arrested?"

"Let's go find Hodges. Ryan's situation is above your pay grade, anyway."

"Right. I don't have a pay grade anymore."

"Zach," Tammy said, "I want you searching the airport cameras. All of them. And call my mobile with anything, and I mean any little thing."

***

Future exit 27B was just as Zach described. Incomplete. Finding the reflective tape Hodges must've driven through, and the orange cones he'd driven over at the bottom of the ramp, indicated to me that he'd been in distress when he exited the highway. Hodges never disobeyed traffic laws; a legacy from his father, an Arkansas State Trooper. The Hodges I knew wouldn't drive through a barricade.

Wakefield parked our van at the edge of the asphalt.

"Take a look around. Maybe we'll get lucky."

The dirt road resembled a South Georgia hunting trail. It was overgrown with dead weeds made brown from the nightly cold temperatures. There were a couple of excavators and one bulldozer parked and waiting in a small clearing about five hundred yards past the end of the asphalt, but nothing else to indicate work being done.

"Look," Leecy said, pointing toward the ground fifty feet from the edge of the asphalt, "fresh tire tracks."

"He was here, then."

"Yes, it looks like he drove along the trail for about a hundred yards," she added, squatting to look down the right-hand rut of the two-rut trail.

"Come on, kid," I said, patting her on the shoulder. "Let's see what else we can find."

"Follow me and pay attention," Wakefield said to Leeds, who was leaning against the hood of the van. "You'll want to see this."

"See what?" he asked, walking beside Wakefield.

"Just watch."

Squatting where the tire tracks ended, I stared at the dirt, then looked right. "Here's where it happened," I said.

"What?" Leeds asked.

"The van stopped here," Leecy said, showing him the abrupt nature of the front tire marks and the slight skidding action of the rear tires.

"Okay, so the van stopped," he said, rubbing his face with both hands. "So what?"

"Just listen," Val suggested.

"See how the weeds are mashed down in this area? Someone was lying down here," I said, waving my open right palm over the dead weeds to the right of where the van had come to a stop.

"See the blood?" Leecy asked, pointing to the dark brown dots on the ground. "And look at these boot prints."

"Too deep to be one guy," I said.

"One guy carrying another guy, maybe?"

"Yep, I think so."

"What are you saying?" Leeds asked.

Ignoring his question, I stood shoulder to shoulder with my daughter, surveying the area for a few seconds.

"I don't think so."

"Me, either," she said. "Too risky to dump the body out here."

"Will one of you be so kind as to catch me up as to your current line of thinking?" Leeds asked.

"Sure," Val said. "I'll be happy to. See, there was a fight. Someone was knocked down near the side of the van and killed, but the body was moved."

"We know they went to the airport because we saw them on the CCTV cameras. And you two think the body is in the van?" Tammy asked.

"Not the body," Leecy said, "bodies. You're forgetting about the pilots. Leeds told us the plane Hodges was supposed to board with the three prisoners is still sitting empty on the tarmac. Where are the pilots, and where are the prisoners?"

"You've got to be bloody kidding me," Leeds said before the ringing of Tammy's mobile cut him off.

"Wakefield, here," Tammy said, placing the call on speaker. "What've you got for me, Zach?"

"Not much, I'm afraid. It's like she knew where the cameras were at the airport and did everything she could to avoid them. There are no cameras on the tarmac. The cameras I did find with partial views of the planes are too far away to do us any good."

"So you've got nothing," Leeds said.

"I didn't say nothing. What I do have is a blurred image

of a man driving away from the FBO office last night on a golf cart, and behind it, way off in the distance, I think I can see the van we're looking for. The timing is right in our window of events, and I think the guy could be Taka."

"Thanks, Zach," Wakefield said. "I know where to look next. Get in your electric car and bring your gear. Meet us at Laird's hangar."

"What?" Leeds asked.

"Come on," Tammy said, running toward our van. "We might still have a chance at finding someone alive."

"Where?" Val asked.

"Hangar 17 is owned by Laird. I went there looking for you three yesterday."

Arriving a few minutes ahead of Zach, we didn't jump out of the car and hurry to look inside the hangar. There was no reason to. The hangar doors had stopped a foot short of being fully closed, and we could see the rear of the van clearly through the opening.

Zach arrived, and Wakefield told him to hack the keypad so we could gain entry. It took him longer than normal to perform what he'd always called an easy hack, but maybe that was because the kid's hands were shaking the entire time.

"Okay," Wakefield said, "let's see what we've got."

Opening the doors of the van Hodges had been driving we found the three bodies as I'd feared. Hodges and the two pilots were unceremoniously dumped on top of each other. The duffel bags of money were gone, as were the highly-coveted MI5 computers.

"Where's Ryan?" Zach asked.

"Where are Tia and Lee?" Leecy asked him by way of an answer.

Leeds' phone began ringing and he said, "Excuse me a

moment," before walking away to answer the call.

"I suspect Lee is either with Tia or running from her," I said.

"And Ryan?" Zach asked again.

"Leecy," Val said, ignoring Zach's question for a second time, "check Hodges' pockets for his personal effects."

"Sure," Leecy said, walking toward the van. She reached around Hodges' legs, patting down his pants pockets and his jacket pockets. "Nothing here."

"And the pilots?"

"Just a second," Leecy said. "Phones, wallets, and keys all present and accounted for."

"Sorry about that," Leeds said, rejoining the group, "but the locals picked up Lee a few hours ago hitching on the highway. They've got him in a holding cell if we want to talk to him."

"He can't help us," I said. "You did say you tried calling your pilots earlier, is that right?"

"Yes, I did."

"Did you try Hodges?"

"Yes, several times. No one answered."

"What are you thinking, Ron?" Wakefield asked.

"I'm wondering why the other guys have all their personal stuff and Hodges doesn't. I'm wondering if someone is trying to tell us something."

"Tell us what exactly?" Leeds asked.

"I don't know, but let's see if we can find out," I said, pulling out my cell.

Dialing Hodges' number, I put the phone on speaker and waited.

"Damn," Ryan said, answering the call, "that's impressive. You found him in less than eight hours. You guys work fast. I told the little lady you were real good."

Wakefield motioned to Zach to start a trace as Ryan said, "Don't waste your time trying to trace this call. Tia's got this thing bouncing off satellites. So let's just talk. You got me on speaker?"

"Yes," I answered. "Why'd you kill Hodges?"

"Whoa. Hold on, Big Guy. I didn't kill Hodges, but does that really matter now? I mean he's dead; we can't change that. Let's talk about something we can control, okay? Before I get started, tell me, is everybody there and listening?"

"Yes."

"Okay, good. Here's how it's going to work. You guys are going to forget about me."

"I can't do that," Wakefield said. "You have to answer for Hodges, Franks, the pilots, and so much more."

"No, I don't. Focus, Tammy. We're not talking about the dead guys right now. No, I want to talk about your boy, Peter. I want assurances he isn't coming for me, and I'll even tell you why you're going to do what I want."

"Go ahead," I said. "We're listening."

"I have a head full of secrets. Secrets I'm more than willing to share for the right price. You guys come after me, I start the bidding. I start selling your real identities to people. For the right price, I'll tell people all about you, Peter Heely, and your crew. I've read your file, and I know exactly which people to approach with the information I have. There are people out there that would kill you if they knew who you really were and where to find you. Now, I ask you, is that a good enough reason to leave me alone?"

"No," Wakefield said, "it's not."

"Shut up, Tammy; I'm not talking to you. If the CIA wants to send Tammy Wakefield after me with a bunch of dipshit agents like Hodges and Franks, 'cause that's who they hire nowadays, then fine. I'll see you coming a mile away. I know how you operate, but that's not what I'm talking about. I'm only talking about Heely and his crew."

"You don't need to worry about me, Ryan. I've been terminated."

"Good. What about the other two?"

"I'm out, too," Val said.

"I resigned this morning," Leecy added.

"Wonderful, then you three have nothing to worry about, and neither do I. Looks like we've run out of things to talk about."

"It does?" I asked, "I have to admit I'm curious."

"About what?"

"Is whatever Tia promised you really worth betraying your country?"

"Yes, it's worth it, and do you know why?"

"Can't wait to learn."

"In a few months, you won't recognize that country."

"Ryan, what does that mean? Ryan? Are you there?" I asked, looking at Zach.

"He's gone," Zach said. "He ended the call."

"Now what?" Leeds asked.

"First thing we need to do is accept that he's already talked," I said.

"You don't know that, Ron," Wakefield said.

"He's told Tia and Ilion. I guarantee it. They paid him to roll over on the three of us."

"He said he *would* tell, not that he had," Wakefield argued.

"No, I disagree. In his way, I think Ryan regrets giving us up and he used the phone call to warn me. Think about it, Tammy; he needs money. He doesn't have any resources. He wouldn't go on the run empty-handed, and don't forget, there were two million reasons for him to talk inside that van."

"What does that mean?" Zach asked.

"It means," Leecy said, "that this is far from over."

"We've got to find Tia and this Ilion, and stop the hacking operation," Val added.

"In Russia?" Leeds asked. "This is a right bloody cock up, this is. How am I going to explain this?"

"You don't," Wakefield answered. "We don't. We clean it up."

"Zach," I said, "trace the planes that left here last night. We're looking for the one that landed in Russia. Do you still have that card I gave you?"

"Yeah, sure."

"Good. Trace the number and the address."

"What are you thinking, Ron?" Wakefield asked.

"That we'll find the hacking operation at the address," Valerie answered for me. "And Tia and Ryan and maybe even Ilion wherever the plane landed."

"Fingers crossed it's just that easy."

"Can someone please catch me up?" Leeds asked.

"I think I can help with that," a voice said behind us.

We turned to see Mr. Furukawa standing in the open doorway of the hangar.

"What are you doing here?"

"I've been waiting nearby," he said, his Asian accent no longer present, but replaced with a hint of a British accent. "After I left you three last night, I came to the airport. I was planning on intercepting Tia when she tried to board the plane she flew to Geneva the other day. I knew she was planning to take the money and run. Then to my surprise, she shows up here with one of your guys. He *was* with you, correct?" he asked, looking at me.

"He was."

"So I surmised. I assumed you'd beaten me to her. So I just kept my distance and watched your man approach the silver Gulfstream 6."

"That's the plane I arrived in last night," Leeds interjected.

"Right. Your man approached the plane and called to the pilots to come and help him transfer the prisoners."

"How could you possibly hear that?" Wakefield asked. "Where were you?"

"I was wearing a maintenance uniform, working on a plane less than twenty-five feet away."

"Bloody hell," Leeds said. "Who the hell are you? And why didn't you stop them from killing those agents?"

Ignoring Leeds, Furukawa continued. "What happened next was so fast. Your man led the pilots to that van," he pointed at the van with the dead men in it. "He led them around the van to the other side where I couldn't see. I heard four pops and then the van drove away. Not having any transport at the ready I had to acquire some, but I eventually sped off in the same direction. It took me another hour to find the van stashed inside here. By then I knew I'd lost them. I returned to where I'd last seen the plane Tia flew to Geneva only to find it was no longer there. That's when I decided to wait and see who showed."

"And that's it?" Leeds asked. "That's bollocks."

"No, it's the bloody truth. I'm sorry about your men, but there wasn't anything I could do to prevent what happened. Believe me; I would've stopped him had I known your guy had turned."

"So you didn't see who killed the pilots?" Wakefield asked.

"No, they were on the opposite side of the van. Like I

said, I couldn't see. I only heard the shots. May I join you? I'd very much like to help."

"Sure," I said extending my hand toward him. "The man that saved my wife and child's necks, not to mention my own, is welcome in my book."

"Hold on a second," Leeds said. "Will somebody please tell me who this chap is, and why the hell we believe anything he has to say?"

"This is Mr. Furukawa," Val said, looking at Leeds. "He helped us escape Tia's torture chamber."

"He what?" Wakefield asked. "I thought he was the mastermind behind the kidnapping."

"I was," he admitted, "just keeping up appearances. I prevented anything too bad from happening."

"And a good thing, too," I said. "Nice trick with the jumper cables, making sure everyone was behind you so they couldn't see you never touched me."

"Yeah," Leecy agreed. "The same can be said for leaving us loosely tied to the stairs down in the pit."

"And telling us it was just a family of raccoons living down there," Val added. "But I'm not as trusting as Ron. Tell me, Mr. Furukawa, or should I refer to you by another name? Who are you working for?"

He smiled, unbuttoning the black overcoat to reveal the Blues Brothers suit he was still wearing, and said, "Furukawa is fine, Valerie. I, like you and your husband, am a freelance operator, currently under contract with MI5."

"Bollocks. Why in the hell would MI5 contract work they can easily handle internally?" Leeds asked. "Or turn over to Special Branch or MI6?"

"Robert, may I call you Robert?" he asked, but not waiting for an answer. "The reason is plausible deniability, as always. MI5 let the components be stolen in the first place. They didn't want to be associated with a botched attempt at effecting their return."

"I still say bollocks."

"Understandable. But if it helps, I can also tell you that I've done business with just about every agency in every country. I've even worked for the Mossad. What matters here is I can help. I've been embedded in Tia's operation since shortly after her purchase of the MI5 components last year. My assignment from MI5 was monitoring her work and, when the time was right, shutting down her operation, which is what I was about to do when you showed up," he said, looking at me, "and blew my chance. That was my device she found that day."

"What in the hell have you been waiting for?" Wakefield asked. "She's been hacking US companies for over a year. What more did you need?"

"MI5 gave me very specific orders. I haven't yet acquired the item I needed to complete my mission."

"What item?" Leeds asked. "Are you referring to the computers?"

"No," I answered for Furukawa. "He's after Tia's hacking algorithm." I shifted my gaze to Wakefield. "The one Tia used to hack the CIA."

"Yes," Wakefield admitted, "she did hack the CIA, but I was ordered not to mention it."

"Granger's correct," Furukawa said. "The end game for me was possession of the algorithm."

"You say you've worked with Mossad?" Val asked, walking toward him. "If you were ever contracted by them, then I know the man that would've been your handler." She said un-holstering her Glock. "Tell me the name of your Mossad liaison officer."

"Yes, I understand you need verification," he said,

staring at the weapon. "I worked for the same man you worked for during your time with Mossad, Ira Wenzel. Would you like to speak with him right now? I can give you his personal mobile number."

"Sure, lets…" Leeds started to say, but Val interrupted.

"Hold on, Robert. Tia could've gained access to a phone number. No, instead, describe Ira for me."

"He's a diminutive man that favors dark gray fedoras during the winter months. He uses a cane and has for thirty years. He looks fragile, but that's because he prefers out of date three-piece suits that are wrinkled more often than not. But one shouldn't be fooled by his appearance as his voice is still commanding and authoritative."

"And what's Ira known for doing?"

"Spilling food on his shirts and ties."

"Welcome to the team," Val said, returning her gun to its holster and shaking his hand, "And thanks for helping us last night."

"Thank you for welcoming me. Helping you three out of the situation I created was the very least I could do. Now, I heard some of the conversation you were having as I entered the hangar. What were you discussing?" Furukawa asked.

"Tia," Leeds answered. "But before we go a step further, I want it made crystal clear that you will not be fulfilling your assignment. The algorithm, if we succeed in locating it, is the property of Interpol."

"Hey, you'll get no argument from me," Furukawa said. "I've informed my contact at MI5 of the current situation, and he's ordered me to help you, Mr. Leeds, in any way I can."

"Great," Wakefield said. "Now that we're all on the same page, any ideas on where Tia might be heading?"

"We know Ilion Volodarsky's plane was waiting to fly her somewhere," Leecy said. "And Zach's attempting to track the plane's destination."

Holding up a hand, Furukawa said, "Excuse me, but if Zach will check the St. Petersburg airport in Russia, I'm sure he'll find that the plane landed there."

"He's right," Zach agreed, looking up from his computer. "Using the tail number of the plane we identified last night, I tracked it to Geneva, and from there to St. Petersburg. The address on the card is also in St Petersburg."

"What about the microdots we planted on the cash?" Wakefield asked.

"Too far out of range. Well, if I could boost the receiver, maybe, but not realistically. We've got to be within a mile of the microdot's transmission signal for the receiver to work."

"So what are waiting for?" I asked. "Let's go."

"What?" Leeds asked. "You're not suggesting an unsanctioned mission."

"That's exactly what I'm suggesting. I'm going with or without Interpol or the CIA. I don't report to either organization anymore. Please tell me you're not thinking of trying to stop me."

"Ron," Tammy began, "I appreciate your wanting to help, but I..."

"We're not asking to help you," Leecy said. "We're asking to borrow the plane. We don't need any help."

"If they won't lend you theirs," Furukawa said, "you can use my plane, as long as I get to come along."

"To hell with it," Wakefield said. "Let's go. Come on, Zach, grab your gear. We're going to St Petersburg. Robert,

I'll call you if we locate the hackers, and you and your Interpol agents can swoop in and make the arrest."

"Bloody hell. You're not leaving me here to explain all this. I'm coming with you."

Walking toward the hangar's exit, Wakefield said, "I'll phone the local authorities about the bodies. Leecy, gather all personal effects from the pilots, and anything left inside the van. Zach, follow SOP for dead agents. Let's go, people; wheels up in twenty minutes."

"Hold on," Furukawa said. "I was told to be of assistance in any way, and if you, Tammy, would allow me, I can have a cleaner come and take care of the van and the bodies inside. I can even arrange for the bodies safe transport back to your country."

"Do it. I'll arrange the reception on my end."

"Very well, and I'll have the plane met in St. Petersburg with ground transportation. One van or two?"

"Two," I said, walking toward the open hangar doors.

"Come on, Furukawa," Wakefield said. "We'll talk weapons in the air."

C H A P T E R

THIRTEEN

ST. PETERSBURG

"This is the address on the card Tia gave you," Zach said, pointing at the TV screen mounted on the cabin wall of the Gulfstream G550 airplane, where the satellite image of a mansion filled the screen.

"I ran a records check on the property," Zach continued, "and it belongs to the Volodarsky family."

"She was telling the truth," Leecy said.

"Yes, she was," I agreed. "Question is, did she tell Volodarsky what she divulged to us?"

"I think we check out the house regardless," Val said. "We don't have anywhere else to start looking."

"Having spent a year with Tia," Furukawa said, "I don't believe she would own up to doing anything as stupid as having given Ilion Volodarsky's name and address to the authorities."

"And why is that?" Leeds asked, looking more himself after spending some time washing up in the plane's lavatory.

"She's in love with him, that's why," Leecy said. "She's not about to admit to anything that might jeopardize the relationship."

"Just so I understand," Wakefield said, getting our attention, "we're placing all our eggs in this one basket and betting Tia and Ilion are at this location?"

"Yes," I said, walking toward the flat screen. "Zach, tell me everything you've got on the house."

"I'm looking at the plans I found on file with the city," Zach answered. "The home was built sixty years ago."

"Entrances?"

"Six," Zach said, studying the architect's designs. "The main entrance faces the front garden. There are two side entrances located at either end of the house. If you're facing the house, the side entrance on the left will put you in the kitchen and the other in a solarium that's connected to a library. Then you have three entrances across the back of the house. Two are on the main floor. One connects the formal living area to the back garden and the other does the same through a downstairs bedroom. The third, I now realize, isn't an entrance but access to the upstairs patio located off the master bedroom."

"What about alarm systems?" Leecy asked.

"If one's active, I can disable it."

I was still studying the satellite image when Valerie said, "Leecy and I will provide cover from the hillside overlooking the back of the house. Furukawa, can you get your contacts on the ground to provide us with two sniper rifles and ammo?"

"No problem," he said. "You have something specific in mind?"

"Yes," Leecy answered for her mother. "Russian-made, with noise suppression."

"Anything else?"

"No," I answered.

"If you'll excuse me," Furukawa said, moving toward the rear of the plane. "I have a call to make."

"Me and Furukawa are the entry team," I began. "We'll approach from this wooded area near the solarium. Val and Leecy will provide backup on the hill overlooking the back of the house, covering the most likely escape routes. Wakefield, you and Leeds will cover the front. Tammy, you're here in this thicket of trees on the eastern corner of the property, covering both the solarium and front exits. Leeds on the opposite side near the kitchen exit, cutting off that escape route and any cars inside the detached garage."

"And what about me?" Zach asked.

"Don't worry, Zach," Leecy said, "when we find the hacking operation you'll have plenty to do then."

"You'll have plenty to do at the house," Valerie said. "You'll be watching the road for us and keeping us apprised of any approaching vehicles."

"Two vans and more than enough weapons will meet us when we land," Furukawa said, rejoining the group huddled around the flat screen.

Wakefield was looking at her watch. "Zach, issue everyone an earpiece and run diagnostics. We're live in fifteen minutes."

***

"Okay, team," I said, approaching the solarium with Furukawa at my six. "Anyone seeing any movement inside the house or on the grounds?"

"No," Val said, followed by the others reporting *all clear*.

"Here we go," I said, trying the handle of the glass solarium door. "It's unlocked; we're inside. Furukawa will check the main level and the basement. I'm heading upstairs. Any movement detected?"

"No, it's all clear," Val answered.

"Nothing," Leeds said. "I don't think anyone's home."

"I've got Furukawa in my sights moving toward the kitchen," Leecy informed us.

Furukawa's voice broke in. "Sorry, but I'll have to disagree with Agent Leeds. I've got dishes on the table and shoes by the back door. They're here. Checking the basement next."

"Car approaching," Zach informed us. "Green five-door Citroën wagon passing by the van now. It's turning into the driveway and coming your way, Leeds."

"Got it. I see it. Parking. It's a delivery boy. Take cover inside the house; he's ringing the kitchen bell."

"I'm taking cover in a bathroom just off the upstairs landing near the master," I said. "I can hear voices. Bedroom door's opening. It's Tia. She's heading downstairs to answer the door. Do not engage. Let her come back up stairs, Furukawa."

Silence

"Furukawa?" I repeated.

Nothing.

"Damn it," Leeds said. "We trusted the wrong bloke. It's a trap."

"I've got two trucks coming my way," Zach said.

"Keep calm," Valerie ordered. "Furukawa said he was checking the basement. He could be out of range, or the signal is jammed. Ron, I'm moving to you. Leecy, cover me."

"No, Valerie," Wakefield broke in. "I'm closer. Ron, I'm coming to you."

"Best make it quick," Leeds said. "Tia's with the delivery boy at the kitchen door."

"Cancel the trucks. They turned off before reaching my position," Zach said.

I left my hiding position and peeked inside the bedroom.

"Either of you ladies on the hill have eyes on the naked man standing in front of the window?"

"Roger that," Leecy said. "I've got a clear shot."

"Okay, just hold that firing position till I tell you to shoot."

"Roger that."

Wakefield joined me in the hall and said, "I hear Tia coming our way."

"Yes, she is," Val agreed. "I've got her moving through the house in your direction."

"Anyone got eyes on Furukawa?" I asked.

"No," Val answered.

"Holding on target," Leecy said.

I could hear Tia on the stairs below us and gestured for Wakefield to join me in the hall bathroom. By keeping the door slightly ajar, we could see the entrance to the master bedroom. We heard Tia's approaching footsteps before we saw her. She was wearing a mid-thigh length silk bathrobe, walking toward the bedroom at the end of the hall. I watched her enter the bedroom and whispered, "Now, Leecy."

Wakefield and I were out of the bathroom and running toward Tia as the sound of breaking glass erupted from the master bedroom, followed by a heavy thud on the floor.

We found Tia frozen in place. I walked around to look at her face and could see she was in a state of shock. Her mind was struggling to process how what had just happened had, in fact, happened.

"Hello, Tia," I said.

She cut her eyes in my direction, then closed them. "How did you find me?" she asked.

Holding up one finger, I said, "Just a second." Addressing my team, I said, "All clear."

"Well?" Tia asked, turning around to see Wakefield aiming a Glock 17 in her direction. "Did you bring everybody?"

"Not everybody," Wakefield answered. "You killed two of my men, remember?"

"And turned a third," Tia said, smiling. "May I sit?"

"Sure," I said. "Have a seat on the bed."

Leeds was the first to join us, but Leecy, Val, and Zach quickly followed him. "Anyone see Furukawa?" I asked.

"No," Leecy answered.

Looking at the sniper rifles Leecy and Valerie were holding, Tia asked, "Which one of you shot him?"

"I did," Leecy said.

Smiling, Tia said, "I was right about you. You're very good, young one. I think we are very much alike, you and me."

"Leecy," I said, interrupting Tia, "I want you and Leeds to find Furukawa and take Zach with you." I waited while the three of them left the room before turning my attention back to Tia. "You're going to tell me what I want to know."

"Sure, we can make a deal. That's how you people work, right? I mean, that's what your man Ryan kept trying to get that guy Hodges to do last night."

"What?" Wakefield asked.

"Hodges didn't make a deal. I mean, that's obvious, but Ryan worked on him really hard, promising him a share of all that cash that was in the van with us."

"I assumed you killed Hodges," Wakefield said.

"Oh, I did, but only after Ryan made Hodges so mad that he missed the exit for the airport and pulled off the highway to put a gag on Ryan."

"Jesus," Wakefield said.

"Where's Ryan?" I asked.

"Deal first."

"Okay," Wakefield said. "What do you want?"

"I know my freedom is too much to ask, but I think minimum security prison and some creature comforts we can agree to later isn't. But those, along with length of sentence, will depend on what you want from me."

"Ryan. Where is he?"

Laughing, Tia said, "Wherever two million dollars can take him."

"We're not playing games with you, Tia," Valerie said.

"I don't think you are," Tia responded, looking at Valerie. "So you don't need to pop my eyeball out to make me talk. No reason to get excited, I just don't know where Ryan went."

"Tell us about the last time you saw him," Wakefield said.

"We landed early this morning. I gave him the duffle bags full of money, and we parted company. That's it."

I looked at Val and she said, "I'm on it," and ran from the room.

"Where are the MI5 components?" Wakefield asked.

"Here in the house."

"Where in the house?"

"Ilion had me set them up and connect them to the servers in his basement." Tia said.

"Shit," I said. "Did you load your algorithm?"

"Yes, of course I did. Why?"

"And the hacker operation? Where is it?" Wakefield

asked.

Smiling, Tia laughed and said, "Everywhere."

"What?"

"There isn't a hacker army, okay?" Tia said smiling and laughing. "That was all propaganda, but Ilion and Putin were planning to build one. Like Ilion told me, if the world thinks we have one, why not give them one?"

"That's why you bought the MI5 components?" I asked.

"No, I bought those because I wanted to use them for the work I was doing. I'd beaten the Russians to the components and Ilion contacted me about working for them. I put him off for over a year, but," she paused, looking at Ilion's dead body, "he was very persuasive. He convinced me only recently to help the Russians build a global network connecting all the top hackers, and to use my algorithm as the main software platform for the operation."

"Dad," Leecy said, entering the room, "you need to come with me."

"Yeah, sure," I said, and looked at Tammy. "Can you get her dressed and ready for transport?"

"I can," Tammy said. "You two go ahead. I have a few more questions I'd like to ask Tia."

I was following Leecy down the stairs when we heard the shot ring out from the bedroom. I was turning to run in that direction when I heard Tammy's voice in my ear.

"Tia decided not to cooperate." I looked up and saw Tammy at the top of the stairs. "So I changed the terms of the deal."

"Agent Wakefield," Leecy said.

"Let it be, Leecy," I said. "What's going on? Why'd you come get me?"

"The earpieces won't work in the basement so I had to

come for you, but I'll let Zach explain what's down there."

"Did you find Furukawa?"

"He's with Zach in the basement."

***

"Zach," I asked, entering the basement, "tell me what I'm looking at."

Zach was standing next to Furukawa, and both men were typing feverishly on keyboards wired directly into the computer servers.

"We've got half a dozen server stacks connected to the MI5 systems, creating a super computer. The system is online and active."

"What does that mean?" Wakefield asked.

"It means," Leeds answered, "the hacker army is very real."

"That's right," Leecy said. "And once the MI5 computers were hooked to the servers, thousands of hackers across the globe downloaded Tia's algorithm."

"The same one she used to hack the CIA," Valerie added.

"That's correct," Furukawa answered. "The algorithm is out in the open."

"Now what?" Wakefield asked.

"Zach and I," Furukawa began, "have corrupted the algorithm by uploading a virus. We're sending viruses disguised as updates to each hacker that downloaded the algorithm. That should take care of most of the hackers' ability to use the algorithm. Once we're finished, we can dismantle the system, and Mr. Leeds, you can have the algorithm and the MI5 components."

"And the overall success rate of this virus disguised as

an update?" Leeds asked.

"Ninety-nine percent," Zach said.

"Well then we at Interpol will just have to keep vigilant won't we?"

"Any luck finding Ryan by tracking the microdots?" Wakefield asked.

"Yes, hold on," Zach answered. "Just one more thing...and done. Furukawa?"

"Yeah. Me, too. I'll start taking this stuff apart. Robert, you want to give me a hand?" Furukawa asked.

"Yes, sure. I'm beginning to like getting my hands dirty," Leeds answered.

"Zach?" Wakefield asked again.

"Yes," Zach said, turning his attention away from the computers and focusing on Wakefield. "I used the servers to boost the signal of the microdot tracking program. He's still in possession of the bags, and he's here in St. Petersburg. I emailed you the address ten minutes ago."

"Leeds," Wakefield said, "we'll meet you, Zach, and Furukawa at the airport at midnight. The Grangers and I have some business to attend to."

"I understand, but don't you forget you still owe me a coffee."

***

"What's this place?" Wakefield asked as she eased the van to a stop half a block from the entrance of a drab, three story concrete building in southwestern St. Petersburg.

"It's the kind of place where no one comes looking for you," I said.

"Cash only hotel, and they probably only charge by the hour," Valerie added. "Check the ladies hanging around the front door. Working girls."

"So," Wakefield said, staring at the building, "three floors and twenty rooms to a floor. How do we find him?"

"I know where I'd be," Leecy replied.

"Enlighten us," I said.

"I'd select a room closest to the exit, but not the ground floor, and definitely not near the front entrance. There's too many people hanging around there. No, I'd be in a room at the end of a hall near the stairs on the top floor."

"Makes sense," Val agreed. "Ryan pays off a guy at the door to alert him if anyone out of the normal crowd shows, and Ryan makes his escape via the stairs."

"What's our approach?" Wakefield asked.

"We access the stairs through the emergency exit doors at either end of the building," I said. "Then sweep the rooms closest to the stairs first, meeting in the middle till we find him. We work in pairs—two teams of two. Leecy, you and me enter the left side of the building and Val and Wakefield, you guys take the right. Got it?"

"Don't forget who we're going after," Wakefield reminded. "He may be a traitor and an asshole, but he's also a highly trained CIA operative. He speaks fluent Russian, so don't let your guard down."

"What are we waiting for?" Val asked. "It's not getting any darker. Let's go."

"Earpieces on," Wakefield said.

***

Ten minutes later, we'd bypassed the alarm of the exterior doors, entering the building. The heat from the overhead vents exacerbated the smell of moldy carpet and cigarette smoke.

"This place is disgusting," I said, climbing the stairs to the third floor. "We should all see a doctor after this."

"Stop being such a baby." Wakefield replied. "You're wearing gloves."

"If he's not up here, then we'll check the other floors," Valerie said.

Leecy's hand was on the door leading to the hallway and she said, "Ready?"

I nodded yes, and she pushed open the door and entered the hallway. I could see Val and Wakefield working back-to-back, checking rooms at the opposite end of the hall. After the first five rooms, I said, "Looks like this floor is being used for storage."

"Yeah," Wakefield said. "Same thing on this end."

With nineteen rooms cleared, we met in the middle of the hallway. We were standing on either side of the door for room 301.

"Quiet," I whispered, trying the doorknob. It was locked.

I smiled, knowing that was a good sign, because every other room's door had been unlocked. Picking the lock of the cheap doorknob, I held up my hand, counting down with my fingers from 3...2...1, and opened the door.

We entered using a standard single file formation. I broke left. Val, now familiar with the layout of each room, found the light switch by the door, and Leecy broke right. Wakefield entered the room, walking between us toward the bed in the middle of the room just as Val turned on the lights.

"What the fu..." Ryan said, reaching for the weapon on the nightstand.

"Please," Wakefield said, standing at the foot of the bed. "Just give me a reason. Pick up the gun, you piece of shit. I'd love to have the excuse to put a bullet between your eyes. You did nothing while Tia killed Hodges and those pilots. Please do something now."

Ryan's hand hovered calmly above the weapon. His eyes were blinking rapidly, adjusting to the light.

"I figured I'd see you again, just not this soon. How'd you find me?"

"Microdots in the money bags," Leecy answered.

"You find Tia?" he asked.

"Yes," Valerie answered.

"I guess you took her into custody, then."

"You'd be wrong," Wakefield said.

"You kill her, Granger?" he asked, looking at me, his hand inches from the gun.

"I did," Wakefield answered.

"I see. So the rules be damned. Is that what you have in mind for me? An execution?"

"I won't waste my breath reminding you of all the charges pending against you," Wakefield said, ignoring his question, "but I'll be adding murder to the list. You're going to answer for Hodges, those pilots, and Franks."

"But you know I didn't kill those people."

"That doesn't mean you're not complicit."

"Last time I checked," Ryan said, "I'm the only person still alive when Hodges and those pilots were killed. Who's going to challenge my version of events?"

"And you'd be wrong again, dumbass. There's a witness. So if you thought you were going to claim Tia held a gun on you and threatened to kill you if you didn't help her, forget it. That argument won't hold water." Wakefield said.

"I didn't know what she was going to do."

"I find that difficult to believe, given your profession. You'll be hard-pressed trying to convince anyone that a man like you, with your catalog of life experiences, didn't know a crime was going to be committed when you goaded Hodges into stopping the van. Even if you didn't think he was going to die, you knew Tia was going to try and take advantage of the situation, which means you're guilty of aiding and abetting, and maybe even felony murder, Ryan. The same argument can be made regarding the pilots. That's three life sentences at Leavenworth, and I've only scratched the surface on the charges I'm prepared to bring against you."

"That's it, then," Ryan said.

"Let's go, Ryan," Wakefield said, watching his hand closely, as it was still hovering above the gun. "There's no easy way out of this for you."

Ryan made his move, and the ear splitting shot reverberated off the walls of the small room.

"Son of a bitch!" Ryan screamed. "You shot me in the hand!"

"Yeah, I know," Leecy said. "That's where I was aiming."

"Wrap the hand up with something, grab the money, and let's get out of here," Wakefield said. "The local police will be here soon."

Ten minutes later, I was closing the van's side door in time to watch the police charge through the front entrance of the hotel.

***

"The pilot assures me we should enjoy calm conditions all the way to Cologne," Furukawa said.

"Smooth sailing all the way?" Leeds asked.

"Yes, but there's something else," Furukawa said.

"What?" Wakefield asked.

"I've spoken with my contact at MI5, and there's news coming out of Russia. Anyone care to watch it on the television?"

"Are you having a laugh? Of course we want to see it," Leeds said.

The familiar face and dark hair of the English-speaking, female MSNBC reporter that reported the explosion in Sevastopol filled the screen.

"We now go to Moscow for this breaking news story and President Vladimir Putin."

"Valerie?" Wakefield asked, leaning across the aisle. "Do you mind translating?"

"No, not at all. Putin is saying a tragedy has occurred, that a member of his cabinet has been killed. Ilion Volodarsky was discovered murdered in his home in St. Petersburg. He's saying Ilion recently returned from a peace-seeking mission to Geneva, where he met with strong resistance from the Ukrainian Nationalists. Putin fears Ilion's death is directly linked to these peace-keeping efforts, but also, he believes the murder is related to something else. Putin says Ilion uncovered the true origins of the alleged army of hackers, and it was this very discovery that led to his death. Ilion had proven beyond doubt that the hackers responsible for causing havoc all over the world, were and continue to operate freely inside the Ukraine, and are receiving the full support of the pro-Nationalist party. Putin is blaming the pro-nationalist Ukrainian forces for Ilion's death."

"Wow," Zach said. "You gotta hand it to the guy; he never misses an opportunity to blame someone else for the shit he stirs up."

Turning off the TV, Furukawa asked, "Why didn't he mention the girl?"

"Tia didn't fit in with the new narrative, I guess."

"I don't know," Wakefield chimed in, then turned to Leecy. "Check the prisoner's restraints one more time, okay?"

"Sure thing," Leecy said, leaving her seat next to Wakefield and walking toward the back of the plane.

I watched her check Ryan, who was shackled and cuffed to the jump seat at the rear of the plane, and was turning back around in my seat when Zach stood and walked towards Leecy.

"Hey, Zach. Sit with me?" I heard Leecy ask. She sat down on the couch that ran along one side of the plane. "What's our flying time?"

"We'll be in Cologne in three hours," Zach answered, sitting down next to my daughter. "Then nine or ten more hours, depending on headwinds, till we reach DC."

I was still looking over my shoulder when I saw her take his hand in hers. I allowed for a slight smile, then felt Val's gentle but firm elbow in my side and turned to face her. "What?"

"You're wasting your time worrying about her."

"I'm not worrying."

"Well, you should be worried, but about him," Wakefield said from across the narrow aisle.

"Is that so?" I asked, looking from one woman to the other.

"Have you ever stopped to consider what Leecy would do if Zach ever got out of line with her?" Val asked.

"Now that you mention it, no, I haven't."

Furukawa turned around to face us. "I've been waiting for the right time to talk to you about Leecy," he said. "I understand the CIA no longer employs her. Would..."

"No," I said, cutting him off. "Don't ask that question.

She's already informed us she wants to finish college. So, that's that."

Patting my arm while flipping through the pages of a magazine, Val said, "Take it easy, big fella."

The End

EPILOGUE

LATE OCTOBER 2016

I raised my glass of champagne for one final toast and said, "To Leecy, Yale graduate, I'm so proud of you. Congratulations."

Touching champagne flutes and glasses of sparkling water together again, Val added, "Me too, sweetheart. I love you."

"Really great, Leecy," Zach said, leaning over and kissing her cheek. "Congratulations."

"Thank you again," Leecy said, taking a sip of sparkling water before continuing, "but I think they want us to leave. We're the last ones here."

Downtown New Haven was closing up after a long day of celebrating. Seeing a couple of inebriated graduates walking arm and arm in the middle of the road, I was about to offer them a ride home when the campus police appeared, and I could hear them doing the same. With that one exception, the streets of New Haven were relatively quiet, though I thought I heard the sounds of a couple of late night revelers crossing the quad before we turned off the main drag onto our street.

Watching Zach and Leecy walking together ahead of us, holding hands...well...the relationship was something I was getting used to. She was taller than he was, and wearing heels with her jeans made the difference in size even more noticeable, but Zach didn't seem to notice or care. He was a good kid, but, more importantly, I knew Leecy. I trusted my daughter's judgment.

"Can you believe it?" I whispered to Val.

"What?"

"She's finished with Yale at eighteen."

"Oh, that. I thought you were talking about her and Zach."

Smiling I said, "Yes, well, that also crosses my mind from time to time."

"I bet it does," she said, tugging on my arm. "You know he reminds me of you when we first met. Do you remember?"

"I remember, but I don't agree."

"You were as smitten with me as he is with Leecy, and I was out of your league, too."

"Yes, I did marry above my station," I said, squeezing her hand.

"I love you," she said, reaching up and kissing me.

***

The short walk from the restaurant to our front door was soon over, and I was inserting the key into the deadbolt when something occurred to me.

"Zach, it's too late for you to drive back to your parent's house in Boston. Why don't you call them and let them know you'll be staying here on the couch."

"Sure thing, Mr. Granger," Zach said, a little too enthusiastically for my liking, but I let it go.

Turning on the light in the living room, I asked,

"Anyone want to catch the late news with me before lights out?"

Valerie brushed past me and whispered, "You just earned some brownie points, mister." Then louder, she added, "Sure, I'll turn on the TV. Coffee?"

"Decaf, please, and thank you," I said, watching Zach follow Valerie toward the kitchen with his phone to his ear.

I turned to lock the door and came face to face with my daughter.

"So does this mean you like my boyfriend now?"

"It means I love my daughter."

"Dad."

"Yes," I said, hugging her. "Of course I like Zach, but he stays on the couch."

She slapped my arm and walked around me toward the kitchen. "I know that."

I checked the deadbolt and then heard the TV come to life. The words "Breaking news," caught my attention.

Looking at the TV, I saw flames and black smoke filling the screen and heard the disembodied voice of the reporter.

"Continuing our report on our top story tonight," the female voice began, "it's been confirmed that the explosion in a downtown Washington, D.C. office building was the result of a bomb being detonated, and not a gas leak as reported earlier. The explosion has claimed the life of an as-yet-to-be-named member of the Intelligence community. As you can see from the images we're bringing you tonight, the three-story building has been completely destroyed. Dozens of people are seeking medical attention here in the street."

"Oh my God," Leecy said.

I glanced away from the TV to look at her, Valerie, and Zach standing in the kitchen, and when I looked back at the screen, a young, black female reporter's face filled the screen. She was holding her finger to her ear and nodding her head, then faced the camera again.

"Sources have confirmed there was a meeting of high-level government officials here tonight. I'm being told the meeting had adjourned prior to the explosion and only one of the participants was still inside the building. We're trying to verify that person's identity now." I watched as she paused, placing her finger to her ear again. Then she nodded and continued.

"If you're just joining us, a bomb has exploded in downtown Washington, D.C. tonight, killing one and injuring others. Sources are now confirming the possible target of the bombing was Senator Savid. Yes," the reporter said, nodding her head, "that's now the official word. Senator Danielle Savid, the front-runner in this year's Presidential election, was the target of tonight's bombing in Washington, D.C."

I felt my cell phone vibrating in my back pocket and reached for it.

"Valerie, can you believe this?" I asked. Then I looked at the screen of my iPhone and added, "It's Wakefield."

"It's never good news when the Deputy Director of the CIA calls in the middle of the night," Valerie said.

"What do you think she wants, Dad?"

I shrugged my shoulders and answered the phone.

"Tammy. To what do I owe this pleasure?"

"Ron, are you watching the news?"

"Are you okay? You sound like something's wrong."

"Just answer the question. Are you watching the news?"

"Yes, we're watching the news its all about some explosion in DC. Why?"

"The director of the CIA was killed in that explosion."

"Jesus, Tammy, what're you guys into?"

"That's why I'm calling, it's literally blowing up in our face. I'm in trouble, Ron. I need your help."

"Just tell me where and when."

BEFORE YOU GO

Thank you for reading this Granger Spy Novel.

Write to me at info@johnjdavis.com and tell me what you liked, which characters you'd like to see more of, even what you didn't enjoy so much about the book. I'd love to hear your thoughts and feedback.

You can keep up with the series and all its characters in the following ways:

- Purchase the first novel in the series, **Blood Line**, at http://a.co/ie0ebI0
- Sign up for *The Granger Report* for sneak peeks, freebies, giveaways and periodic news about new releases: www.johnjdavis.com

If you think your friends would enjoy the series, I'd be honored if you'd spread the word. Books also make great gifts!

If you feel particularly motivated by your reading experience, please take a few minutes to post a review on your retail site and/or Goodreads. Reviews tell other readers what's worth reading and I'd appreciate it if you'd leave a few words.

Many thanks,
John

ABOUT THE AUTHOR

In 2014, John released his first novel, Blood Line, part of his Granger Spy Novel series. Blood Line was an immediate success, and, to John's surprise, an award winner, gaining four awards in 2015 - Killer Nashville Silver Falchion Reader's Choice Award, Reader's Favorite Gold Medal and eLit Awards in two categories. John credits the years of sitting in lobbies and airports for honing his skill of human observation, which feeds his talent for writing fast-paced, character-driven stories. The newfound success lead John to write the second installment in the series, Bloody Truth, and the upcoming third.

John is currently at work on the accompanying screenplays for the Granger Spy Novels.

Author Website: www.johnjdavis.com